TO TOUCH A REAPER

R.R. MANGOLD

ISBN 979-8-9897340-0-9 (Paperback Edition)
ISBN 979-8-9897340-1-6 (Ebook Edition)
979-8-9897340-4-7(Hardback Edition)

This book is a work of fiction. Names, characters, places, and incidents either are products of the author's imagination or are used fictitiously. Any resemblance to actual persons, living or dead, events, or locales is entirely coincidental.

Cover Art by Adam Mangold
IG @a_roth_mangold
Interior Design and Formatting by Talia Aden
TikTok @taliaaden

Second Printing, 2025

TO TOUCH A REAPER

R.R. MANGOLD

To anyone that would trade immortality for one more day with those they lost.

CONTENT WARNINGS

This story carries strong themes of death – including child loss & suicide.

Mention of domestic violence.

Many religious characters and beliefs are mentioned in this story.

Mention of the attacks on a mosque.

This book is recommended for 18+ due to sexually explicit scenes.

1
Reaper

I'm usually standing next to a person who is moments away from dying, instead I jumped at the opportunity to watch the cause up close. A lone sniper. It's not the violence that fascinates me, but the methodology. People pass this man on the street every day and wouldn't assume he is capable of a deadly shot from this far away. In a few minutes I will head over to his target as he bleeds to death on the steps of the New York Federal Courthouse. It is my job to detach his soul from his body, allowing him to cross over. Wherever the soul goes is beyond my pay grade. *Not that I get paid for this.*

The sniper cannot see me, even as I stand less than a foot away in this bleak unfurnished apartment. He smells like cigarette smoke and leather. I leaned close and peeked through the scope when he pulled his body away. He is not watching the courthouse steps but staring at a flag on top of the building. Curiosity bubbles within like an overflowing cauldron. The numbers and equations he is writing in a little notebook are fascinating. Scratches of measurements, equations, and wind direction. Little pieces to a deadly puzzle.

He unzips the jacket that was tight against his back muscles. I copied his look today. Tight grey washed jeans, a black tee under a leather jacket. I could have been straight out of a 60's musical. The sniper didn't hear the creaking of my jacket as I moved closer to the window. Nearly touching the barrel of the gun. He could stare directly at me and see nothing.

He took a sip from a paper coffee cup. It smelled divine. A reminder of what I cannot have. This is not my world. Not really. I only exist in it to assist Death.

Death, who is the worst boss ever. Every conversation is one sided, and less of a conversation. More of me waiting to be summoned day after day without any say in where I go.

I have no home, no belongings, and no family. My body is not even real. Reapers, like me, are lesser angels. We have none of the angelic benefits. No wings. No opportunity to visit heaven. *If heaven does exist.* Most annoyingly, no paintings or statues depicting us as beautiful beings with glowing light around our heads.

Instead, reapers often have skulls for heads and wear hooded robes. I in fact have not worn a hooded robe daily since the mid 1700's and have never carried a scythe. I did twirl a lion topped cane in the early 1900's, but that was very fashionable for the male exterior I wore back then. Conveniently, I can choose to look like whatever I want, and I usually choose to blend in. Even though I am only seen by fellow reapers.

Currently, I project the image of a sun kissed young woman. I have grown very fond of this face. I like my brown eyes and deep chocolate colored hair. I've kept this look for three decades now. Changing my attire and hair to match the trends I see in magazines. I first saw this face on a stage in Rome. Sometime towards the end of the sixteenth century. She was a young Italian actress that commanded her audience with her natural beauty. I adjusted my hair to mimic the large waves I see that are popular in modern times and may have made my eyelashes longer. Some reapers have kept the same image for centuries. I cannot help but attempt to fit in, it's a habit I have yet to break.

When I am alone, and there is no human in sight, I can interact with this world. Picking up books or magazines. Or changing the channel on a TV left on. Finding things to read in abandoned places was a lot easier before cameras were invented. Death does not want us making books float on a security camera leading to hysteria amongst the humans. They are always quick to blame ghosts. In fact, ghosts are rare.

The sniper shifted his long rifle down. The crowd of news reporters and protestors grew louder as the large double doors of the courthouse flew open.

"Showtime." the sniper said to himself.

A man in a perfectly fitted navy suit stepped out with his arms up. He wore a huge grin and was accompanied by a team of lawyers. The newspapers predicted he would walk free due to a technicality. I read from a discarded paper yesterday. Something to do with false witness statements. It was not my job to judge.

The sniper let out a slow calm breath and squeezed the trigger. The head of the man on the steps snapped back. Screams filled the air. That was an amazing shot. We were at least seven hundred meters away on the ninth floor in a shitty apartment building.

The man in the suit hit the ground hard. Blood was already pooling around his head. The sniper began packing up his rifle and supplies by the time I left the room. I can go anywhere with just a thought, and I found myself standing behind a crowd of police officers hovering over the body. I waited with my thumbs in the pockets of my tight jeans and glanced in the direction of killing shot. A tiny window in a brick apartment building that was only open a few inches. The sniper's aim really was impressive. In all my existence this was my third sniper assassination. By far the longest distance.

I found myself distracted when a translucent man appeared at my side. It was the man in the suit without his fatal injury.

"What is happening?" he said.

"You're dying."

"But I just got free." His spoke through clenched teeth. "This can't be real."

When people die, they are either angry or in denial. I imagine the sadness comes later. I usually get bombarded with the "this can't be happening" or "put me back" or just a lot of groveling. I have had many wealthy people try to bribe me. As if I would have a use for their possessions or money.

"Take my hand." I extended my left hand to him. The one with my gold soul ring on the middle finger. He examined it quickly and shook his head. "Take my hand." I say again.

"Why? Who are you?"

His blinks were rapid, his face was questioning whether I was sent to harm or save him. The articles I've read about him did not paint him as a good man. At least by my own standards. I kept my face hard and expressionless. Acting is a good skill for a reaper to have. "Your time here is done. The afterlife awaits."

"Is it heaven? Cause I am catholic. I have been baptized." He huffed.

The dying always says the same thing. "I am a Christian I should go to heaven. Take me to Jannah, for I am Muslim. I am a Mormon, therefore heavenly father will bless me with a planet of my own." I miss the old Gods. The Egyptians were way more creative. I will say the Gods from Eastern Asia are quite colorful and impressive. Too bad the primary influence on a human's religion is location. Most don't learn about the other faiths in the world. They stick to what the people who raised them taught them.

My favorites are people with no religious belief at all, and how stunned they are when I appear before them. The shock on their face always makes me smile. Most of them are pure skeptics of anything beyond what can be scientifically proven. Reapers have no answers for them either.

"Take my hand." I repeat scrunching my brow until two faint lines form between them. He tilted his head down to his body, watching it take its last breath. Slowly he placed his palm in mine. Shrugging his shoulders with defeat. His hand felt solid in mine. The only part of this I enjoy, that moment where my body connects with another, and I feel real.

A moment later, he faded like a grey cloud entering my ring on an unseen wind. Chatter and cries enveloped me from the crowd being pushed further back from the body. After collecting his soul, the ring warmed the way metal would in the sun. I rubbed it with my thumb. He will stay in the ring with me until I unload it. Sending it through the final gateway of the living world.

I turned from the courthouse steps as chaos erupted behind me. Cameras were flashing and news reporters were live on air. Describing the horrifying scene on the courthouse steps. I passed in front of a camera knowing it would not detect me. There was not even a ripple in the light detected by the cameras. No breeze as I passed the anchor preparing to go live on TV.

Soul collections are rarely back-to-back. Death is not as common as one would expect with millions of people living today. The population increase also increases the population of reapers, but still I have never felt overwhelmed. I should have some free time before Death summons me again. It feels like the perfect time to go see a movie. The smell of popcorn always gives me comfort after a day filled with so much blood.

2
Reaper

I sat behind a couple nervously sharing a popcorn bucket. They would flinch every time their fingers touched. I leaned my face between them inhaling the buttery scent. The crunch of them biting has me considering what it feels like. If I were able to taste anything I would grab a piece for myself. Even if I managed to get some into my mouth, I would have no sense of feeling. It would just fall through me. A reminder that this body is only an illusion created by my mind.

I am more than a ghost though. They are avoiding a purpose whereas I spend every second fulfilling mine. Waiting for the next soul to guide to their afterlife. Ghosts are merely imprints of a soul with a strong tether to earth. Playing out like a scene from a movie. Humans were close when they guessed that ghosts have unfinished business, but they are more like a memory of a soul that used to be. Repeating a scene frame by frame. Eventually they fade. Some take months, others may linger for a whole century.

The movie is nearing its end. The male character is giving a heartfelt speech from a dock as the love of his life drifts away on a boat. Any minute now she will dramatically jump off into the water and swim towards him. If my calculations are correct, she has only known him for two weeks. I have seen love encourage powerful things, but I find romantic comedies to be the least realistic.

You can't motivate a reaper with love. Our emotions are like dull knives. They still cut, but with less impact. We are not judged by how many souls we collect or by the speediness that we send them off. Once they enter my ring, time stops for them. Death has not promised us an eternity in paradise. Not in the way religious humans are motivated towards a promised afterlife.

I get called many things in different languages while reaping. People tend to find my existence as proof of their personal beliefs. When in fact, reapers are not attached to any religion. We separate the souls and move on to our next assignment. Never knowing what waits for them beyond the gateway. I can't even tell you if there is a single God in charge of everything. The only thing I know for certain is Death is real. They hold the strings to the reapers like a puppet master. If the rumors are true, Angels are also real. Although I have yet to meet one. Demons might be real, but as far as I know they are not part of the Angel family, and do not associate with us. They belong to whoever oversees the dark afterlife. Some call them Lucifer, Hades, or the King of Hell. I gave up trying to figure out who they were. Who the creator of all is.

I got lost in thought and the theater was cleared of people. Choosing to walk slowly to the sidewalk instead of just appearing there. If I were human, I would be heading home. In a way I was. My eyes searched the skyline for an inviting rooftop. One where I could see people living their lives. A quiet place I could wait until my next assignment.

3
Jimi

The air in the children's hospital smelled like the usual cleaners and a hint of cotton candy. A machine was installed a few months ago for the volunteers to use when a patient needed cheering up. I flattened the tuck of my scrubs into my pants as I walked towards the room of a patient that arrived today.

The child was sleeping when I walked around his bed. I initialed on his chart next to 11:00pm check. Then replaced his IV with fresh saline fluid. I left the room of our new patient and allowed his parents to get settled in. The boy was not yet five years old. I left a bag of play-dough of various colors on his bedside table. Attempting to be as quiet as possible.

The Saint Grace Children's Hospital is the leader of leukemia treatment. Working closely with New York's medical Universities. His parents drove from two states away hoping to receive the best care without having to take out a second mortgage on their house. I understand the fear. The only way I can afford my apartment is with a trust that was left by my grandparents. Even an apartment with leaky faucets and single pane windows that let the cold seep through.

It was never a question that would end up working at a hospital. I spent time at SGCH recovering from broken bones and a collapsed lung when I was a teen. I remember being embarrassed that I was in a children's hospital. Thinking I was practically a man. I denied their paper and colored pencils as long as I could until boredom won the battle. I sketched my view from the hospital bed and every nurse that worked there. I always doodled in the paper margins at school, mostly faces. Trying to get the details of the peak of their lips and slope of their noses. One nurse suggested I had a future as an artist, but the wheels in my head were already spinning. I wanted to be a nurse like her. After a nine-day stay, I showed my gratitude by gifting the staff all the portraits I had finished. They succeeded in keeping my mind distracted when my parents couldn't visit. Having me focus on what I had and not what I lost. Making this temporary home feel warm.

Since then, I wanted to be a Nurse Practitioner myself. My sights were set on SGCH after high school graduation, and they never changed. Although my father reminds me every day that I am so close to being a doctor. A fact he counts it as a failure. *"Your grandparents didn't come from Korea with nothing in their pockets and knowing only ten words in English for you to give up, son"* he would say. It doesn't feel like giving up. A bit like settling, but that does not bother me in the slightest.

I am moving at a snail's pace and am emotionally drained. Putting on a big smile throughout the day wears me down more than walking on the hard laminate floors. The fluorescent lights hum as I glide down a quiet hall. Today was a long eleven-hour shift that was supposed to be only eight. I flinched as a soft hand with manicured nails gripped my arm and pulled to the side. I found myself inside a supply closet. The door shut and the light flickered as if preparing to go out. The shock wore off quickly. I've been here before. A petite woman with blond hair pulled into a high ponytail stood before me. She wore the same blue scrub pants as I did, but her top was printed with tiny colorful balloons. My body recognized her as she pressed palms against my chest.

"Serena! What are you doing?" Stupid question. I knew what she was doing. We used to hook up in college and then it started again a few months ago when I transferred to SGCH.

She pushed up on her toes and kissed my skin just above the V of my neckline. "I need to blow off steam. It's been a stressful day." Her hands found their way under the shirt of my scrubs. I grabbed her wrists.

"Not now Serena." I tried to push her off, but she held her arms outward and pressed into my body. The familiar feel of her curves against mine made my resistance fleeting. I rolled my head back and shut my eyes. Tension already releasing from my shoulders.

"Why not?" She wiggled out of my grip and ran her hands up until my shirt lifted off my stomach. Instincts had me lowering my hands to her hips and leaning down until my lips met her neck. It is not advised hospital staff to wear perfume or cologne, but her apricot body scrub always left a lingering scent on her skin. "Jimi, you look like you need this as much as I do."

I did. I really did. This hospital has consumed my life for the past four months. I have become very comfortable closing myself off to the world. Having nothing but my patients and my cat to keep me company.

Serena's lips were warm and soft on my neck. A low moan sat in the back of my throat. A sign that I was losing the battle. I tightened my grip on her hips. *Maybe just a quick one.* Sensing the change in my body she removed her hands and untied her pants. The bottoms of her scrubs fell to the floor, followed by white silky underwear. I reached over to check the lock on the door. We found every lockable closet the first two weeks I was here. Both of us easily falling back into our college habits of using each other's bodies as stress release.

Serena and I never dated. Never asked for more or expected more. Something was missing between us to ever cross that line into a relationship. We don't even kiss on the lips, just fuck. My mouth has been on every inch of her body, yet I resist her lips even now. She seems to do the same, so I never pushed it.

"I'm ready." she said, turning around and bending with her legs wide. She handed me a condom over her shoulder. Serena gripped the metal frame of a shelf filled with linens and towels. I dropped my pants to my ankles and pulled my cock out, sliding the condom over my shaft. I rubbed the tip over her entrance and found she was in fact already wet. As I slid into her, I wrapped an arm around her front to play with her clit. After dozens of hook-ups, I could make her come easily. I know exactly how she wants to be touched and fucked. Release always came for both of us, there was no surprise there. No surprise at all. No mystery or wonder. No time trying new things or finding out what your partner likes or dislikes. We had it down to science.

Just strong thrusts behind her as I circle my fingers over her clit. Her internal muscles are flexing around me. I increase my rhythm causing the shelves to rattle. Stacks of linens are silently wobbling. Serena moans with her mouth closed, attempting to be as quiet as possible. It's 11:45pm and we operate on a skeleton crew in the evenings. There is little risk of us getting caught, which would cost both of us our jobs. So, why risk it at all? We have no love for each other. We hardly speak now that we are not in classes together. *This will be the last time.* I decide as I feel her climax. *I need something more real than this.* I thrust quickly. Sinking inside her as deep as I can. My stomach muscles flex. Serena feels great. *Why do I have no desire for more than this with her? She is beautiful. Intelligent.* She comes undone. Her knuckles go white gripping the shelf. My head falls back as I spill into the condom. We paused only for a moment, until I released her hips. Checking to see if I left finger shaped bruises on them. She wouldn't mind if I had.

We both pause with our heavy breathing the only sound. After a few moments I grabbed a hand towel from the shelf and held it between us as I slid out of her. Peeling the condom off and wrapping it in a section of rough brown paper towel I ripped from a roll that fell over on a shelf.

I cleared my throat. "Let's call that the last one." I say while pulling my pants up.

"Why? You plan on getting a girlfriend for once?" Serena smiled over her shoulder. She had already wiped herself with a towel and was putting her clothes back on.

"Someday." I roll my eyes. "But mainly, I like this job."

"Boo." She said with a pout.

"Look, I know you only went to medical school to find a rich doctor to marry, but some of us actually want this career." She swatted playfully at my chest. My scrubs were lightly damp with sweat and stuck to my chest.

"Don't forget hot. A rich hot doctor." She smirked. "Plus, I saw this hall's camera was on the repair schedule for tomorrow. That's why I came here to find you. One last supply closet rendezvous before eyes are back on it, and we have to find a new location."

I could have told her I only live a few blocks from here, but that felt too intimate. Too much like the start of a relationship. I smiled flatly in agreement. She fanned air towards her face hoping her reddened cheeks would fade in color.

"Are you still down in emergency?" I wrapped our dirty towels with a clean one and tucked them under my arm. Then nodded towards the door. With intentions to hide the evidence in the laundry right away.

"Yes. It may have more blood and gore, but I don't know how you handle it up here. All these sick kids and sad families." She opened the door and peaked to make sure the hall was clear. We both walked out towards the employee elevator. Serena scanned her badge. We did not have to wait long for the elevator to arrive. She pressed B for basement.

"If I can give the patients a few happy or comforting moments while here and make them forget that they are dying. Then it's worth it. Trust me." My eyes trailed the blinking numbers. Serena reached out and touched my arm, but swiftly dropped it as we reached the basement.

She smirked over her shoulder as she walked out. "It's too bad you're not rich Jimi. You're too good for this world."

"So, you think I'm hot?" Serena winked and walked to the left towards the women's locker room. I turned right. This would be the part where I should yell something flirty back at her. Instead, I exhaled at the floor. I've lazily created an "out of sight- out of mind" way of thinking with Serena. With most things these days actually. Nothing has made me feel excited in years.

The shower pressure was terrible. Either too soft or hard enough to remove a layer of skin. I chose to go with hard. I squeezed the shampoo suds in my thick black hair and let the hot water of the shower blast my chest. *Too good for this world.* What makes someone good? I'm good at my job but nothing that the hospital couldn't replace. I am sure not going out of my way to make a difference in the world. I feel like that makes someone good. Monotony feels natural to me. Settling comes easy for me. I've yet to find something or someone worth taking a risk on if the outcome is not perfectly clear. My friend, Dante, would call me a coward. My father would call me smart.

I have never tried to find a greater purpose or meaning in this life. I am not a religious person. Which is odd considering my father met my mother at a church. She was raised going every weekend. My father was fueled by curiosity. My Korean immigrant grandparents had no knowledge of western religions to teach him when they arrived. He was so desperate to fit into their small town that he wandered through the doors of an Episcopalian church one Sunday. Only knowing it was a gathering place of worship. He did not understand most of what they were saying, but there was one outgoing girl that would sit next to him and explain.

They became close friends and then high school sweethearts. My mother made the decision to stop attending church once she moved out of her parents' house to attend college. Neither of them has returned or tried to make me or my sister attend. Two years into college, my parents eloped at the Albany courthouse and moved into a small apartment. She became pregnant with me and never graduated. Something she will never admit has caused regret, but it's obvious in her eyes. My father went on to become a pharmacist. A path he tried many times to push me into.

The pressure to succeed was drowning me. If I could just focus on saving a few lives. On being a better nurse, then maybe I could make up for the life I let slip through my hand's many years ago. Maybe there is a scale I can balance out.

4
Reaper

The hours between 1:00a.m. and 4:00a.m. were always my favorite while being stationed in New York City. Small groups of people in their twenties stumbled home from a night of drinking and dancing. Most of the businesses were closed, but the lights were bright in the backrooms of bakeries where bagels and donuts were being prepped. I keep finding my way back to this bench in Bryant Park. It was across the street from a small pink cookie shop. According to the sign they make the best cookies in New York. That's a pretty big claim for a small shop to make. If I were able to place a bet, I would say it was true. The smell of the melting chocolate and sweet dough baking is the most divine smell I have ever experienced.

I was bursting with envy at the thought of the taste of those cookies. Death did not grant us the luxury when creating us. He allowed us to see, hear, and smell. Being able to taste would open us up to a primal temptation and to reapers becoming thieves or interfering with the human world. I am sure cookies would go missing if I had my way. Judging by the effects of alcohol, which would go missing too. I, myself would have consumed many bottles of champagne in the roaring twenties. Our existence is relatively boring.

Sure, I can travel the world and see any sight. I can sit at the top of the tallest mountain and not feel cold or be affected by the lack of oxygen. It sounds lonely, but I am not always alone. Wars and other tragedies summon more than one reaper at times. We catch up like old friends. Old friends that only see each other in fucked up situations.

Death muted most of our emotions when we were created, but the legend of our origin states we were something before reapers and whatever that was remains a part of us. Somewhere deep inside.

My earliest memory was coming together like mist. I remember hovering above the earth. A thought came to my head that I needed to form a body. I observed the group of humans walking barefoot on red dirt. I mimicked their dark skin and blended the facial features of a few of the males. I planted my feet on the ground and followed behind. They were people living in a land now called Ethiopia during the Zagwe Dynasty. I could understand their language and spent my first day just observing.

When night came, I felt the tug. An invisible pull inside my chest. It was Death giving me my first assignment. I followed it into a tent where I found a large man standing over a sleeping woman. His face twisted in the light coming from a small candle that was shaking in his filthy hands.

I flinched when a body appeared standing next to me.

"Reaper." She said with a smooth voice. "I am here to walk you through your first collection."

I nodded. I was given a general knowledge of my purpose before sent to earth, but a description of my role is hard to understand until I see how humans live. Understanding I was created to only see the end of life seemed dreary. I now see I will get to observe a bit more than I expected. "Which one is it?"

"Can't you see?" The reaper rocked on her heels. Her dark hair was twisted together and hung in two sections bouncing on the front of her shoulders. Her skin color and eye shape did not resemble the people of this land. Or the image I created for myself. "Concentrate young reaper."

I squinted at the man hoping it would reveal something. He was moving closer to the female and set the candle down on a low table. Her bed was nothing more than layers of stuffed fabric on the dirt floor. I was looking so intensely at him that I almost missed the glow coming off her body.

"No. Not the female." I groaned. "She seems young by human standards. Sleeping hardly seems like a risk to end her life. Death must have made a mistake."

"Death does not make mistakes. You will learn to accept that."

"The man looks evil." Something in his dark eyes felt empty. Void of what makes humans different from a reaper. In reality I was the one empty. Without a soul. But this man seemed hollow. I tried to step closer, but the reaper put an arm in front to block me.

"Death does not choose based on good or evil. They could be young or old. It can be drawn out for years with illness or quick with something spontaneous. You must not let your emotions cloud your ability to do your job."

I tucked my arms close to my chest. My muscles were lean, and they flinched watching the man creep closer to her body. He did not approach her the way a lover would. He seeped towards her like a shadow.

The man had a hand over the woman's mouth now and he moved himself on top of her. She tried to let out a scream, but it was muffled. Her eyes were so wide I could see white all the way around her dark iris.

"I can't watch this." I said moving outside the tent. The reaper appeared by my side in a blink. "This is not how I expected it to be. When I was told I would be sent to earth as a reaper it sounded beautiful. This feels..." My words faded into the night. I shook my head at the ground.

"My first collection was a mother during childbirth. Soon after that I walked a battlefield and collected multiple souls in one day. I was envious of the humans." The reaper dipped her head low as muffled screams came from the tent.

"You want to live like a human?"

"No, young reaper." The air went silent. "I wish I could die like them."

I didn't understand what she meant that night, but I do now. After walking the earth for centuries. Immortality can feel like a curse. There are days when I see so much suffering that I want to cease to exist. Anything must be better than this. This purpose of collecting souls for Death. It wasn't until the late 16th century that I began enjoying the world. I spent my time between reaping watching people live. Watching them create art, sing, or make love. The Renaissance was quite invigorating. I visited as many theaters and musical performances as I could.

Humans have invented so many amazing technologies. I am thrilled by their inventions. The average life span has increased immensely thanks to medical advancements. Even visiting the children's hospital seems less dreary than it did a century ago. These children would have been taken much sooner by illness if it were a century ago. Fuck, some only a decade ago.

A man walked quickly past the bench where I sat. He had his umbrella low enough to cover his face. I felt a tug summoning me and stood. If I didn't know any better, I would have thought the man flinched, but it is nearly 2:00am, and he is walking alone in Manhattan. Any shadow could make him flinch.

I took a few unnecessary steps before vanishing to my destination.

5
Jimi

Another late shift at SGCH. The lights over the nurse's station are dimmed to help create a sense of calm in the evening. The top of a fuzzy head peaked over the tall counter. Tight curls pulled up into a puff on top of her head. Cassidy was a shy nurse and rarely spoke a full sentence to me. She was completing our patient assignments and leaving the papers on the counter for us to grab.

I pounded the last sip of coffee from a paper cup while swiping a paper with my name on it from the counter. I folded it twice and put it in my pocket. Cassidy looked up quickly before returning to her illuminated computer screen. Two other nurses were huddled in the corner comparing paper. Half of the night nurses were still in the program to become Nurse Practitioners. Suffering through the night shifts hoping it will pay off in the end.

If I wanted to get there in under two years, there would have to be a cut to my hours in the hospital. I'm racking up my residence hours quickly but have left very little time in my schedule to study for finals exams. My mother suggests I work less and that I find a girlfriend. *"I would like to have grandchildren before I cannot keep up with them on my bad knees."* Is what she always says.

Dating has never been my strong suit. I was a geeky kid. Girls didn't look in my direction and I attended most school events alone. College allowed me to bloom, as one would say. Thanks to a gym membership and a good haircut, I found college women were far more inviting. It helped me that K-pop became extremely popular in America. Twenty-year-old me did not mind being a sudden fetish. I made some questionable decisions asking my father to teach me a few phrases to pick up women.

I am not opposed to a relationship right now. If I could find someone willing to handle my work schedule. Someone who was willing to hear me talk about death and illness all the time. *Life with me sounds mighty cheerful.*

I am on my last round in the Leukemia wing. Checking charts and giving low sedatives to those that need it. Jasmine is a six-year-old who is fast asleep. She had long black hair that was spread like a wing across the pillow. I moved the coloring book and handful of crayons by her side. Just before they fall to the floor. She must have fallen asleep in the middle of coloring a unicorn with rainbow hair.

Her parents take turns sleeping on a pull-out cot, but tonight I found it empty. Earlier in the evening I sat with Jasmine playing board games while they took a night off. Having a family member with an illness can put strain on every marriage. Especially if it is your only child. Jasmine benefits from seeing her parents in good spirits. Having them away for one-night may look lonely, but it benefits her in the end. I am far too familiar with what guilt feels like at a young age. I wouldn't wish that upon anybody.

I signed the chart and went to put it back in the sleeve at the end of her bed when movement caught my attention to the corner of the room.

Legs were illuminated by the low lights of the hospital room. The curves of a body with the knees crossed told me it was a woman.

"Who are you?" I turned in her direction. She did not answer, but her leg stopped bouncing. As if frozen by my words. I squared my shoulders. "Do you have a visitors pass?" The woman leaned forward. The leather from her jacket creaked as she moved. Her face came into view. Lit by the soft glow of a single wall sconce to her side. My breath caught when I examined her mere perfect features. Warm olive skin and dark eyes. One arch eyebrow lifted. Dark thick waves frame her face. I blinked awkwardly and hoped she didn't notice me staring at her soft pillow like lips. I wanted to lay mine upon them and live in their plumpness. Her dark eyes watched me with wide amazement.

"Are you talking to me?" She uncrossed her legs and moved to the edge of the chair. I clenched my jaw, not sure if I should call security or not.

"You're the only other person in here." I took a few steps in her direction. This caused her to open her mouth to respond before closing it silently. "Can I see your visitor pass?"

The tilt of her head was unsettling. This woman could seduce me or kill me with the look she was making. I glanced at the sleeping child. Something didn't feel right. My training told me to call security and get her out. An odd heat inside me was pulling me closer to her. Longing to wrap my arms around her. Probably testosterone.

"I don't need a visitors pass." She stood. "You can see me?"

"Miss if you don't have a visitor pass to see this child, I will have to call security." I moved towards the phone mounted on the wall.

"Don't bother." Faster than seemed possible the woman darted past me and out the door.

I ran after her but found the hall empty. My own footsteps and beeps of machines are the only sounds. I considered my lack of sleep and too much caffeine responsible for a hallucination. That the shadows in the hospital room were playing tricks on me. No, she had to have been real. My mind could never have dreamt up someone that beautiful.

Moments later, I did call security and gave them a full description of the women. Two security guards checked every room. No one matching her description was found. Worried she went to a different floor, they proceeded to check the security cameras, but all they saw was me running out of the room and looking confused.

Did I make her up? The guards made a note to pass on to future shifts. In the end, they blamed it on insomnia. A common problem among night shift employees is that they are not good at balancing sleep during the day. I continued to look for her my entire shift. Knowing she was most likely long gone by now. I ended with a burning shower and headed home.

6
Reaper

My toes hung over the edge of the roof across from the Hospital. Mid-size buildings are my favorite. Between ten to twenty floors. Not too high for people watching. The tallest roofs are for when I need a break from this world. The closer to the clouds I can get, the more at peace I feel. This building was twelve stories high. Giving me a perfect view.

I tucked my hands into my front pockets while waiting for a familiar face to appear. After about two hours, I saw him exit the employee door to the hospital. No longer wearing his scrubs. He changed into a denim jacket with a hoodie underneath. As he passed me, I moved to another roof ahead of him. He pulled the hood over his dark hair to block the drizzle.

He saw me. He spoke to me. In all my existence that had never happened. Not from a human. I watched him take his phone out and flick his thumb over pictures. I could not tell what he was looking at from up this high, and I considered moving next to him. *Would he see me? Was it a glitch of some kind?*

I followed him from the rooftops as he crossed the mostly empty streets. At one point I watched him from a fire escape. A woman was inside making tea and didn't flinch when I appeared next to her window. Confirming she could not see me. I kept my distance from the man walking below. Clearly something was wrong. He disappeared into an old apartment building. The sign was mostly faded, and piles of trash sat on the sidewalk waiting for morning pick up. A few minutes later a light went on behind tall brick trimmed windows.

I was grateful Death did not summon me for the rest of the evening. I sat on the rooftop across from his apartment building. My legs dangled off the ledge. I couldn't keep still and found myself pacing on the rooftop. He stayed up for an hour longer. Eating in front of a TV while a fluffy white cat sat at his feet.

The curtains were ill-fitting on the tall arched windows. They could very well be a bedsheet hung over a curtain rod. From my vantage point I could see over them because the fabric only covered the lower half of the window. He has stripped down to just tight shorts and slipped under his comforter too quickly for me to get a good look at his body. What I did see looked like toned muscle. I pushed down the urge to get a closer look.

All the lights in his apartment went out. I appeared on his fire escape. Once there were no more rustling sounds from him tossing and turning, I risked being seen by putting my face between the gap in his curtains. I peered through the window. His legs were still. The cat was nestled near his head. I breathed a sigh of relief. Maybe this human has a connection to reapers. There could be a clue in his home. I must know.

When I popped up in his apartment. I stayed by the door. It was an open studio space. Everything in one room, except the bathroom. The windows were tall and rounded at the top surrounded by red brick. It was very quiet. I hesitated at a sound until I realized it was a steady quiet drip from the kitchen faucet. I walked slowly around the room. I have never tried to be quiet before. It was a strange sensation, to fear being seen or heard. Part of me wanted to laugh. His breathing remained steady allowing me to relax while I snooped.

There was a short bookshelf with a record player on top. I recognized most of the names. Mostly indie rock bands and soul artists from the seventies. Music has always been a treat for reapers. I have run into many reapers standing against the back wall of concert halls. He mostly listens to indie folk rock, but his collection of classic jazz albums is quite impressive.

The next day I was summoned twice to collect souls. Afterwards, my soul ring throbbed with slight pressure. Indicating it was full and would need to be unloaded soon. Every free minute I have, I spend trying to find the attractive male nurse. I got close enough to reach his employee badge when he was showering. Jimin Seong. I whispered it aloud. "Jimin Seong. What makes you so special?"

I found myself completely infatuated by him. His schedule made him very easy to follow. The way his clothes hugged his shoulders a bit too tight had me imagining his flexing muscles as he moved around his apartment. While at home he relaxed with a beer and rock music. Occasionally he drew in a small sketch-book. I could not see where he kept the book and admit that I searched for it while he was at work.

Jimi looked just as natural in his blue scrubs as he did in ripped jeans and a t-shirt. Watching him in the hospital was harder to do without him seeing me. I changed my appearance so I could walk close to him. At one point he was close enough that I could have reached out and grabbed his arm. Me looking like a teenage boy grabbing him randomly was not the introduction I was hoping for. I did love watching him work. He made all the children smile and eased worry for the families. A natural.

I observed something sad when he left the patients' rooms. His shoulders hung low as he walked down the halls of the hospital. His spirit dimmed slightly. May-be he was just a good actor, and I am a victim to his charms like everyone else. Without hesitation a bright smile filled his face when he entered a patient's room. Oh, he's good.

After watching him for three days, I decided it was worth seeing if he could still see me. I needed to test it fully. Not in another disguise lurking around him. The face he first saw me with. A face he would recognize. While he was at work, I found a calendar in his apartment. He only worked late shifts and had nothing scheduled outside of work other than one date with a doodle of a guitar with stars around it. *Smith's Bar 9pm* was written in swooping handwriting. It was marked on today's date. Smith's bar, which sounded familiar. I am certain I have seen that name before.

I appeared at Bryant Park and scanned the surroundings. People were gripping scarves to their necks trying to keep the cold wind off their skin. It was rush hour and people were scurrying to and from the nearest subway stations. I walked in a spiral circling the park. I could have sworn I saw that sign on a building near here. *Smith's Bar.* I repeated in my head as I walked. Sure enough, after two short blocks and two long ones I saw a red neon sign on a corner pub. Smith's Bar.

I walked towards the entrance to scope it out for tonight. There was a tingling tug in my chest. I let out a groan that no one heard. After I collected the soul tugging me away, I will return. I will wait. Tonight, I will confront Mr. Seong and find out why he saw me. If he still can.

7
Jimi

Finally, a night off. I spent most of the afternoon in sweatpants curled up with a book. An epic fantasy that I traded for at the used bookstore. The handful of self-help books given to me by my father have their value. Two equals one book that I actually want to read. I can get a decent summary of the books from the description. Enough to trick my father into thinking I am reading them. Who would have thought so many doctors are heroes with perfect marriages and genius kids? He must be trying to tell me something.

My old roommate was performing tonight nearby. Most of the time, I have excuses not to go. I was work-ing too late or did not have the energy to travel into Brooklyn. But this show was a few blocks from my apartment, and he has been texting me reminders for weeks. My HR was shocked when I requested the night off. Usually, I am picking up extra shifts.

I switched my sweatpants out for grey plaid pants. I picked them up at a thrift store last week. I cuffed them so they sat above my black converse. Then tucked in a band tee with a group from his college days that no longer exists. It was speckled with tiny holes and stains just like a well-loved shirt should be. I layered my favorite denim jacket on top. Choosing three pins to add onto the left pocket. Rarely these days do I spend time not wearing scrubs. Regular clothes have begun to feel like a costume. Nabi curled around my legs. She left traces of her white fur on the cuffs of my legs. My stomach growled. I should have eaten more than one slice of leftover pizza this afternoon. The sun had already set, and my body would be expecting dinner in a few hours. It would have to settle for bar nuts and beer.

After checking the automatic cat food feeder. I took a shot of gin to warm my stomach, then headed out the door. I am clearly forgetting how to live around people because I caught myself looking over my shoulder multiple times as I walked down the sidewalk. The feeling of being watched lingered around me and has for the past few days. Although I found no one when I searched the shadows.

The bar was filling up when I arrived at 9:15pm. I ordered a drink and found Nina sitting at the bar.

"Where's Dante?" I said to the curvy black female. She sipped on a beer and eyed me through thick lashes.

"Hi, Nina. How are you?" she said mimicking my greeting. "You look fucking fierce tonight, Nina."

I rolled my eyes. "Hi Nina." She cleared her throat. "You look fucking fierce tonight."

"Thank you, Jimi. Dante is setting up the stage with the rest of the band." She nodded in the direction of the back of the bar. Dante was hunched behind an amp messing with a tangle of cords. He was trying to concentrate. I decided to wait until after his set to talk to him. Nina kept our conversation in a steady flow. She is never short of words. She described in detail the couple Halloween costumes she was planning. Nina would be Glinda the good witch and Dante would be the wizard in an emerald suit. The image in my head gives me plenty of fuel to tease him later. Badass punk rock star in a velvet green suit and matching top hat. Classic.

"Will you have a date this year at our Halloween party?" Nina poked my arm with a sharp manicured nail.

I finished off my beer and nodded towards the bartender for another. "Probably not."

"I can hook you up with one of my hot friends. They love doctors." She beamed.

"I'm not a doctor."

"You will be." She smacked my arm playfully. I rolled my eyes.

"No, I will be a Nurse Practitioner." I tapped my beer against the side of her fruity cocktail. "You sound like my father."

"Daddy Seong is a smart man."

I shivered. "Please don't call him that." We laughed together mutually teasing each other about who had the more attractive parents. I was mid joke about taking her mom as my date to the party when a group of three people walked up to Nina like it was a high school reunion. I found myself pushed out of my bar seat. Replaced by one of the band members' girlfriends. The two women and one man clearly knew each other well. When the first song started a loud whoop came out of their mouths in unison. As the music continued, I drifted farther away from Nina's back. The group was screaming and singing along with the band. I had heard Dante's music before, but this was my first live show in almost a year.

The vibrations of their pop-rock filled the bar. I moved away from the crowd and found myself up against the wall. Which was covered with posters and writing. When I turned to read a dirty poem written next to my head, I saw movement in the dark corner. I squinted to see through gaps in the crowd. Big brown eyes were watching me. Her body turned away from the stage. Full lips turned up slowly when our eyes met. It was the woman from the hospital. From Jasmine's room. She was leaning against the wall on her shoulder. Did she know someone in the band? If so, she was not watching the show. She was watching me.

I pushed my way behind people, walking along the back wall. My feet lead me in her direction almost by instinct. As if she threw a rope around my waist and was reeling me in. The room was so loud I had to lean in close to speak to her.

"I have been looking for you." I said. She scanned the room then her eyes landed back on me. Her lips opened, ready for words but nothing came out. "You were at the hospital, right?"

She nodded slowly. "I was."

"Why were you there? And how did you leave without any of the cameras seeing you?"

Her eyes glinted as a laugh escaped her luscious mouth. The amused expression on her face made me furl my brow. She looked at me like I was a toy, and she was a cat. "I was working." She huffed.

"I have not seen you there before." Instinct told me to stand tall over her, but the booming music forced me to lean closer to her ear. She did not flinch as I got closer. Instead, she studied me through her thick lashes.

"I would not be good at my job if I was seen." She smiled with teeth this time.

"What does that mean?" I braced myself against the wall when I was knocked into by a man moving through the crowd. That time she took one step back. Keeping her body away from impact. Part of the man's drink spilled onto the toe of my converse sneakers. I groaned and saw her smile slightly out of the corner of my eyes.

The crowd hollered as the song ended. I clapped my support for Dante. They were halfway through their set. When I glanced back towards the wall, she was gone again. I found myself distracted during the rest of the show as I scanned the crowd for my mystery woman. Maybe she is an undercover cop or spy. No, my life could never be interesting enough to meet a gorgeous international spy. There obviously is something unusual about her. It is more than just being mysterious. Every word out of her mouth felt like half-truth. A professional highly trained in the art of seduction. That woman spoke three sentences to me and that was all it took. I was hooked. Desperate to continue our conversation. To learn everything there is to know about her.

Most of the crowd cleared out after the live music ended. Songs shuffled from a digital jukebox mounted on the wall. I joined Dante and Nina at a table with a large plate of cheese fries in the middle. I rolled a fry in my fingers until it got cold. My eyes scanned the dark corners of the room and checked the door every time someone walked in.

"Are you looking for someone?" Dante smacked my arm causing beer to spill on my chin.

"Sorta. I was talking to this woman earlier and she just disappeared." Nina squeezed Dante's arm and gave me a cheeky grin.

"Did you approach her first?" Nina asked.

I emptied my beer bottle and placed it on the table. "Is it so hard to believe I would approach someone? I have swagger."

"No one says swagger anymore." Nina responded. I stuck out my tongue at her like we were in grade school. Dante reached back and grabbed two beers from the server's tray. He traded her for our empties. His bushy dark eyebrows bounced while he flashed a cheeky smile then placed a full beer in front of me and tapped the top with his own.

"Did you get her number?" He kissed Nina's cheek and took a swig of his beer.

"I didn't even get her name." Nina's jaw fell open. "She only said three sentences to me."

"I think I hooked Nina after three sentences." Dante bragged.

Nina rolled her eyes. "I remember it a bit different. You gave me a bad pick-up line. I thought you were cheesy." She rubbed his arm over his newest tattoo. A gerbera daisy. I was a jackass for teasing him last month for the flower choice. Not realizing it was Nina's favorite. "I still think you're cheesy, but now I like it."

"Blame my Italian older brothers they taught me to pick up girls growing up in New Jersey."

Dante's brothers would have probably done a better job than I had. It just occurred to me that I had a woman cornered in the dark at the back of a dive bar. I took a big gulp of my beer. "I think I came on too strong. I was asking a lot of questions."

"Dude, it's not supposed to be like a job interview." Dante chuckled. "I know you are out of practice," I responded to that with my middle finger. "But you are supposed to be charming and get her to talk about herself. Be interested without looking desperate."

"Didn't you practically beg Nina to go on a date with you?"

"Yes, and I'd do it again." He moved her braids aside to kiss her neck. I turned my head not wanting to stare at their PDA. I stopped mid swig of my beer. Long wavy hair hung over the back of a leather jacket. I recognized her even from behind. She was leaving. Had she been in the bar the whole time? I stood up abruptly from my chair catching the bottle before it fell over.

"Guys I gotta go."

"It's still early." Dante said into his beer.

"I have something in the morning." I pulled a twenty out of my wallet and threw it on the table. "Great show man. It was nice to see you again, Nina."

I rushed out the door as they were shouting goodbyes at my back. I checked to my left and only saw a group of smokers. My apartment was to my right. *Please be right. Please be right.* Halfway down the block I saw a woman in a leather jacket walking under a streetlight. I bolted. When I reached her, I cleared my throat loudly. She had the strangest expression on her face. One of complete misbelief as if I was the one that vanished and reappeared.

"You left before we could finish our conversation." I panted.

She blinked rapidly. Her thick lashes shading the moonlight from her eyes. They were so dark I couldn't see the pupils. She paused with her mouth open before responding. "The bar was too crowded."

"Can I walk with you? I promise I am not a stalker." Something about that made her smile. "If it makes you feel better, you can walk me home. I am just a few blocks ahead. Then you don't have to tell me where you live."

"How do you know I am not a stalker?" She tucked her hair behind her ear and peeked at me from the side. She might be the most beautiful woman I have ever seen.

"I am willing to take that chance." Her posture loosened as she chuckled. I took a step to see if she would follow. Lucky for me, she did. "I'm Jimi."

"Hi Jimi."

This beautiful woman is really going to make me work here. I just need to imagine what Dante's brothers would say and do the opposite. Get to know her without interrogating. *Don't be a dork, Jimi.*

"Ok, you don't want to give me your name. I get it. I'm a stranger. Will you at least tell me why you were at the hospital?" That was not as smooth as I would have liked. She probably thinks I am a cop.

"I was there to see another patient. I needed space to gather my emotions and just wandered into that little girls room." She put her hands in her back pockets, and I noticed she didn't have a purse or any sign that there was a phone on her. I wanted to ask who she was visiting, but I reminded myself it was not a job interview, and she had no reason to trust me.

"I work there."

"I gathered that by the scrubs."

Idiot. "Have you heard Virtuous Limbo before?" I changed the subject.

"Who?"

"The band performing tonight." She shook her head at me. Her hair was so thick and perfect I wanted to reach out and submerge my fingers in it. Every cell in my body wanted to pull her close and feel those lips pressed against mine.

I had to dodge a man staring at his phone. It pulled my attention away from her only for a second when she said, "You know someone in the band." It was not a question, but more of a statement. Indicating she saw me when I was sitting at the table with Dante and Nina.

"Yeah, my friend Dante." I shivered from a cold breeze. How was she not bothered by the chill in only a leather jacket? I regretted not wearing something warmer. The news has been blasting concerns of an early winter all week. "We met in college."

"At medical school?"

"Yeah." I shoved my hands into my jacket pockets.

"Is he also a Nurse?"

Part of me wished she assumed I was a doctor. I have been happy not pursuing a PHD up until this point. A women as beautiful as her could get the attention of every successful man in the city. She probably had her pick of rich men able to pamper her.

"He dropped out after a couple years, but we remained roommates." I cleared my throat and considered how to change the subject. "I am still in the program towards Nurse Practitioner. Hopefully less than a year. What do you do for work that had you at SGCH so late?"

Her eyes watched each step she took on the stained sidewalk. She was so smooth on her feet that they made no sound. She inhaled a deep breath before answering.

"Hospice."

"Oh. That must be rough." I frowned.

"Let's not talk about it." She mirrored my hands and tucked them into the pockets of her jacket.

"Of course." We went through the small stuff quickly. She never stayed on one subject for long. I learned neither of us have any siblings. When I probed about her parents, she clenched her jaw and asked to change the subject. I didn't push. I assume her childhood is not something she wants to dwell in.

Every time I made her laugh, I wanted to kiss her. I found it extremely distracting. Is it normal to want to kiss someone so soon after meeting them? It's impossible for someone to be this perfect. She must be married or a serial killer.

The glass doors of my building became visible as we neared. We talked for a good fifteen minutes, and I feel I still know nothing about her. Judging by her sly smile, she wants it that way. Although I don't feel her pushing me away. I feel her being intrigued by me. Even though I have yet to say anything impressive. I paused walking and she stopped, turning to face me.

"This is my building." I waved a hand behind me. Her smile faded. I wanted to kiss the corners of her mouth and wish for its return. "Can I call you? Maybe we can get coffee sometime."

A couple was walking towards us. I reached out to pull her aside, but she moved quickly before they slammed into her. They paid no mind to almost bumping into her, caught in their own conversation. "I don't have a phone." She said with her back now pressed against the brick of my building. Who doesn't have a phone?

"We could meet in Bryant Park and walk to a coffee shop."

"I don't drink coffee." She frowned. No phone. No coffee. She is really making me work. Which I will gladly do to spend more time with her.

"Ok. I will bring coffee for myself to drink in front of you. We can just walk around the park and people watch." I am running out of ways to ask her out.

She laughed. "That I can do."

"How about Tuesday at 11:00am?" My face warmed when she nodded. "Will you tell me your name?"

Strangely she stared up as if her name was written in the night sky. I studied her perfect olive skin in the moonlight. I could have sworn she wasn't wearing makeup. That her skin was perfectly smooth and her lashes that thick. Her dark brown eyes met mine and I took a step closer. She didn't move back. I took another step, and she tilted her head to look up at me. Her eyes were inviting. I am not usually this bold, but then I took a shot of gin that was followed by three beers. I leaned an inch closer. She spoke snapping me out of a daze.

"I will tell you my name if you show up on Tuesday." She said with a coy smile. That smile might be the death of me. It burned something fierce in my chest. Like a fire had been lit after waiting for the logs to dry from years of rain.

"I'll be there." I placed a hand on her waist and leaned down. I heard her breath quicken, but she leaned into me. I wanted to be brave and go for her lips, but I settled for her cheek and pressed a soft kiss to her skin. Her smooth skin that did not bite like the cold air around us. Instead, it was warm against my mouth. I might be lingering a few seconds longer than a typical cheek kiss.

When I pulled away, I noticed she had a hand over the spot where I kissed. Like she wanted to seal in my touch. Like she craved me as much as I did her. Our eyes burned into each other. Exchanging no words out loud. Just a mutual longing. The first link of a chain forming between us. I cleared my throat and turned away. She finally lowered her hand leaving a closed smile on her face.

I entered the code for my buildings door and walked backwards. Not wanting to take my eyes off her. Wishing I had gone for her lips instead. She gave me a small wave and mouthed "good night" as the door shut. I gave her a smile far too big to look cool and turned towards the elevator. After pressing the button, I turned back. She was already gone.

8
Reaper

When I was in his apartment before, I noticed the scent of bergamot and citrus. A mixture of lotion, candles, and the large bowl of fruit that always seems to be fully stocked. It clung to his clothes creating a personalized cologne. The scent has lingered in my nose ever since he approached me at the bar. Then it almost overtook my senses when he leaned in close and pressed his lips to my cheek. I almost vanished away that second. Ran away to the nearest rooftop. I felt it. Felt him. His warm soft lips pressed against me. *How is this possible? A human touching a reaper.* It was crazy enough that he saw me and spoke to me, but touch. That has never happened before. At least I have never heard it from a reaper. Maybe it does happen, and they choose to keep it a secret. Fear of it being taken away like a gift mailed to the wrong person. The need for connection is not just a human thing. Reapers are curious beings. We can form friendships. I have met many reapers that I visit from time to time. In a way I have romantic exes. Though no feelings were hurt with our parting. We mutually mimicked acts of lust out of curiosity and nothing more.

Most reapers are not prudes. We have seen everything. *Everything.* I have been known to watch people have sex every now and then. Even reapers have preferences. I have seen so much violence that I am thrilled to find a couple truly making love. Passion, that's what I want. There's no passion between reapers if we try to be intimate. We lack connection and it feels artificial. Somehow our ability to feel pleasure is even lessoned. Another curse when Death created us. Keeping us from getting swept up in pleasure and forgetting our purpose. A constant reminder we are not human, and this world was not made for us.

When Jimi placed a hand on my waist and kissed my cheek, I had never felt anything like that before. Warmth grew all over my body and I tingled inside. It was like having a thousand hands touch me for the first time. I was grateful that I chose this beautiful body. I heard his heartbeat race when he looked at me. Such a strong heartbeat. I wanted to place my ear to his chest and drink in the sounds.

He was asleep now in a tangle of sheets on his bed. A poster hung on his wall with Korean calligraphy. I stood in the middle of his living room trying to read it. The Word of the Wind by Mah Jonggi. I rocked on my heels, reciting the beautiful words inside my head. I became painfully aware of my surroundings when footsteps sounded outside his apartment door. *I shouldn't be here*. The cat stirred and he shifted in bed. I should have left, but I froze for three seconds too long. His sleepy eyes opened, and he jolted an arm out to turn on his lamp. I had jumped onto the roof across the street by the time the light came on. From there I watched him look around his room before turning the light back off. That was close.

See you in three days, Jimi.

Bryant Park was not busy at 11am on a Tuesday, but I chose a bench that was out of the view of the yoga class and blocked by a wall of trees. Jimi would appear to be talking to himself. I owed it to him to avoid making him look as crazy as possible.

I studied myself and realized I was wearing the same outfit when he last saw me days ago. What are people wearing in NYC these days? Layers because of the unusually cold October weather the news had been talking about. But this is a date. I should wear a dress. That's typical among human females. At least now they are not pared with a hat or corset. Modern clothing is much more comfortable. I kept the leather jacket but materialized a long grey maxi dress underneath. Something I saw in a store window last week.

I checked the time at a nearby bank then quickly returned to the bench. The inability to wear a watch was another gift from Death. I could mimic the look of one on my wrist, but it would not work. The watch hands would appear frozen, or the digital numbers fade to nothing. The eldest reapers claim we live outside space and time. That time is for the living. Seen as a gift by our creator. You would think having endless time would be a great gift, but we are just shadows, our time has no purpose.

"I was afraid you wouldn't show." Jimi walked towards me with a single coffee cup in his hand and a white paper bag in the other. He had a strong walk. Lika a leading man in a movie that was either about to bend a woman backwards and kiss her or possibly grab a chair and hit someone in the back to start a fight. Everything about him felt safe. His tall stature and wide shoulders. His muscles were lean, and I considered what he would look like out of all his clothes.

I smiled and crossed my legs towards him when he sat down on the bench. Reminding myself to act normal. "You said no coffee, but I did get a couple pastries if you want one."

"They smell divine, but I already ate." The lie came out too easily, considering this is the first human I have spoken to that could hear me. I glanced around the park. A woman walked by with a dog. She probably thought Jimi was insane. Talking to an empty bench.

"So, mystery girl, where are you from?" He sipped his coffee. I knew he would ask this. I have observed thousands of dates, and they always ask the same thing. I came into existence in Africa. Modern day Ethiopia, but I cannot say that. I took my look from a few different actresses in Italy.

"Rome." I settled with.

"Wow, really?" He shifted and our knees touched. The sensation sent a shiver of heat up my body. "I have always wanted to go to Italy. You don't have an accent. How long have you been in the states?"

Lying was going to get exhausting. I needed to change the subject. "I have been here for a long time. Which one of your parents are Korean?"

He almost choked on his coffee.

"Good guess. Most people think all Asians look alike. My father is Korean. My mother is white. A *"European mutt"* she calls herself." He flashed me a bright smile and my heart speed up. A strange sensation considering I manifested this body, and it functions as an illusion. Somehow, he makes it feel real. The closer he sits to me the more this body feels solid.

I couldn't tell him that I already knew his parents' ethnicities by snooping in his apartment. He had an old graduation photo on his fridge, and I assumed it was his mom and dad. He had the Korean poster on his wall and a row of tassels hung above his front door. All clues that I recognized immediately.

Our conversation kept a steady pace. We shared our favorite places in the city, and I didn't have to lie. I told him about my favorite theaters and the seats I thought had the best views. He had a favorite donut shop in every borough of NYC. Which I found surprising since there wasn't an ounce of fat on his body.

The park was getting more crowded, and I caught a few odd looks in Jimi's direction. He didn't seem to notice. His eyes stayed on me most of the time.

"How about you walk me to the subway station." I stood from the bench. He tossed the empty cup into the trash bin and held out his hand.

"Lead the way." His smile was sweet in a way that would bring light to a dark situation. I can see why he became a nurse. The energy around him was pure and joyful. I slid my hand into his and interlaced our fingers together. My breath caught at the sight. Of holding his hand like it was normal. "Have I earned your name yet?"

I smiled and lifted my gaze from our hands to his eyes. I thought about this question earlier in the day. It was inevitable that he would ask my name. The only name that stuck out to me was a shortened version of the first name of an actress I remember seeing decades ago. I shaped the angle of my nose and curve of my cheekbones after her.

"Mila."

"Mila. I should have known it would be something beautiful." Jimi squeezed my hand. I pointed in the direction of a subway station, and we began walking. It was difficult to keep him from swaying his hand and looking like a fool. I had to press my body close to him to avoid being walked into by pedestrians. Surely the sight of someone passing through me like a ghost would freak him out.

On the real tough days, the days spent collecting the souls of civilians caught in a war being fought for greed or religion, I like to stand in the middle of a crowded sidewalk and let everyone pass through me. I plead to Death to let me feel something. It never works. Their bodies pass through me like I don't exist. I guess in their world, I don't.

I wanted to keep talking to him. Forever if I could. Unfortunately, a summon tugged inside me and I groaned through my teeth.

"What's wrong?" Jimi said as I pulled him into an alley.

"I have to go." I hoped people walking by would think he was just talking on the phone. I turned him until his back was against the building. The last time we were this close he kissed my cheek. I felt alive then, and I wanted to have that sensation vibrate through my body again. "First I want to try something."

"Ok." he said in a deep whisper.

I scoured the area. The alley was shaded and most people walking by were too busy to look in our direction. I stepped closer to him and placed my hands on his chest. His firm muscles flexed under my fingers. He placed both hands on my hips and pulled me in until I was pressed tight against his body. "Hold still." I said leaning up on my toes. Usually, I would make my body taller, but I needed to keep the illusion that I was human. I remained the height he first saw me as. His body went stiff then relaxed as I pressed my lips against his.

He melted into me, and I tilted my head to be even closer. I've kissed other reapers, but a reapers kiss feels cold and numb. This was filled with heat and made my body ache for more. I felt the tug inside me, pulling me towards a soul collection. I frowned against his lips and pulled away. I could feel Death's grasp on me. When a reaper does not show up, they can be punished. Usually by spending time in a space that lives between the living and the afterlife. I would simply cease to exist until Death sends me back. Not wanting to risk never seeing Jimi again, I separated our bodies. His cheeks were flushed. I added a little rose color to my own to match.

"I really have to go, but I would like to see you again." I said quickly, feeling the summons grow stronger. "Tomorrow?"

"I work. Real late. Won't be off until 1:00am."

"What time do you eat dinner?" I already knew because I have been watching him for nearly five days.

"10:00pm usually." He rubbed his hand down my arm. I wanted to explore more of his touches. I wanted to see how real he could make this body feel.

"I will wait for you outside the hospital." Turning towards the subway entrance leading down into a bustling station. I need to get out of his sight before I can vanish away.

"Wait!" He yelled through a bustling crowd. Jimi took a few steps down the stairs after me, but I was already running. I round the corner and then jumped to an elderly care facility miles away in Vermont.

9
Reaper

I found myself in a very common location. The lobby of a nursing home. It smelled like disinfectant and something that I could only guess was pureed peas. I changed into a long flowy white dress. I have found older people don't react well to a woman all dressed in black showing up after they die. I walked past the front desk in the direction of the tug. Halfway down the hall was a room with a calendar held on the metal door by flower magnets. The picture on the calendar was a collage of children. The words "Grandkids 2023" framed the bottom. I sighed and walked into the dim room. A woman lay sleeping. The glow coming off her body was strong.

Dying in your sleep is always the best way to go. I moved to her side and was about to take up a seat in the empty chair when a man came up behind me. He was moving slowly with a crocheted blanket draped over his arms. He seemed older than the woman lying in the bed. I moved to the corner and just watched. The man covered her legs with the blanket and sat in the chair. He scooted it closer until his knees touched the metal frame of the bed.

"Moriah, my love." He covered her hand with both of his. "You scared me today." He pressed his forehead to his hands. I could see him stroking her paper-thin skin. The wrinkles moved like waves in the ocean. "I am not ready to let you go."

Her body stopped glowing, and I found her standing at the foot of the bed.

"We had fifty-three good years." She looked at me with no shock in her down turned eyes. I shifted awkwardly on my heels. Her shoulder's slumped when I didn't respond immediately. I opened my mouth and shut it quickly. Her grey eyes dimmed when she looked down at her husband still holding her body's hand. "Can you tell my husband Everett that I am ready to go. It's my time."

I shook my head. "I cannot."

She reached out to touch him, but her hand passed through his body. The older woman, Moriah, whimpered once with disappointment. "It took you long enough. I hated living here."

I couldn't help but laugh. "Sorry for that. It's not up to me." She moved closer towards her husband. We both noticed her chest stopped rising and the monitor beeped a steady tone. "Take my hand." I held out my hand with the eight-pointed star ring. She reached out and paused before touching me. Her eyes darted to her husband.

"How long before he joins me?"

"That's above my paygrade." My words made her scrunch her brow.

"Are you an angel?"

"I am not." I grabbed her hand and felt her soul lighten. "I am just a conduit for Death. Here to deliver you to your final resting place."

She nodded. "Do you have a name?"

It was not the first time someone asked me while they were dying, But it was the first time I had an answer.

"Mila."

"Thank you, Mila." She disappeared in a cloud of mist being pulled into my ring. Her husband, Everett, was standing. Tears ran down his sagging cheeks. A nurse rushed through the door. I moved outside the window and watched as the nurse attempted to revive her. The husband crumpled over her body, squeezing it like a life preserver.

Moriah was the last soul I could carry before needing to unload. I whispered goodbye to Moriah while standing outside the window and vanished.

The best place to unload souls is quiet and secluded. I appeared seconds later in a forest outside Wrigley Canada. It was raining and the trees were not thick enough to keep the ground dry. I left no steps in the mud as I walked, and the rain fell right through me. To match my mood, I changed into dark jeans and a black hoodie. I pulled it up over my head pretending I needed cover from the rain drops.

When I was ready, I planted my legs firm and raised my hands out in front of me. My feet barely making an imprint in the lush forest moss. A pulse vibrates off my palms. The ring warmed on my finger. Quick as a blink, a flash of Deaths form appeared quickly. A dark shadow figure towering over me with large black wings. Then it was gone. Replaced with dark smoke, and I watched it solidify into a doorway with nothing but blackness beyond it. The frame was dark marble. Smooth with rounded edges. No sign it was met to have hinges and hold a real door. It was meant to remain open. A gateway to dark void.

I always wondered what would happen if I stepped inside. Would I cease to exist? Would I arrive in the afterlife? Or would I just pass through it like water through a sieve? One by one the souls flew out of my ring and into the void. Forty souls. That was all I could carry. I asked another reaper why it was forty souls, and they had no answers for me.

I spoke every language created by man. I have seen every continent and stood on the tallest mountain peaks. I have seen childbirth, first kisses, and every crime that could be committed. The only answers I do not have are those surrounding my own purpose. Will there be an end for me or is the life of a reaper an eternity? Could we be granted a human life and get the chance to find a love like Moriah and Everett? Can I get fifty years with someone who will hold my hand when I die?

My mind went to Jimi as the door dissipated like steam before me. The seclusion of the forest felt lonelier than usual as I remembered the feeling of his hands on my body. The warmth of his kiss. The forest seemed to have woken from a stagnant silence. Wind sang through the trees and somewhere high birds were talking to each other.

I wandered through the peaceful forest for a few hours. Inviting the sounds of nature to ease my emotions. Get my head back to the base level a reaper is supposed to be at. I tried to suppress everything Jimi was making me feel, but inevitably every thought found its way back to him.

I appeared on the roof across from his apartment. He was asleep on his sofa with the Tv still on. Moving blue light lit up his face. I couldn't help myself but go to his apartment. I stood over him and breathed in the musky smell of bergamot and citrus. His cologne has become my favorite scent in the world. I leaned down and ran a hand over his jacket. I wanted to wrap it around me. To cover myself in his scent.

He was still asleep. With no human eyes on me I picked up the jacket and covered my shoulders. I closed my eyes and took a deep breath.

"How the fuck did you get in my apartment?"

I froze as Jimi's eyes pinned me to the floor. Something dropped in my stomach.

10
Reaper

Oh no. I fucked up. I am not used to the risk of being seen and I got distracted by the scent of him. Lost in the memory of his touch. Hoping it would wipe away the darkness that I bring. My mouth hung open. Hundreds of languages in my head and I can't think of the right words to say.

He stood and gripped the TV remote like the hilt of a sword pointed in my direction. I took his jacket off my shoulders and placed it back on the chair. I put my arms out in front of me like I was approaching a feral animal.

"I didn't mean to wake you." That did not sound right. I flinched.

"What does that mean?" He took a step back. His jaw tightened. "You wanted me to stay asleep?"

Yes. I thought. I wasn't ready to have this conversation. To reveal everything. To have him tell me to leave him alone forever. He was so kind and good. He brought happiness to people in the hardest times of their lives, and

I was a soldier for Death. I crept around the shadows waiting for people to die and collect their souls like trading cards. Instinct told me to leave, but I stepped closer. Only a few feet separated us. I saw his eyes dart to the cellphone sitting on the coffee table.

"I didn't want to tell you this way." These were not the right words. I could see it on his face. He was terrified of me. I can't image what he would think of me in my intimidating reaper form. With full robe and glowing eyes. I would tower over him. He probably senses the monster in me. The way his eyes narrow looking at me standing in his apartment. Jimi took a step back from the couch, keeping the front of his body angled towards me. He looked at my empty hands before he spoke again.

"Tell me what? That you are some kind of psycho stalker or burglar. Are you here to rob me? Cause look around, I am a poor nursing student living in a studio apartment." He backed up until his legs hit the foot of his bed. The commotion startled his cat, and it jumped off the bed in my direction. Animals cannot see or sense reapers, so I didn't flinch.

"I am not human." I said each word slowly. The cat passed through my legs like I was nothing more than a shadow. Jimi started shaking the remote at my legs.

"What the fuck?" He sat abruptly on the bed. It was practically a fall, as if his legs gave out under him. "Are you a fucking ghost? Am I going crazy? Have I been talking to a fucking ghost?"

I moved slowly towards the bed. I made sure to walk and not just vanish or reappear. He would probably check himself into a hospital if I did. He let me approach and I sat on the edge of the bed the furthest from him I could get without falling off.

"I am not a ghost." He put the remote down and scrubbed his face with his hands.

"This is insane. I am going insane." He repeated it a few times. I wanted to reach out and touch him. I wanted to bring back his smile and feel human again. I needed it. I needed him.

"What I am has many names around the world, depending on culture, religion, and other folklore. You probably know me as a reaper." I spoke looking at the floor. Tension was building in my chest with each second he didn't respond. He turned slowly. His dark eyes going wide. The color of his face paled, and his shoulders slumped. "Say something, please."

"You are death?"

Obviously, he would think a reaper is the cause of death. That we are the ones to end lives. He probably thinks I am here to take him That I am no different than a cat playing with a mouse before they eat it.

"No. I am a conduit for Death. You can say Death is my boss in a way."

A frown filled his face. "Are you here to take me?"

As expected, he will now wonder if he is about to die every time he sees me. That look of attraction will be filled with fear and disgust. I shake my head. "No. I have no indication your time is near."

He shifted to face me directly. He pressed his lips together. I could tell he was holding back words. "You were in the hospital. Are you going to take Jasmine soon?"

I have never had a conversation about death with a human before. Well, a live human. There must be rules I am breaking. Will Death show up and stop me. Would they take Jimi early if he gained knowledge about reapers? I took a deep breath and tried to feel the world around me. I sensed the usual reapers in the area. They were moving around like usual. None of them in my direction. I rubbed my ring and felt my connection to Death themself. They were still there, but I felt no tug.

"I was in the hospital for someone else." Our eyes met. Oh, how I wanted to kiss him again. Heat burned inside me, low in my abdomen. How is he making me feel so human? He caught me staring at his lips and I shuttered away.

"What do you want from me?" he whispered into the heavy air of the studio. Thickening with everything unsaid.

"Nothing." *Lie.* I wanted everything from him. His shoulders eased. "I have been around for centuries, Jimi. I have seen every corner of the developed earth. And you-" There was a lump in my thought. An odd sensation I have not felt before. I swallowed it down. "And you are the first and only human, alive, to have ever seen me. To touch me. I don't know how it's possible or why it's you. That's the truth."

Jimi stood slowly and walked to the middle of the studio. He ran a hand through his hair that was already messy from sleep. He opened his mouth a few times to speak but shut it quickly.

"What you're saying is crazy." He paced in a small circle.

"I am sorry. I can leave you alone." *Please say no. Say you need me. Say you want me.* Then he stepped towards me, and I shot up to my feet. Desperation melting off my body. *Touch me. Kiss me.* My eyes were begging. He stopped close enough that our toes touched. My breath caught when he placed a hand on my arm and rubbed it down until our fingers touched.

"How are you not real? I can see you." He stroked my arm. "I can feel you."

I leaned slightly into his touch. Grateful for the pressure of his hand. "I have no answers for you."

He brought his other hand up to cup my cheek and I practically whimpered with my eyes shut. He brushed his thumb over my bottom lip. His eyes were filled with words he was not saying.

"I don't see how you are not human."

I smirked against his thumb and vanished before him. He cursed and I appeared behind him with my arms wrapped around his waist. Jimi tried to spin in my arms and face me, but I vanished again. I watched his search for me while I hid in a dark corner. I made my body solid black like a shadow. He spun around calling my name. The fear had seemed to fade and replaced with worry.

"Mila!" There was panic in his voice. "Mila, this is really weird. How do I know you are still here." I laughed and it made him jump in the direction of the sound. I appeared on his bed laying down on my stomach with my legs waving in the air. I gave him a cheeky smile. "What the fuck. You're like a Cheshire cat."

Despite his shot he was taking this better than I had hoped. Jimi appeared amused by my party tricks.

"I never thought of that. I do love Alice in Wonderland."

"You watch movies?" He sat back on the bed.

"I watch movies, but I prefer plays. I read books, when I can. I have read The Adventures of Alice in Wonderland in three languages." I boasted.

He lay down on the bed on his side, facing me. I rolled until our faces were inches apart. His expression was hard to read. He focused on what I was saying. Awkwardly, I continued. "Theaters are easy. I can stand in the back or sit in an empty seat. But I cannot interact with objects with human eyes watching. That's how you get conspiracies about ghosts. Too many movement sightings will get a reaper reprimanded." I propped my head up on my palm. Some of my hair fell onto my face. Jimi brushed it behind my ear. I closed my eyes at his touch and resisted leaning into it. *If I cling to him too fast, will it scare him away? I am already hooked.* I heard him sigh.

"How does your boss reprimand a reaper?" His palm lingered on the side of my head. Looking up, I found the familiar warmth in his dark eyes.

"We are sent to a void for however long they decide." My hand fidgeted with the soft fabric of his comforter. Such a human habit. Nervousness was not something reapers usually struggled with. I felt my stomach tingle like something was flying around inside. All of this is entirely new. My hips scooted an inch closer to him. Jimi ran his hand down my arm and rested it on my waist.

"Will you be punished for talking to me?"

Will I be punished? Jimis brows were knitting together. It was a question I had no answer for. Part of me was relieved to hear worry in his voice. He cared if I disappeared. This sweet and sexy man cared for me. Me, a reaper whose business is death and nothing more.

"I don't know." I shrugged. "I have never heard of it before. A human able to see or touch a reaper. Like I said before, it's different than anything I have experienced. Different than how other things feel."

His hand moved to my back and pulled me in closer until our bodies were flush with each other. "How so?"

Our hands were roaming now. Exploring the silhouettes of each other's bodies. I tucked my face against his neck and breathed in his cologne. My hand roamed up his chest admiring the firm muscle under the fabric. "When you touch me, I feel real." His hand slipped under my shirt and traced up my spine. My body reacted by warming inside as he trailed up my back.

"How are you not real?" He moved his hand from my shirt and grabbed my jaw, tilting my face towards his. We both paused. Heat burned low in me. His cock stiffened in his pants, and I pushed body against it. His lips met mine softly. Moving with the rhythm of a somber song. A small moan filled my mouth. I had never made that sound before. It sparked something in him, and our mouths opened. Tongues twisting together. I moved my body against his with desperate need. His hands tightened in my hair on both sides of my head as he rolled me onto my back.

We kissed feverishly, grinding our bodies together. I willed my jacket to disappear. He sat up, kneeling between my legs. His unkept hair fell above his eyes.

He tensed. "What the fuck? Where did your jacket go?

"Um, sorry I should have warned you." I leaned up on my elbows. "I could put it back if it freaks you out." I paused. "Or I can make the rest of my clothes disappear."

Jimi's eyes darkened. The twitch of his cock against me told me he was more interested in the second option.

"You can do that?" I nodded. He scrubbed his face, and mumbled into his palm, "This is crazy. I must be going crazy." He took a deep breath and steadied himself with hands on either side of my body pressing into the bed. "I guess just warn me next time." He nipped a kiss on the tip of my nose. A simple gesture of affection that was foreign to me. It was playful and had me capturing his lips for an equally quick kiss.

I nodded. Jimi leaned over and kissed me again. Deeper. Letting us live in this moment of confessions. He broke the kiss to say, "And for the record, I prefer to take your clothes off myself."

11
Jimi

This was insane. I was acting insane. Kissing and rubbing the body of a woman I barely met. And she is not even a woman. Not entirely. Well, I am not sure how it all works. She's a reaper. I wonder if she considers herself a woman. Her lips are so soft and her hands in my hair feel real. The thunder in my chest sure feels real. Something has woken, and with her this close it will never slumber again.

She has me nestled between her legs and is grinding up against me. I am so hard. I have to reach down and adjust myself. The head of my cock slightly poking out of the top of my sweatpants. Pressing onto her feels like a dream. Like I made her up from a list of perfect things.

Her body is vibrating. I think actually vibrating. I wonder if she can feel that too. The sputtering tension pulling our bodies closer. When I break off our kiss and peek at her face there is an expression of sadness.

"Are you okay?" I ask against her lips.

Mila kissed me softly and sighed. "You're effecting me in ways I have never felt." I smiled at that. "I don't know what our connection is, but I have never felt-" She trailed off.

I wanted to hear the rest of the sentence, but I also wanted to rip her clothes off. I lifted her black t-shirt and kissed her stomach. "Go on."

"Alive." Her voice shook. "I have never felt actually alive."

"You feel alive now?" I slid my hand to the side of her breast and trailed over her nipple with my thumb. I felt it stiffen through the fabric. She nodded and my question and shut her eyes briefly. This is the start of a greater conversation, but for now I need to feel more of her.

With that I pushed her shirt up until she let me slip it over her head. She had on a black lace bra. My eyes went wide taking in the sight of her olive skin and full breasts. The bra looked like it was made for her. Hugging every curve with scalloped edges of lace.

"Did you make that for me?" I traced the edge of the bra with my fingertips. She nodded with a coy smile. "I love it." I slid a thumb under the lace and circled her nipple. Moving the fabric aside I replaced it with my mouth. When I sucked on a nipple her back arched. I moaned onto her skin. She squeezed her legs around my waist, and I considered asking her to make her clothes disappear. But this was a new experience for her, and it should not be rushed. It should be savored.

I needed more. I needed to taste her.

Kneeling between her legs I took my shirt off, throwing it to the wood floor. She leaned up on her elbows. Her face was unreadable. I froze, contemplating if she wanted this as much as me.

"Is this your, um, first ya know?" I nodded between her legs. Her smile was almost wicked with a chuckle behind it.

"With a human, yes."

My hands turned to fists for a brief second. "What do you mean human?" I took a half step back. "You fuck a vampire or something?"

Mila fell back onto the bed and put her hands over her face. "Are we really discussing this now?"

"Holy fuck! A vampire!" A million images flashed in my head of every vampire movie or Tv show I have seen in my life.

"No, Jimi. Vampires and other monsters aren't real." She laughed and a weird sense of relief filled me. "I've only been with other reapers. Reapers get bored, and curious." She raised an eyebrow. I nodded slowly. "But no reaper has ever felt like this with me." She motioned between us. I leaned my body closer. Fear and worry melting away with the warmth in her eyes.

Her palm traced down my stomach. This time I think I vibrated when she cupped my hard cock through the fabric. My head fell back, and I gritted my teeth. This is insane. There must be consequences if I fuck a reaper. Death could show up mid thrust and kill me. We need to figure out this connection first. Before we risk it all, but a little taste couldn't hurt.

"Let me worship you." I unzipped her jeans and tugged them down to her knees. She had on matching black lace underwear. I bit my bottom lip. "In case you get banished for this. I want to make it worth it and give you the biggest orgasm any reaper has ever had."

Her tough exterior melted, and she let out a low whimper as I tugged the pants and underwear off completely. When I threw them to the floor they vanished. A million questions flashed in my head, but they floated away when I took in the sight before me. She lay in just the lace bra, the rest of her bare. I gripped her ankles and bent her knees. I cannot wait another second. First, I kissed the inside of her knees, then I kissed her thighs. I was caught off guard when she whispered "Oh no."

"What? Is something wrong?" I said between kissing her body.

"I'm not sure. I feel like I am dripping. Down there." She was covering her eyes with her arm like she was ashamed.

"That's never happened before?" Mila shook her head. I placed my mouth hovering over her folds. They glistened with her arousal. I stuck my tongue out and licked from bottom to top. She tasted like salted honey. Her body tensed and I could feel her legs try to press shut. "You look normal to me. Actually," I licked her again. "you look perfect. Try to relax. Let me pleasure you."

Her body eased and she let her legs fall open. I spread her open with my fingers allowing me to take her clit fully in my mouth. I licked it and rolled my tongue around it. Every flinch of her body was encouragement. Mila was gripping the comforter with both hands. She was so wet. I could feel her need. I needed it too. I dipped my tongue into her, letting my thumb take over playing with her clit. She moaned my name. I thrust my tongue as deep as I could get. Her inner walls clench around it. I could tell she was already close.

I replaced my tongue with two fingers and increased my speed. I licked her clit, and she bucked under me. I added a third finger, and she bucked against my mouth. With my empty hand I held her stomach down, keeping her on the bed. She released my name on a scream. Her body shook and I lapped my tongue faster.

Fuck, she tasted good. If I died between her legs, it would be worth it.

Her climax fought against my fingers as she leaked onto me. I didn't remove my mouth until the flexing stopped and she sunk deeper onto the bed. I sat up with my fingers lingering inside of her. Our eyes met and she appeared to have just run a mile. Panting and cheeks flushed. Just how I wanted her. When I slipped my fingers out, she flinched at the sudden emptiness. I couldn't stop staring at her brown eyes and the satisfaction that filled them. Mila shut her legs. Locking me out.

"Something wrong?" I said getting up to grab a towel from the bathroom. My cock was straining hard against my pants.

"Nothing is wrong. Everything is too right." She said rolling onto her side.

"Then why do you look sad all of a sudden?" I washed my hands in the sink and splashed water on my chin. Ignoring my toothbrush. Not wanting to lose the taste of her on my tongue. When I entered the room, she was already dressed in the same outfit as before and standing up. I spread my arms out in confusion. "Leaving?"

The pink was fading from her cheeks. The lust in her eyes was replaced by panic. I could feel her pulling away from me. Emotionally and physically. She opened her mouth and shut it a few times before answering me.

"I am not supposed to be able to feel," She pointed to the bed still crumpled, "that. I am a reaper. We have limitations on our emotions and sensations. Every day in this world is a reminder that we are not human. That this world was not made for us, and we are just servants to Death."

I walked up grab her. I wanted to hold her close, but she stepped away. No, she teleported it seemed. Jumped back four feet in a blink. My shoulders dropped.

"There must be an answer why we are connected like this. Mila, I feel it too. Like you were made for me." Her jacket appeared on her body, and I frowned. Confirmation she hasn't decided to stay.

"Before I risk your life, I need answers." Mila appeared before me and placed a soft kiss on my lips and vanished. I stood in the middle of my studio replaying the moments since I met her. My feet didn't move until that odd sensation, that vibration in my chest, faded to a low hum. I moved closer to the large window and studied the skyline. I'm frustrated, I can't call or text her. I'm worried, I will never see her again. But mostly I'm confused. Am I falling for a woman that is an instrument of Death themselves? Am I chasing a dream that could end in a nightmare?

12
Mila

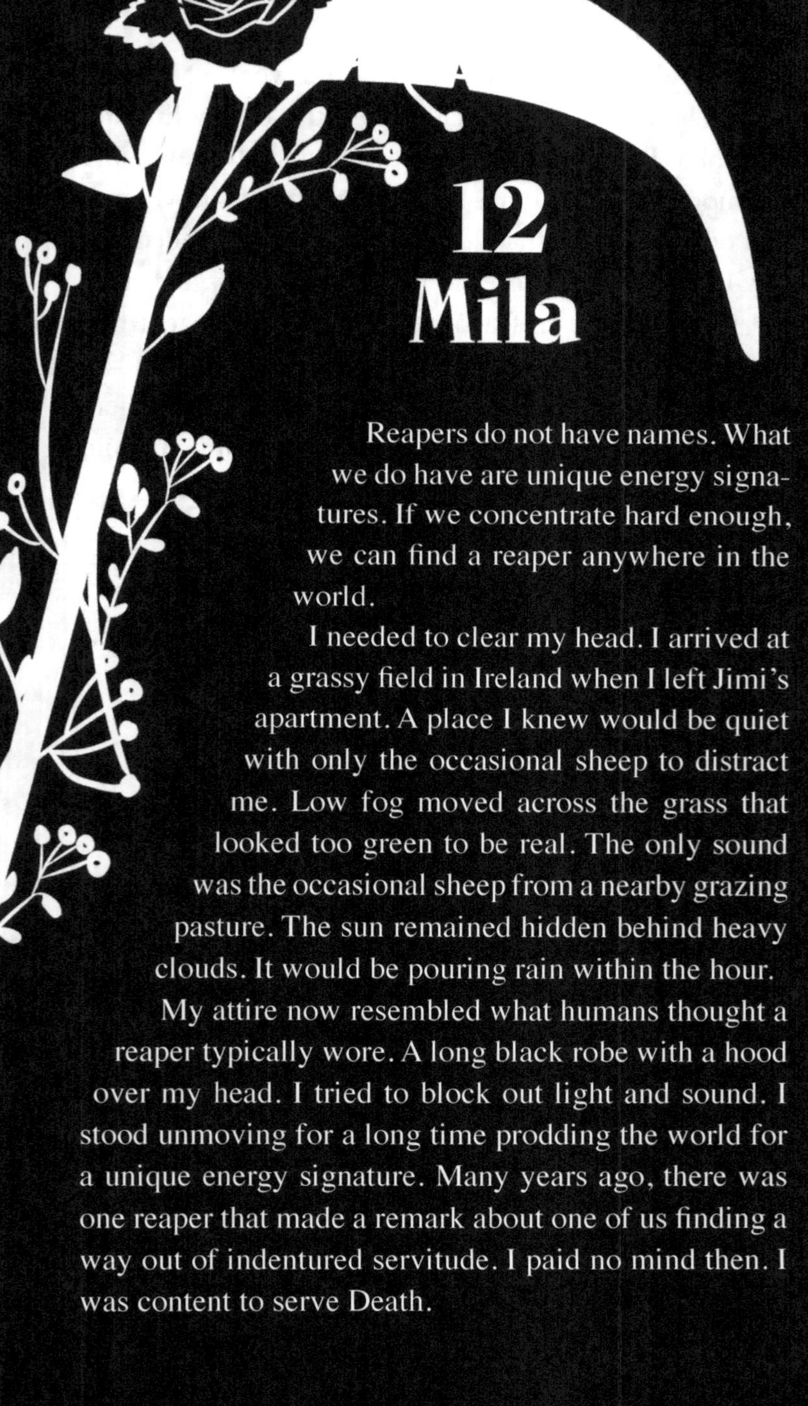

Reapers do not have names. What we do have are unique energy signatures. If we concentrate hard enough, we can find a reaper anywhere in the world.

I needed to clear my head. I arrived at a grassy field in Ireland when I left Jimi's apartment. A place I knew would be quiet with only the occasional sheep to distract me. Low fog moved across the grass that looked too green to be real. The only sound was the occasional sheep from a nearby grazing pasture. The sun remained hidden behind heavy clouds. It would be pouring rain within the hour. My attire now resembled what humans thought a reaper typically wore. A long black robe with a hood over my head. I tried to block out light and sound. I stood unmoving for a long time prodding the world for a unique energy signature. Many years ago, there was one reaper that made a remark about one of us finding a way out of indentured servitude. I paid no mind then. I was content to serve Death.

Wind whipped the tall grass around me. I closed my eyes to focus on the reaper's connections. They felt like little strands of silver thread tying us together. I began to feel reapers everywhere. I picked through them like sifting through sand, until one stood out. East of Africa mainland on a small island. The Seychelles I realized.

"There you are." I whispered to the wind.

I was not surprised to find the reaper on the beach. Beaches are a favorite spot to watch the world shift amongst our kind. Something about the sunrise felt like home no matter where in the world we are. The sun was rising now sending a blend of oranges and pinks to dance on the waves. I walked up to the side of the reaper. She was in female form with long hair in golden box braids. Her skin was warm brown and smooth. We both have a habit of trying to blend into the area where we are working. She even made her clothes match the native people. A long wrap dress hung stagnant even with the wind. I remained in my black robe but dropped the hood onto my shoulders.

I flashed a closed smile. "Reaper." Spoken as a greeting.

"Reaper." She smiled back. "When did you arrive? This is such a small island. Death rarely has more than one of us here."

"I came here looking for you." I motioned to an empty bistro table. The café on the beach had not opened yet and not a soul was around. We took up two chairs across from each other. I wasn't sure where to begin and glanced down at my hands.

"How are you, reaper." She asked. I could have sworn she made her facial features soften with the question.

"I am doing good." I wished I could eat or drink something to distract my hands. *Could Death hear our conversations? Do they already know what happened?* "I have been thinking about a story you told me centuries ago. The one about the reaper that stopped being a reaper and found a way to be something more. Something human."

They blinked at me and gave me a moment to explain myself. I just swallowed my words waiting to see if she was open to the conversation I was starting.

"Are you tired of this life, young reaper?"

"I would not call what we have 'a life'." I crossed my arms. I rubbed the underside of my ring. Which felt more like a tiny shackle now. Once a sign of honor and duty.

She sunk into her chair and peered at the sun. It had fully risen over the horizon and made the white sand beach glow with light. "We will be rewarded. That is all you need to know."

"Rewarded how?" I slouched. "What if I wanted to pick my own reward? What if I wanted to live a human life?"

"Human lives are short." She said flatly.

"It would be worth it." There was a lull in our conversation. She scanned my face trying to evaluate my thoughts. I leaned on to the table. "Please, tell me everything you know. I have found something worth wanting to be human for. Worth fighting for."

"Worth going against Death for?" She snapped.

"Yes." I whispered. Her eyes went wide understanding the meaning behind the single word. We talked once about the one thing we would want to experience if we were human. After the list of amazing foods and exciting adventures we both agreed on one thing. *Love*. Love is the greatest gift given to humans. Not a greedy love or a jealous love. A love without conditions or expectations. A love that is rare. When it seems like the whole world worked to bring two people together. That is the love we both desired.

"Reapers can't love. We only obsess. It can only be one sided." The reaper placed a hand over mine. My eyes followed the numbing touch. I felt pressure but there was nothing more. No heat or vibration. Not like when Jimi touches me.

I shook my head. I might regret speaking this aloud. This reaper might communicate with Death and get Jimi killed? Would Death do that? Did I find a glitch and they would correct it by taking him from me? Or will I just be thrown in a void? An endless darkness. Never to return to earth. The salty air was suffocating. I forced myself to be honest. To take a chance that this reaper believed in friendship. In a bond between us. "He sees me. He can hear me. Maybe it is the kind of rare love we talked about."

"What you are saying can't be true. Death would not allow it." Her brow furled. She moved her hand from mine and was tapping her fingers on the table but made no sound. I could have sworn her eyes went one shade lighter until they were hazel with gold flecks.

"Maybe whatever is happening is out of Deaths control." I spat. We both paused to stare at each other. I took a deep breath that was completely unnecessary. I went to speak but the reaper interrupted me.

"There was a reaper before you were around. They claimed to have met an Angel. A real Angel. The Angel claimed we could become human; all we must do is claim our assigned soul." She turned to look out at the beach before returning to meet my eyes. A million questions flashed in my head. *Our assigned souls?* I suddenly felt empty.

"We don't have souls." I said shaking my head.

This is not where I expected this conversation to go. What does Death do with the souls of reapers? Where would they keep them? A bird's caw snapped me from my spiraling thoughts.

"That is because Death sent us to earth without them." My chest beat in reaction to a clanging sound. A man flipping up the wood awning of the café and propped it up on a metal bar. He was humming a tune. Neither of us turned our heads. There was no worry that he could see us. "Can your human see all reapers? This special human that you believe could be," she paused, "a very rare kind of love."

"I don't know. He seemed completely shocked when he found out what I was." My eyes darted around the beach.

"Maybe I should pay him a visit and see." she said with a slight smile tugging the corners of her mouth. How would Jimi react to seeing another reaper? Perhaps I am taking this too far. Perhaps she will show up in a form more desirable than mine and he will want to pursue her instead. This might all blow up in my face. *Unless*, I thought. *Unless I can become human.* If I can be with him completely and not under Deaths orders.

"How does a reaper claim their soul?" It was the only answer I needed. If I could be with Jimi, grow old with Jimi, live with Jimi. All costs would be worth it. A short human life would be worth it. Foregoing my reaper reward would be worth it.

"When you open the gateway to release the souls you have collected, you call out to your own soul. The same way you found me. You search in the darkness, in the eternal emptiness until you find the familiar vibration that is unique to you. If it enters your body, you will be stuck to whatever form you currently take. Then voila, you're human."

It took concentration to keep my feet on the ground. The idea of a life with Jimi has my head floating. Remembering the feeling of his arms around me sent heat to my cheeks.

"It seems so simple. Why don't more reapers do it?" A sluggish customer walked up to the café window to order. We both stood and strolled down the beach.

"Life is a gift. We are never given the answer to why we are chosen to be reapers and not born as humans, but to question it is to go against the creator. Death answers to someone more powerful. To defy Death is to defy the creator, and their plan. Death will punish you. I am not sure how. Maybe they will give you a shortened human life with illness and suffering. Maybe you will not be at peace in the afterlife. But I am certain there will be consequences."

All it took was one night with his hands on me and I was contemplating risking a lifetime of suffering for him. If I could talk to Death. Maybe plead with them. If I could convince them that I was meant to be human. That I belonged with Jimi. *Did I belong with Jimi?* We did just meet.

"Could you visit me tomorrow in NYC? We can see if Jimi can see all reapers or if it's just me." She nodded and I placed a hand on her shoulder. I am going to take this leap. Let the reaper see Jimi. Risk them telling Death. Risk Jimi being more intrigued by her. I have this odd sensation of the ground moving under me. I mimicked a deep breath to stable myself. The reaper raised an eyebrow. Surely noticing my emotions were running high. "Thank you, friend." I nodded and vanished back to a rooftop in Manhattan. It was the middle of the night, and the Chrysler building was illuminated with a blue light. I could see Jimi asleep in his apartment. Could I slip under his covers without waking him? I took a step closer, as if I was going to float off the edge and into his arms. I felt deep tug inside. Someone was dying and I was being summoned.

13
Jimi

I hoped to see Mila when I woke up, but my apartment was empty. Not wanting to miss the opportunity to see her, I cooked at home instead of grabbing my usual bagel sandwich on my way to work. I glanced down every alley that I passed wondering if she would be hiding in the shadows.

I should be way more freaked out learning a reaper has been following me. Since the night in the hospital. That was two weeks ago. Then I saw her at the bar for Dante's show. I realize now, she was there to see me. Mila was standing in the dark corner so no one would see me talking to myself. I ran my hands through my hair. *This is crazy. I must be crazy.*

Every time I entered a room in the hospital, I scanned for her. I was completely distracted and had to push the image of her naked on my bed out of my head. Not think of the strange sensation when I touched her. Like I was complete. Like a missing part of me was found. It was 10:00pm when I got a text message from Dante. He had just finished a show nearby and wanted to meet up. He offered to bring slices of pizza. I waited in the cafeteria.

Dante walked in with a paper plate in each hand and a can of coke stuffed in each coat pocket. My stomach growled when I smelled the sauce and melted cheese. His jeans had the usual ripped knees, and I could have sworn he was wearing the same studded belt from our college days. Looking down at my pale blue scrubs I suddenly felt like I was in a costume. Dante was a bad influence in the sense that he tried on multiple occasions to convince me to walk away from medicine and pursue art. I knew there were no jobs in art and the life of a starving artist was not what I wanted. So, I settled for the life of a sleep deprived nurse that survives off vending machine snakes and food to-go.

"You're a saint." I huffed while grabbing a paper plate from him. I wasted no time taking a huge bite of the pizza. He laughed when I moaned onto the food. Raising one eyebrow as if he was holding back a comment about me getting off on a slice of pizza. He is always trying to break my empty bed streak by setting me up with one of Nina's friends.

Dante shook his head slowly. "How's life? We didn't get to talk much the other night." He cracked open his coke and took a deep gulp. Simultaneously while burping he added, "Any chicks letting your boring ass get in their pants."

That didn't take long. I rolled my eyes. "I am not boring, asshole, I'm busy." A lump sat in my throat. There was nothing I could tell him about Mila without him having me committed to the psych ward of the hospital. "I've been talking with someone, but she lives far away." *I will regret this lie later, I just know it.*

"Yeah, where?" He pulled the slice of pizza away from his mouth until a thin string of cheese stretched out. Dante snipped it with his fingers and dropped it into his mouth. His expression was urging me to give him details. I shifted in my seat. The plastic creaking under my weight. *I wonder if it's too late to back track what I said.*

Fuck. "She travels for work allot, an international flight attendant." I crammed more pizza into my mouth to stop myself from speaking. Dante's eyes went wide with excitement. *Yup, I am already regretting this.*

"That's fucking hot, man. Does she get free flights?" He had only his crust left and pointed it at me like a wand when he spoke. "Is there a romantic vacation in the near future?"

"I haven't asked. We are still getting to know each other." Understatement of the century. I was still learning about what it means to be a reaper. Still grappling with the fact reapers exist amongst other things. That she is not a real human and what I see is a projected image. Mila's words flooded my head. *She felt real with me. Only me.* I could never introduce her to my friends or my parents. We could never have normal dates in public. Fuck, would she age? She will watch me grow old and die.

"Ok dude." He pushed his empty plate aside. "I came here for a reason other than to ask if you're getting laid."

"Fuck I hope so." I laughed. Dante straightened in his chair as if starting a job interview. The formal posture caught my attention. This man only behaved this way when parents are involved. Always able to lay on the charm when needed.

He reached into his quilted puffer coat and pulled out a small leather box. He placed it on the table in front of me. We both stared at it for a moment in silence.

"I love you, man, but you're not my type." I said through a low laugh.

"It's for Nina, asshole." He opened the box. I picked it up carefully. Feeling unworthy to hold it. Inside there was a yellow gold ring with diamonds in an art deco design sitting in the center of a velvet pillow. My eyes went wide. I have no words. No way he is mature enough for marriage. We are just kids. Or we were kids. Now in our mid-twenties I suppose we should have more of our lives figured out by now. Dante clearly does not feel like he needs more time. I gulped. I was still at a loss for words. "I am going to ask her next week."

"Damn, it's gorgeous. How did you afford this?" I raised one eyebrow. "Gigs paying that well?"

"Gigs pay shit. That was my grandmother's. I had to negotiate grandchildren with my mom for her to give it to me."

"Negotiate?"

"Three years or less for the first one. And we must have at least two. If it were up to Nina, we would have five or six." Dante took the ring box from me and turned it to see how it glinted in the light. I watched the glow in his face instead of the ring.

"You've talked about children with Nina?" I asked.

He snapped the ring box shut and stuffed it in his pocket.

Dante gripped the ring box through the outside of his jacket as if fearful it would disappear. "We had the conversation about kids on the first date. She has one sister, and you know how big my family is. I guess Nina has always wanted a big family." He grinned. "I think she would feel different if there were five loud Italian siblings in her house growing up." Dante was raised in the most stereotypical New Jersey Italian family I had ever seen. When I would go home with him on an extended weekend back in college, I always thought his family was putting on an act. He was in the middle. Easily ignored by his parents. Probably why he got away with so much shit. Like dropping out of college to be in a band full time. Yes, he teaches private lessons to kids enough that it pays the bills. Or half the bills now that he is living with Nina.

I laughed. "I can't picture you as a dad."

He finished the last of his coke. "I am going to be a great fucking dad. First things first, I want you to be my best man."

"You are assuming she says 'yes'." I checked my watch. My break was almost over. Dante noticed and checked his phone. I stood collecting our trash from the table. I walked to the garbage can and tossed them inside. When I turned around, I almost jumped out of my skin. Standing in the back of the room was Mila. She wore black leggings, and a black hoodie pulled over her head. I was instantly reminded of what she was.

Dante flicked his attention behind himself, then back to me. Confusion filled his face.

"Just surprised by how fast time went by." I nodded towards the clock on the wall behind where Mila stood. "I really have to get back to work." We walked towards the exit leading to the rest of the hospital.

He punched my arm hard enough to make me stumble. "What's your answer, man?"

"Of course, I will be your best man. There was never any doubt." He hugged me. Like brothers would and punched the air as he walked away. A classic movie of a movie that we used to do in college after we hooked up with a girl the night before. Nowadays it's just a sign that we accomplished something. Or that we drank too much.

When I peeked in the cafeteria, Mila was gone. I felt uneasy not knowing where she was. After washing my hands, I headed to the Leukemia floor. It was time for my nightly chart checks. I walked past an empty room and there was Mila standing in the center. I entered and shut the door quietly behind me. Her smile built a fire in me, and I clasped her face in both my hands planting a passionate kiss on her lips. She pulled away and grimaced.

"I'm sorry. Too forward?" I stepped back. "I must have read you wrong. I thought-" She raised a finger and pressed my lips shut.

"It's not that. We are not alone, Jimi." She interrupted.

14
Mila

The reaper stood next to me with a hand on her hip and mouth gaping open. One question answered, Jimi did not see her. Second question answered, he can still touch me. My core was still hot from his friendly greeting. His eyes darted around the empty hospital room wondering who was there with me.

"What do you mean, we are not alone?" His dark eyes scanned every corner. Only seeing dark machines and a polished floor. A bit of his chill exterior melted. I could not tell if it was fear or panic that glinted in his eyes.

"There is another reaper here." I motioned to the space next to me. He nodded slowly. "A friend, you can say."

"Can he hear me?" The reaper asked with a tone laced in curiosity. Jimi's face remained flat.

"Can you hear anyone other than me?" I repeated her question. He shook his head. "Can you sense anyone else in the room? Like an unknown presence."

"Are humans able to sense when a reaper is in the room?" I shrugged. He rubbed a hand over the back of his neck and shifted on his feet. I couldn't tell if he was going to vomit or run. Maybe both. "What's going on, Mila? Why is there another reaper here?"

"Mila?" The reaper cocked her head in my direction.

"It's a name I gave myself. He kept asking my name. And having him just call me reaper seemed weird." They raised both brows at me and huffed out one note of a laugh.

"You didn't have a name?" Jimi's voice dropped deeper. There was pity in the tone. He took a step towards me then glanced at the space where I said the reaper was standing. He refrained from getting closer, but I could tell he wanted to wrap his arms around me. To comfort me.

"It keeps us from seeing ourselves as-"

"Individuals." The reaper cut in.

I looked at her with somber eyes. I fixated directly on the reaper when I spoke, forgetting for a moment that Jimi is only getting one side of our conversation. "Yes, individuals." It will take time to get used to someone hearing me. To just being noticed at all. My eyes met his. "I asked them to come here and help us get a few answers. I needed to know if you can see all reapers, or just me."

"Just you it seems." The reaper said walking closer to Jimi. She stood less than a foot from his face, but he didn't move. Not even the slightest flinch. "That's strange."

"What's strange?" I asked.

"Leave us for one minute. Go somewhere far. Oregon, perhaps." She walked around Jimi looking at his body from all angles.

"What are they saying?" He said impatiently.

"They want me to leave for one minute."

"You are going to leave me here with a reaper." He stepped back accidentally passing through the reapers body. Their body appearing like smoke for a split second. "Is that safe?"

"He knows I can hear him, right?" The reaper laughed. The grey robe she wore trailing behind her like a cape.

"You're safe." I placed my hands on his shoulders, his muscles loosened. Our noses touched when I pushed up on my toes. I gave him a soft kiss. Resisting the urge to linger. "I will be back in one minute."

Before he could talk me out of it, I vanished. Assuring myself that a reaper cannot physically harm a human. The beach I arrived on was dark. The sun had dipped behind the horizon hours ago. The moon illuminated large rock formations off the coast. I wondered what it felt like to be cold. To have the cool ocean mist whip at my skin from the wind. I crossed my arms and paced. Each count in my head was an eternity. Sixty seconds was enough time for a skilled reaper to collect a soul. I shivered at the thought. Could Death find him and take him from me in sixty seconds? Time was up. I appeared back in the vacant hospital room. Jimi was sitting on the edge of the bed. His knee bounced causing the rubber from his shoe to create a steady tap on the floor.

"Are they still here?" He jumped up from sitting. I glanced next to him where the reaper waved her arms around his head and laughed. I nodded, ignoring the childish behavior. Usually, this reaper is stoic and calm, but she has found herself far too entertained by our odd situation. I rolled my eyes. An expression I had seen by humans many times before. It felt right in that moment.

The reaper moved towards me. Her face went still. Void of any clues what they were about to say. "The strangest thing happened when you were gone. Humans have unique signatures just like us reapers. Invisible markers on their souls. That is how we identify who to take. You have felt this many times." I nodded and put a finger up to Jimi signaling that I was listening. He pushed off the edge of the bed.

"I have to go back to work. Come find me." He kissed my cheek and walked out the door. I nodded at the reaper for her to continue talking.

"I focused on his soul markers, getting a good read on him. When you left it was like it weakened. Dimed a bit." The reaper scrunched her forehead until a line formed between their brows. "When you returned it grew stronger."

"What does that mean?"

"I am not sure, but it feels like there is a piece of his soul attached to you. Like a piece of lint stuck to fabric."

I scoffed. "That's romantic."

"Are you sure you never saw him before that night

here, in the hospital." I nodded my response. "Well somehow a piece of his soul lingers with you. I have never seen it before."

I paced a circle twisting my hands together behind my back. *Like lint on a piece of fabric.* I echoed in my head.

"Thank you, reaper. For helping me and Jimi."

"So, Mila." She gave me a crooked smile. "You gave yourself a name."

My cheeks heated. *Did I actually just blush?* I feel like I am blushing. "He wanted something to call me."

A smile filled her face. "I like it." It was approval from an older sibling of sorts. The heat from my cheeks spread into my chest. Who would have thought having a name could mean so much. Build me up in a way. Make me one step closer to being whole.

She turned to the window as if her robe were about to transform into wings and she would simply sly out the window. "Be careful. I don't know what is happening between you two, but it feels like something Death would-" a nervous pause, "have a problem with." She patted my shoulder and vanished.

After filling in Jimi with everything the reaper said, I felt the tug inside. The reminder that I do have a job to do. "I will see you back at your apartment." He kissed me as the tug pulled harder. I groaned when I slipped out of his arms and found myself standing in a prison. I hate prisons. They are always so dirty and depressing.

After centuries of observing prisons around the world I have come to the conclusion that they do not work for what they are intended to.

Well, if your intention is to separate a dangerous person from society, then they work. The belief that they will rehabilitate a criminal is far from the truth. They are more likely to change surrounded by good people or by having something they believe is worth changing for. I have seen evidence of this in all stages of society.

I walked slowly down the hall towards the shouts of a fight.

"Jimi's soul is a part of me?" I whispered to myself. "How is that possible?" If I could just ask The Creator or whoever was in charge, things would be easier. Maybe I can find an Angel. They are rumored to have more knowledge than reapers. We only know the act of dying. The last moments of a human's life. We are moving keys that open the gateway to the afterlife. We know nothing beyond or even before when it comes to souls.

I walked through the bars of a prison cell just as a bloody fight between two men was coming to an end. A large white man with tattoos up the sides of his face was hunched over a Latino man that was laying on the floor. A sharpened toothbrush stuck out of his neck. I was hoping it would be quick, but the man was slowly choking on blood. I cringed at the sight. The Latino man appeared next to me in a translucent form of his body.

The moment I realized I was in a prison. I shredded

my casual street clothes. I was wearing my black robe with the hood pulled up, shielding most of my face. Places like this only feeds a darkness in me.

"Fuck." The man said when he spotted me. "A fucking grim reaper. This is how I fucking die?"

"Yes."

He kicked the man standing over his body and his leg went right through him. He swore again. Angry that he could not inflict violence on his murderer. The corners of my lips twitched up. He was irritated by my amusement. Maybe I was being a bit insensitive.

"I was supposed to get out in three months." He scowled at me like it was my fault. I did not move. "I missed the last two birthdays of mi hija. I promised her I would be at her next party." I remained emotionless. "This is bullshit."

"It's not my decision." I held out my left-hand palm up. "Take my hand."

"Fuck you, I aint dying." His body stopped gurgling and took its last breath. He turned and ran. I hate it when they run. I appeared at the end of the hall before him. I made my eyes go white. Some people need to be scared into submission. *I hate prisons.* He stopped before me and scanned the area. He bolted towards the cafeteria.

"Ugh." I slouched my shoulders back, before chasing after him. When he turned a corner, I was already there. He slammed into me. I was the only thing that would feel solid to him in his current state. "You can't run from me. You can't fight this. It's your time. Your body has already died."

"Fuck you." He spat.

"You want to haunt this prison forever." I made myself grow two feet taller and stalked down at him. My eyes were pure white under my black hood. "You're a fucking idiot."

He trembled and took a step back.

"Take, my, hand." My voice had more grit than usual. I put my palm out once more, "And move on from all of this." I gesture to our surroundings. He started to place his hand in mind and began to change into grey smoke. The man took his hand away and looked up with wavering eyes. I was about to snap at him. To make myself into a monster. Scaring him to grab my hand, but I paused. He whispered a quiet prayer then placed his hand fully in mine. You would think an immortal being would be more patient. I sighed as he faded into my ring. No longer part of this world.

I wonder if his prayer was heard. Who was listening to the pleas of an inmate? Who listens to those that are inherently good? If I prayed, would it be heard. Does anyone other than Death listen to reapers?

15
Mila

I wandered about the city for a while before I returned to Jimi. I felt unclean and didn't want to bring my aura of dying around him. His smile was too warm to be tainted by me. Perhaps I should just stay away and let him live a real life with a real woman.

The ring on my finger tingled. I needed to unload souls again. Death has been keeping me busy. There must not be many reapers stationed nearby. Or perhaps soul collecting feels like a nuisance now because all I want to do is spend time with Jimi. Even if it's just watching him work.

Quickly I found myself back in my favorite secluded Canadian forest. It was raining, and the drops passed right through me. Despite the gloomy weather, I still changed my attire into a sunny yellow jacket and matching boots. A bright reminder of my desperation to be a part of this world.

With my palms out I summoned the gateway. A group of souls appeared next to me in a line. Somber and emotions muted. Being in my ring has kept them in a liminal state. Unaware of where they were and how much time had passed. I ushered them through the gateway with a smile. Although they did not smile back as the void swallowed them up. They disappeared into the blackness. I leaned closer to the gateway. Unsure what would happen if a reaper fell in. *Would Death just kick me back out. Would it be a true death for a reaper? An end to this servitude.* I thought about what the other reaper said and tried to call to my own soul.

How does one call for a soul?

I didn't have much time. The gateway would close after the last soul walked through. Focusing the same way, I do to find other reapers on earth, but this time I pictured myself. That just confused me as images flashed in my mind of all the forms I had worn over the centuries. *This can't be right.* There must be some way to identify me. A way I can feel my own energy signature.

I felt nothing. The gateway closed in a puff of mist. Frustrated, I hung my head low and jumped to the roof across from Jimi's building. He should be returning from work soon. I sat on the edge of the building with my legs dangling off and waited.

He returned looking tired around 2:00am. I gave him time to get settled and changed into sweatpants before I entered his apartment. He ate a piece of toast with apricot jam over his sink while waiting for a cup of tea to steep. Once he seemed relaxed on the couch, I went to him. Choosing to appear by the door, as if I had knocked. He was sinking deep onto the couch. Pinching the bridge of his nose.

He gave me a tired smile. "Mila."

"Rough shift? You look exhausted."

He patted the space next to him on the couch. I curled up with my legs tucked under me. Immediately at ease with his closeness. I bit my lip when he pulled me in against his body. Trying to keep in the squeal I was desperately keeping inside. Some of it escaped and my cheeks heated. *Did I just blush again?* He responded by hooking an arm around my shoulders and twirling my hair around his fingers.

"Yea." He sipped his tea. "I'm glad you are here. Every time you disappear, I am afraid I will never see you again."

It is me who should fear this. I am not the one that can die. I should be worried. Worried that Death will send a reaper to take him from me. I haven't figured out if we are breaking the rules, yet. What are the rules anyway? It's not like I was given an instruction manual when I came into being.

Maybe the Fates brought us together. Maybe we are supposed to be linked. A power stronger than Death is behind out connection.

His dark lashes blinked slowly making his exhaustion more apparent. He works so hard. He has a true purpose and makes a tangible impact in this world. For the good.

Not like me who only takes things away. I need to figure some shit out. Before I make a mistake that will cost his life.

"I'm here." I said looking up at him. Jimi squeezed me into his body tighter. "There is no where I would rather be."

"Not even a beach in the Bahamas." He smirked.

I sat up, away from him and flashed a devious smile. I vanished before him and landed on a beautiful beach on the island of Nassau. Being in the same time zone, the sun has not yet risen. The beach was empty. I popped back into the apartment and was greeted by a cheeky glare filling Jimi's face.

"It's probably seventy-three degrees and a bit windy, but the sand feels nice." The thirty seconds I was gone he shifted to lay on his side. I lay facing him. "I like it here better."

"I'm jealous." He said into my hair as he tucked me under his arm.

"Of what? Speedy travel? It's not like I get to do anything but observe and wait-" I didn't finish the sentence. There must be a way of having a conversation with him without reminding him I serve as a conduit for death every five minutes. *I could talk like a normal human woman.* I sighed.

"Have you been on the top of mount Everest?"

"Yes. I have visited all the major mountain peaks." I slid my hand into the front pocket of his hoodie. Pulling my body as close to his as possible. I could feel him fighting sleep as he spoke.

"Where were you in the sixties?"

"I assume you mean 1960." He scoffed. "What? I was here for 1360, 1460, 15-"

"Ok I get it." He interrupted. "Jesus, yes I mean the 1960's."

I laughed into his chest. His sent filled my nose and I savored it. "I was in Mumbai. Believe it or not, the jazz scene was amazing. The dancers were mesmerizing. Oh, and the movies."

"We should go to a movie." He said with a slur of sleep in his voice.

"Okay." I whispered. The quiet apartment washed over us when we both paused speaking. "I will let you sleep."

He kissed the top of my head and closed his eyes. "Stay."

I don't need to sleep, but I shut my eyes anyway and curled up close to him. The movements of his chest slowed into a steady pattern. I want to stay more than anything I have wanted before. Stay with him in this life. His life. If I could just figure this shit out. Find my soul and make this body solid. If I can just become something real, for him.

What if he gets tired of me? What if I do everything and become human, just to have him leave me? There is a tightness in my chest that I have never felt before. My breath feels stuck in my throat. *Wait, I have no breath. What is happening to me?*

16
Jimi

I woke, still on the couch. Mila wrapped in my arms. I moved slowly then realized she was already awake. Her dark brown eyes gleamed up at me. I immediately continued the conversation from my dream. I would drown in questions if I didn't ask for answers.

"Good morning beautiful." I kissed her forehead. She sensed the shift in my posture and braced herself for what was behind my cheeky grin. "What about were-wolves?"

She laughed. "Not real."

"Mermaids?" I pestered.

"I wish, but no." There was a twinge of a smile on her face. Soft. It drew my attention to those full lips I loved.

"Demons?" That made her tense. I rubbed her arm.

"No, well yes." She drew in a breath. "There are beings that some say are evil, but their power lies in human motive. One person might call them a demon, while another might call them a Genie or Jin. They are separated from reapers, so I don't have any first-hand experience."

Genies. Demons. I suddenly wished I was still dreaming. My questions were making her tense in my arms. I needed to change the subject before she vanished on me again.

"Coffee?"

She frowned.

"Oh yea, you don't drink." She shifted to let me off the couch. I noticed her shoulders seemed low. Invisible weights pushing them down. She shifted straighter when I flashed a big grin. Tucking something sad inside. My hope is that last night is just the beginning of her spending every night here. Waking up to that face every morning might be the only thing missing from my life. Is it too soon to ask about living together? She has nothing to move in. No belongings or clothes. The look on her face tells me now is not the time to point out our differences. I should just savor every moment I have her nearby.

First, I need to get the coffee brewing. Wake up my mind and think clearly. My stomach growled. I suddenly felt bad eating in front of her. When the coffee pot was percolating, I headed to the bathroom. Everything around me was a reminder that we are not the same. She does not use the bathroom, she does not brush her teeth, she does not-" I popped my head out of the bathroom with a toothbrush still in my mouth. Foam lingering on my tongue waiting to be spat into the sink. "Wait a minute, I have a question."

"Anything." She smiled from where she stood by the window. A line of pigeons was watching the street from my fire escape. They paid no mind to her on the other side of the glass.

"You don't eat." She nodded. "So, you don't go to the bathroom. Can you cry? Like, can you make tears?"

"No." Mila tucked her arms crossed against herself.

"So, you can't make fluid." I am already questioning my choice of words. She cringed.

"That's a weird thing to say." She kept her arms folded and moved towards me. Her brows scrunched towards her lashes. I turned to the sink and spit. After wiping my mouth, I found her waiting in the doorway. God, she was gorgeous. Her olive skin and dark wavy hair were perfect. Actual perfection. As if I manifested her from my dreams.

"Well, I was thinking about the other night." I gave her a wink and I could have sworn her cheeks reddened. "When my mouth was on you and my fingers inside you."

She walked backwards, letting me pin her to the wall outside the bathroom. I made sure not to press her too hard into the rough brick. Unsure if she can feel pain. It would be better to ask than test it myself. I ran my hand up from her hip to her waist and pulled her close by the small of her back. Her breath hitched when I leaned down until my lips grazed her ear. "What about the other night?" Her voice was breathy.

"I felt you come." I kissed her below the ear. "You tasted real to me." I kissed her neck. "How is that possible?"

I didn't let her answer. I needed my lips on hers. She ran her fingers through my hair, and it sent a vibration down my spine. Her tongue was real. The firmness of her body was real. Our bodies pressed together seemed real. She was flat against the wall as I ground my hardening cock against her. I want all of her. No, I need all of her. She broke our kiss but stayed pressed against me. Speaking onto my lips.

"I don't know. Many things are different when I am near you." Her lips were pink from our kissing. Swollen. Exaggerating their already fullness. I leaned down and took her bottom lip in my mouth, it needed a little nip. A sultry giggle left her mouth, and I captured it with my own. Swallowing her laugh so it could live on within me. I could live in her kiss. I could die on these lips, and I would be happy.

"Like what?" I asked between kisses.

Her body stilled. I dug my hand into her lush wavy hair and cupped the back of her head. Protecting it from the hard brick. Mila let out a breath. "Sensations in my body that I have never felt before. And-"

I didn't mean to interrupt her, but my lips found hers again. I needed to let her speak. This conversation was important, but I just can't stop touching her. Pressing my eyes closed tight, I pulled away and adjusted my cock. *Focus Jimi.* "And?"

She had the same longing in her eyes that I had. Both of us fighting against a tether.

"Reapers have emotions, but they are subdued. Muted. However, around you it's like I like I get nervous and anxious. Not emotions a reaper should feel. This heart is not even real. Not in the sense that a human heart is real." Mila placed a hand over her chest. "But I swear, I feel it beating in my chest when you touch me. The other night, with you, it was my first real, um ya know."

I could not help the greedy smile on my face. "Your first orgasm." She nodded. "Well fuck. Why me? What makes me different?" I walked into the kitchen. Ignoring my throbbing cock and focusing on my grumbling stomach.

"I am not sure yet. I am going to track down an Angel and see if I can get answers."

I almost fell over at how casual she mentioned a holy supernatural being. "Did you say Angel?" I put two pieces of bread into the toaster and grabbed the jam from the fridge.

"Yea. It's going to be tricky, but I think they have the most insight. Angels have mingled with humans many times in the past. They used to involve themselves in human business all the time. Now I think they mostly observe. I have only heard them answering human prayers in the past. So, I am not sure they will even hear me."

"I can't believe this is a real conversation." Shaking my head slowly, I laughed and spread jam on my toast. "Spend the day with me." Today could be a test. See if we could make it work between us. I took a bite of my toast and hoped it wasn't awkward for her. To watch me eat knowing she cannot.

A smile beamed on her face. She sat onto a stool across the kitchen island. "I might get summoned away, but I will return to you when I am done."

And there it was. The glint in her eyes confirms she wants to test it also. Test me. Test this bond between us. Whatever this is. Fate? An accident? Or some kind of curse? I am grateful it brought her to me. I have seen death at the hospital. It is cold and lonely. Mila is warm and feels like a missing piece of me has been restored. I winked, which caused her cheeks to flush pink.

"No big deal. I will just pretend I'm dating an ER surgeon who is on call." I grabbed her hand with mine. "Plus, I have a brilliant idea that will make us able to hang out in public. Even if many eyes are on us." Her brows raised with curiosity. "Trust me." I winked taking a big bite of toast into my mouth.

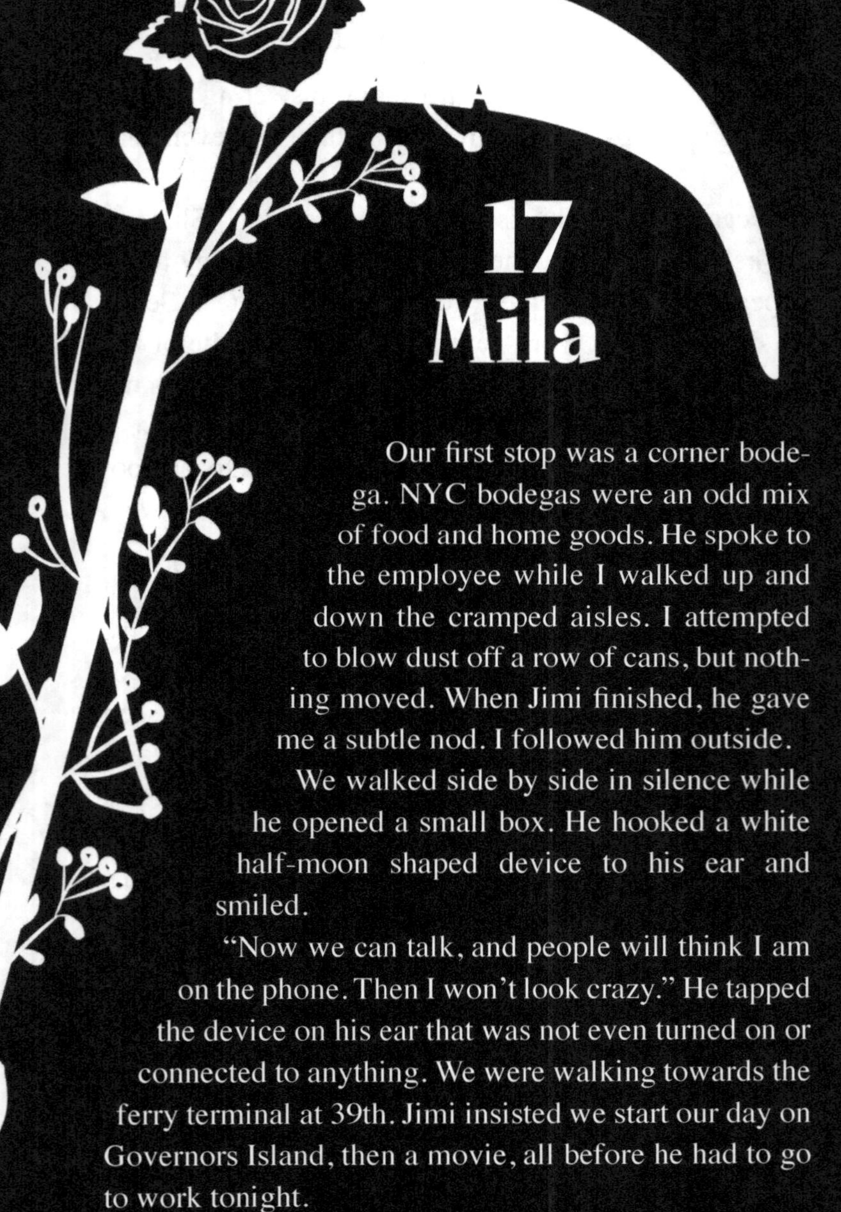

17
Mila

Our first stop was a corner bodega. NYC bodegas were an odd mix of food and home goods. He spoke to the employee while I walked up and down the cramped aisles. I attempted to blow dust off a row of cans, but nothing moved. When Jimi finished, he gave me a subtle nod. I followed him outside.

We walked side by side in silence while he opened a small box. He hooked a white half-moon shaped device to his ear and smiled.

"Now we can talk, and people will think I am on the phone. Then I won't look crazy." He tapped the device on his ear that was not even turned on or connected to anything. We were walking towards the ferry terminal at 39th. Jimi insisted we start our day on Governors Island, then a movie, all before he had to go to work tonight.

"I bet I can make you say something that *will* make you look crazy." He glanced over at me and smirked. "Or just make you smile at nothing. That was easy." He huffed and turned his face back forward.

"I just need to practice not looking at you. With time I can resist the temptation of your pretty face." He wove his body around New Yorkers in a hurry. I could have let them pass through me. Making me temporarily look like smoke, but I wanted to keep the illusion intact. Have Jimi forget what I am and think of me as human. So, I dodge the passerby's before they could get too close.

We walked by a small bakery. "Fuck, what is that smell?" I tilted my head up to inhale more of the scent wafting out of the open doors. NYC usually smells like trash and urine. This was heavenly.

"Chocolate chip cookies." Jimi said with a slight question in his tone.

"I would give anything to taste them." I licked my lips. "What are they like?"

He glanced at me quickly before turning to the bakery window as we passed it. "Hrm, I have never described a chocolate chip cookie before. The chocolate is sweet, and the cookie part is buttery. Sometimes a bit salty."

I frowned. Why did I even ask. I don't know what sweet tastes like, or buttery. I imagine the ocean when I think of salt but have no idea how the ocean relates to the flavor of a cookie. I just nodded. Appreciating that he tried to explain that flavors.

"That would be the first thing I ate if I were human."
I beamed. It was a game reapers would play. If I were
human, I would *blank*. It was mostly a list of things we
wanted to eat or drink. Although many talk about if we
had a human wedding or named a child.

Jimi brushed his hand against mine. "Could you be?
Human that is?"

"I am looking into it." I smirked. I will tell him the
details later. How reapers could get a soul of their own,
but I am unclear on the entire process. That part of me
thinks I should seek an Angel. Since they have more
answers than us due to their closeness with the Creator.
Even though Angels don't serve reapers. They are here
for humans.

On the ferry we found a corner away from people. He
tried to sit in a way that was not obvious an invisible
woman was tucked into his side. I tried to make him
look crazy by kissing his neck or tickling his sides. To
an outsider he would look twitchy and red from blushing. I continued to tease him while he playfully swatted
my hand away. Causing me to laugh because the action
surely made him look more ridiculous. He shot me an
exaggerated glare.

Governors Island was coming into view when I felt
a tug. A very strong tug. I moved my hand off him and
groaned.

"I will catch up with you. I am being summoned." I
kissed his cheek. This tug felt urgent.

"There's an outside art exhibit going on. Find me there." He whispered. I brushed his hand as I stood up and vanished before him.

I have been to this part of the world before. The middle east has the most incredible fabrics. I used to walk through the crowded markets and trace the beaded patterns with my fingers. Curious what they feel like. Envious of the jingling ankle bracelets. The food here has the riches scent and dyes meat shades of red or orange.

Light was shining from above. Coming through seeded glass skylights. I could see tiny flecks of dust floating in the air. It was peaceful. I found myself surrounded by a dozen kneeling men. Their heads were on the floor. I knew if I were to look there would be an equal number of women in the next room.

"Fuck." I said aloud. Not here.

"I know. I am so sick of religious wars." A voice said from behind me. I turned to find another reaper standing there. He was tall with long blonde hair. He was wearing a tan suit with a white shirt. "I came from Sweden. How about you?"

"New York City." I answered. A kneeling man moved his hand, and I moved my foot by instinct. The reaper tilted his head at me. He must have thought me a fool. That man could not have touched me. I shrugged it off and over corrected by walking through a kneeling man on my other side. Positioning myself in the center of the room. There are so many men around us. If there is an attack coming on this Mosque it could mean three or more souls to collect each. I clenched my hands into fists. Trying to control my anger in front of the other reaper.

"Fuck it's going to be bad if Death is pulling us from that far." Both our heads snapped when we heard another voice. They spoke too quickly for us to respond. "Do you not watch the news?" A dark-skinned man with a deep voice chimed in. *Three reapers, fuck, we are looking at mass casualties here.* I suddenly wished we had the choice to opt out of assignments.

"Did you make yourself look like Idris Alba?" Ignoring his question and changing the subject. He flashed me the big smile usually worn by a famous actor. I rolled my eyes.

My stomach churned. Although it was empty, it felt like something was twisting inside. Shaking the feeling off I changed my attire in a flash to mimic the long dresses worn by Muslim women including a matching headscarf all in black.

"I don't watch the news much. I prefer reality shows." The blonde reaper flicked a piece of lint off his jacket. Completely for show because lint cannot stick to us. I rolled my eyes and glanced back to the dark-skinned reaper to continue.

"There has been conflict in this region for decades. These civilians are about to be caught in the middle of a pointless battle over religion and land. Can't you feel how many reapers are in the area?" He closed his eyes, and I did the same. Sure enough, there were many reaper signatures within a few mile radius. Too many. I opened my mouth to speak but was interrupted by a siren followed by a loud boom in the distance.

"Brace yourself." The Idris Alba reaper said just before an entire wall came crashing in filling the room with smoke and broken rock. I stood still as the debris flew through me. The blonde reaper was collecting a soul of a man that died almost instantly in the explosion. Before me were two glowing men. One unconscious and the other attempting to climb out from under a collapsed column. He did not know that the column was keeping him from bleeding out. He wiggled and grunted trying to get his lower body loose. I wish I could tell him to stop moving. If he waited for help, he might survive. If help was coming. He was inches away from being un-pinned by the piece of rebar stuck in his femoral artery. He will bleed out fast and I will just have to watch. I sighed when I heard his scream. He was loose from the rebar but still pinned under the column.

The man appeared next to me. He was in his forties. Most likely a father and a husband. His wife might be in the room next to us for all I know. I greeted him with a smile. *I hated war.*

"Angel." He said to me in Arabic.

I shook my head slowly. "No. But have no fear. I am here to guide you towards Akhirah." I said in his language. His eyes went wide, and he took a few steps, realizing he could move.

"My wife!" He begged, "She was with me. Please, don't take her."

I turned my body towards the wall that divided the men from women and pointed. "You can look for her, but it is not up to me if it is her time." He nodded and swiftly walked towards the wall. I motioned for him to just walk through. He hesitated with his translucent palms on the stucco wall. Slowly he pushed his body into the wall that should be solid, and I followed behind him. This is already more than I usually do when collecting a soul. I found him staring down at his hands when I reached the other side. "You have until your body takes its last breath."

He understood and begun walking through the panicked women and broken bodies. This room was not as badly affected by the blast. The bombs impact must have been to the east. Not directly targeting the Mosque. Women were scattered everywhere. Dust floated through the air. Exaggerating the rays of light from above. Most of the injuries were from parts of the ceiling falling. Sirens already blared off in the distance. Gradually raising in volume. He must have found his wife because he was praying over a woman. She seemed the same age and was helping someone younger that was bleeding from her head. I have borne witness to many people losing the ones they love. It always caused discomfort, but this felt like pain. Actual aching in my chest. I tried to keep my face stoic. Tried to remember the purpose of a reaper. Not to console or help. We do not save people. We do not cast judgement. We are supposed to just collect and move on. But these deaths lately have lingered inside me. Each one imprints itself until I can't handle any-more. I tried not to focus on the changing feeling inside. Tried to push them down.

I felt the man's body die in the next room. I moved to stand next to him. His eyes were tearless, as he could not cry in this form. Though they looked as if a river was about to flow.

"It's time." My voice calms. I placed my hand out, palm up. Bits of dust landed on my gold ring. I didn't have to say anything else. The man examined my hand, whispered something into his wife's ear that was too quiet for me to hear. He placed his hand in mine and turned to smoke. He did not give me his last words. Those belonged to her.

I hate this job.

I need to find an Angel.

18
Mila

Jimi was like a child waiting for their parents to pick them up from school. Bouncing a knee while he sat on a bench across from the outdoor art exhibit. Rows of moving sculptures filled a field of low-cut grass. I wanted to run to him and have him wrap his arms around me. I needed his comfort. His touch.

Slowly, I walked towards him instead of appearing on the bench. It would have been funny to startle him, but I wasn't in the mood for humor. I wasn't in the mood to feel like a reaper.

He was scrolling on his phone when I tapped his foot with the tip of my boot. A smile filled his face before melting away. "What's wrong?"

I pointed to his phone. "Check the news." Jimi read through an article on his phone. *Newsflash: A targeted attack in the middle east. Death toll 14, with 29 injured.* The article claimed it was retaliation. That a group nearby was the target, and the civilians were collateral damage. I hung my head in shame. As if I were responsible for the violent actions.

I sat next to him, unable to feel the cold metal of the bench. Before I came to Governors Island, I changed into jeans and the leather jacket I had grown accustomed to. It was a cool Autumn Day, and I layered my clothes to match the people around us, even adding a black beanie over my loose curls.

Jimi's leg stopped bouncing. A heavy sigh escapes his mouth. He was grinding his teeth together as he read a breaking news headline. My head dropped instinctively. I may not be responsible for humans losing their lives, but I hate being part of it. Hate that the only thing I add to the world is taking souls out of it. He peered up at me. I expected anger to be burning in his eyes. Instead, they softened.

"I'm sorry, Mila." He placed a hand on my knee. Quickly, I moved it off and held his hand to rest on the bench. The last thing we needed was someone to notice Jimi sitting alone with his hand floating over nothing.

"Don't feel sorry for me. Feel sorry for the people that just lost their loved ones over made-up borders and religious beliefs." I huffed. "You humans have always done this. Fought over land. Encouraged separation. Killed each other. Reapers may be servants to Death, but we are not inherently evil like humans."

Why did I say that?

He shifted to angle his body slightly towards me. "You think we are inherently evil?"

"Not you." I pushed the rising pressure in my chest down. Trying to control whatever emotion this was. My lungs tightened, and I was having a hard time thinking of the right words. What the hell was happening to me? "Sorry, I am speaking out of my ass. I am just, ugh, I don't know what I am."

His eyes darted around my face. "Frustrated." He suggested.

"What?" I sucked air into my lungs. Although I had no reason to breathe. It felt necessary at the moment. I wonder if this is what drowning feels like. The desperate need for air.

"You sound frustrated. Have you not felt this before?" He squeezed my hand, and I swore the ring warmed under his touch. I wish I could jump both of us back to his apartment. To have this conversation in private. I wanted to allow him to comfort me. More than just a look of pity that filled his face. Pity I don't deserve. I insult his entire species, and he pities me.

He was so beautiful to look at. The muscles in his jaw flexed. I needed to be close to him. I wanted his lips on me and his hands roaming my body. I craved it. I needed to feel something other than this sadness and anger.

I blinked hard. "Frustration, yes, I have felt that." I observed the statues moving in front of me. "Just never this strong before."

"Let's take your mind off the terrible events of today and go look at some art." He tapped my knee. Jimi hauled me off the bench and pulled me in the direction of the exhibit. Our hands lingered with our fingers interlaced for a few moments before he dropped it. A somber look crossed his face. We cannot touch with people nearby. This was no ordinary date. His smile to me felt forced.

I tried to lighten the mood by linking two fingers into his belt buckle. His smile grew to meet his eyes. My cheeks flushed just by being close to him. Jimi pressed a finger to the device over his ear.

"You're incredible, you know." He whispered.

My cheeks warmed. "I'm really not."

"All you have ever known in this world is death, yet you are still kind and compassionate to humans. Even though you said we are all evil." Jimi winked. "You want the best for us." He stopped in front of a rotating cube with paintings on all sides. The images blended and told a story, but the story was changed depending on which side started facing you. It was either an advanced city burning down, or a city being built from ashes.

"I probably have seen more life than death." He cocked his head at my words. I leaned in a bit closer as if I needed to keep my voice low. I explained. "I have seen so many wonderful things in this world. Amazing feats of engineering. Children being born. Mother's willingness to sacrifice everything for them. I have witnessed people finding their first love, and people growing old and dying together."

"Sounds beautiful." Jimi bumped my shoulder with his.

"But you kill each other. Always have. You can be greedy and cruel. And so selfish. I get so mad watching all the destruction caused by humans. The truth is," I paused. I have had this conversation with other reapers before, but maybe I shouldn't say these things to a human. "The truth is by the time I show up to reap their souls so much damage has been done without them even knowing. The world is a large place. However, most humans live within a small bubble of comfort and ideals. No one has lived a truly good life. They are all complacent if not directly responsible to evil deeds." My hand covered my mouth. I shouldn't be ranting about his own species. Not if I wanted Jimi to like me more than just attraction. This is proving I am not good at communicating with people.

"Even me?" Jimi slid his hands into his front pockets. Looking ever so like the sexy man he is. Making me regret everything I was saying.

"I have not seen any evidence yet to think you are evil. On purpose that is." I nudged his shoulder back. "Although you can do devilish things with that tongue of yours."

I tried desperately to ease the tension. He only partially took the bait when I noticed his body relax.

"Who decides what's evil? I thought you didn't know if there was a God." He asked. Voice getting low.

A small part inside me flinched in fear I would be struck by lightning for having this conversation. What do I even know to tell him? Not much outside of the duties of a reaper. Keeping us ignorant makes us easier to control.

"There is definitely a creator. I don't think they are as involved as religions paint them to be though." I shuffled away from the rotating cube statue.

Jimi just hummed and accepted my vague answer. He followed me towards another statue. This sculpture had two people that were linking hands. As you moved around the carved stone a story changed. When one figure was on top it appeared like they were pulling the other up to safety, but as we walked it shifted to look like they were both falling. Falling together.

"Tell me Mila. If you could be human. What would you do?" Jimi surveyed the area and placed a hand on the small of my back gently. He held it there until we got too close to another couple before removing it. We wove through the statues while I thought hard on his question. I have had many answers to this question throughout the past seven hundred and sixty-three years. It has changed many times.

"If I were human today, I would live in a smaller city. Less noise. I would love to be a stagehand in a theater. I think it would be fun to learn to cook."

"A stagehand." His eyes widened and he couldn't help but look down at me. Forgetting he was speaking to someone invisible to those around us. I pointed forward and he laughed. "You have probably seen every profession in the world, and you want to be a stagehand."

"I like the theater." Going to the theater was like returning home. He raised a brow and peeked at me from the corner of his eyes. "You should have been there when it was evolving."

"When? The height of Shakespeare?" I nudged him and he stumbled. A couple noticed he tripped, and their heads whipped in our direction. I skipped away to a large tree while he picked himself off the ground. The tree blocked us from the view of the exhibit patrons. He caught up with me flashing a playful glare. Dusting dirt off his pants.

"Way before the hack you know as Shakespeare." I sat down with my back to the tree, and he copied my movements. "The English renaissance around 1565ish had some great political dramas. They loved to use comedy to make their monarchs look like fools. The stages were just square platforms that had draped fabric behind, but it was a thrilling time. I was in France for part of the 16th century. Artists were still afraid of being accused of blasphemy. Most plays were used to teach morality, or they were approved farces. But the underground plays were my favorite. Makeshift stages were built in the basement of wineries or in the back of a tavern. They were lewd and vulgar and I loved it."

Jimi laughed so hard it shook the tree. I couldn't help but grin at him. Our conversation was so natural. So normal.

He pressed a kiss to my forehead. Before he moved out of my reach, I leaned up and pressed a kiss to his lips. Quick, but rewarding. Static went through my body. He coerced my lips apart with his tongue deepening the kiss. My hand went up and racked his thick black hair.

A ferry horn blared behind us. We'd forgotten where we were for a second. Both our eyes snapped open. I pulled apart. Already missing his touch. I attempted to look down, but he caught my chin with his fingers and forced my attention to him. His dark brown eyes pierced me. He saw me. All of me.

A chirping melody came from the phone in his pocket. He slid it out and frowned before answering.

"Hi mom." *Pause.* "Yes, I will be home next weekend. I promise." *Pause.* "I already put in my time off request, and it was approved. What is dad yelling in the background?" *Pause.* "The train? No, I will be driving." *Pause.* "Tell him my car is fine." *Pause.* He glanced at me. "It will be just me." *Pause.* He rolled his eyes. "I'm twenty-six, mom. I think I have time." *Pause.* His posture went rigid. "I love you both. Bye" He slipped his phone into his pocket with an awkward stillness and glanced at me from the corner of his eye. Jimi let out a dramatic sigh. "My parents."

"I guessed." Tucking hair behind my ear. "You are going to visit them?"

"Yes, next weekend." Jimi checked his watch. "We should get back. Let's try to see a movie another day. I should eat a full meal before I head into work." His words were rushed and cold.

"Ok." He turned on his heel and walked towards the ferry dock. Suddenly in a hurry. Had I taken too long with my soul collection? I did have to collect multiple in one visit. He took his long strides quicker than usual. I had to use my ability to jump closer to him to keep up.

I looked at the side of his face as we walked. He was clenching his jaw. Maybe his parents said something to upset him. Was it impolite to ask? Humans are so very emotional. It's hard to tell was causes them pain. Or was this anger?

"Are you riding the ferry with me, or are you just going to meet me at my apartment?" His body seemed tense. I wanted to grab him and make him look at me, but there was a crowd coming towards us that had just departed the ferry.

"I want to ride with you." I answered. He pushed a hand through his black hair. I watched his mouth open and shut without saying anything. I glanced around wondering if something else could have upset him. Something other than me or the phone call. He gave a shallow nod. I shrunk into myself. "Did I do something wrong?"

His shoulders sank. "No." His voice flat. Void of the warmth it usually has. Jimi pulled a single ticket from his jacket pocket and handed it to the ticket agent on the dock. The attendant notched the ticket before handing it back to him. They moved aside long enough to let one person pass. I just passed through the attendant's arm when it came down behind Jimi. We both stepped onto the boat and took the seats furthest from anyone else.

He scrubbed his face with his hands before speaking again. "You did nothing wrong. You're wonderful. Perfect even. You might be the most interesting person I have ever met. And Mila-" He grabbed my hand with both of his. My eyes felt wet. *What is happening to me?* "Mila you are the most beautiful person I have ever met. I want to introduce you to everyone, my family, my friends. I want to brag to the world that such an amazing person is interested in me. That you think I am worthy of you. But-"

His pause said it all. The silence screamed the words he didn't say. I finished the sentence for him.

"But I'm not a person." A drop of liquid slid down my face. He lifted a single finger to wipe it away. I looked at the tip of his finger. Wet from a tear. A tear that came from me. *How?* "I'm not a person." I repeated softer.

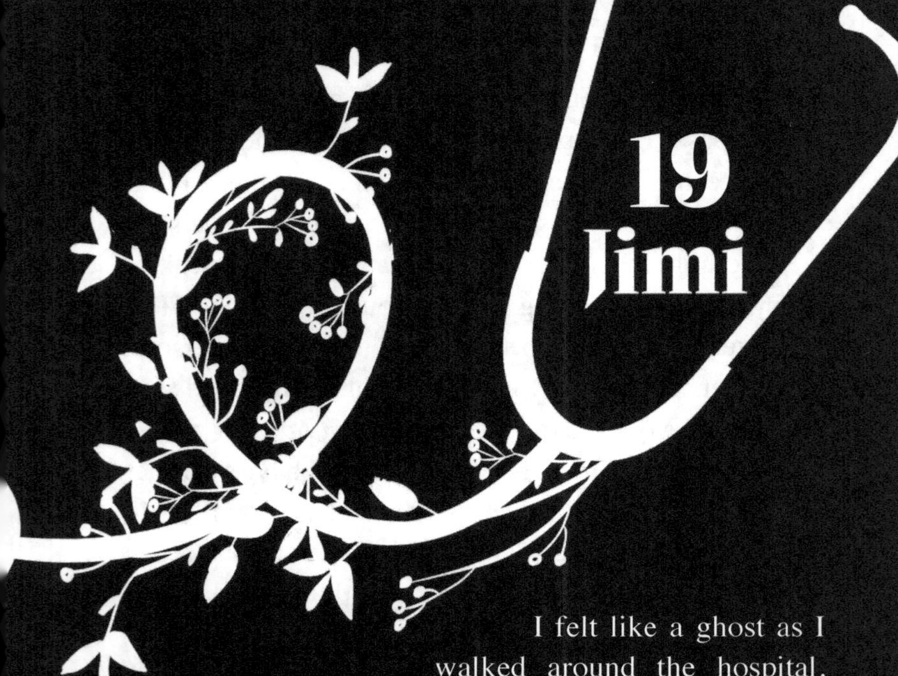

19
Jimi

I felt like a ghost as I walked around the hospital. Mindlessly checking charts and greeting the night staff behind the desk. Clouds filled my head, and my face remained numb. Not the way it goes numb from smiling too much, but as if it couldn't smile at all. Never before have I felt blissfully happy and also devastated at the same time.

Mila's words kept echoing through my mind.

"I am not a person."

"I am not a person."

Taunting me to give up. Persuading me to walk away from her.

My heart has been closed for so long that I forgot what it meant to let a person in. No, that's not correct. *"I am not a person"* she had said. She was a reaper. An instrument for Death. A tool used to collect souls. She could never have children or meet my family. We can't be a normal couple in public. I spent the whole afternoon pretending to talk into an earpiece. Somehow, I was fine with that. I accepted what she was without fully questioning what she is. I let her gorgeous eyes and full lips pull me in before I sank into her completely.

Maybe I am getting ahead of myself. We haven't known each other that long, and she seems to be under the impression that there might be a solution that allows us to be together. A way to make her human. What if she regrets it? There must be benefits to being an immortal being. What if she ends up resenting me for making her give up everything she has known? Worst of all, what if Death is angry and comes after her or me.

I shook my head hoping the spiraling thoughts would fall out. If I continue my mind will break. I've been hollow for some time now. Like something is missing. Going through the motions of life as if it mattered, but a small voice in the back of my head chants that I shouldn't be here. That I am a waste of breath.

I need answers. I need to see Mila.

She was waiting outside my apartment when I returned at 1:00am. The air was cold enough that I pushed out white puffs as I approached. Fall will be ending soon. Mila was wearing jeans and a T-shirt under an open leather jacket. The same jacket I first saw her in. At first glance, she was ordinary. Completely stunning but resembles an ordinary human. People would pass her on the street and never think she was not born like everyone else. Well, if they could see her.

"I didn't want to just pop into your apartment." Her eyes fell to her feet. "I wasn't sure if you wanted my company."

I did this to her. Made her want to shrink away from me. Let my own anxieties push her away. Created a one-sided conversation inside my head. I should tell her I want to fight for this. For us. Tell her every minute of my night spent wondering what life with her as a human would be like. I softened my stance.

I moved in close to her and grabbed her chin with my thumb and pointer finger. That small touch tore down my wall and I was defeated. Immediately winning the war with my anxiety. Noting the light blush that adorned her cheeks.

I lifted her face until she was looking at me with those big brown eyes. She picked this face. It was entirely her creation. Not passed on by parents. This beautiful face. She selected each feature, from her doe eyes to her full lips. I would not have chosen differently if I had picked it myself.

She opened her mouth to say something, but I interrupted by pressing my lips to hers. Capturing the unnecessary apology, I knew was coming. Heat rose in my body. Forget all my worries, I needed this. I needed her. She has become closer to me than anyone in the world. So quickly. I've concluded that I didn't want to live without her. I can't live without her. That sounds dramatic even in my head. Now I just need to figure out what living with a reaper looks like. How we can blend.

I pulled back and kissed her forehead. "I want you here. Always." Her cheeks reddened. Who would have thought a reaper could blush. The perfect shade of pink. "I am sorry for earlier. I spiraled with stress and was not very kind to you."

Her eyes were glossy. It looked like a breath was being held in her throat.

"I am scared too." She cupped my face in her hands. "Just talk to me. I don't know how to do this." She motioned with one hand between us. I tilted into her hand that remained on my cheek.

A car rattled by when it hit a pothole, and we realized we were on the sidewalk, out in the open. "We can figure it out together." I grabbed her hand and entered the door code. She quietly followed me into the elevator. I immediately pushed her against the wall and kissed her deeply. Grateful this building was too old for cameras. She moaned when I pressed our bodies together. Our tongues fighting for space. The kiss was sloppy and full of need.

The elevator beeped and my willpower strained to push off her. Already missing the feel of her body underneath me. It was then I noticed.

"You don't have a reflection." My voice hitched. I probably could have said that with more tact.

"No." She glanced over her shoulder at the mirrored wall of the elevator. "Another quirky trait of being a reaper." She shrugged. Her eyes were waiting for my reaction. To see if I was going to freak out. With a laugh I pulled her out of the elevator towards my apartment.

While I got settled into my studio after a long night at work, she paced around the room. There are no pictures of my family or friends. Just stacks of papers and small statues meant to invite luck. Her hand brushed over my albums. I watched closely to see if she picked one up, but instead Mila moved to enjoy the view from my window. This studio was in an old building and lacked most modern amenities like a dishwasher or washer and dryer. What it did have was character. Original brick walls and large windows. Out of my price range if my father didn't know the owner personally. Mila has never had to pay for things. I wonder if she understands the concept of money. If she were to become human, would she want a job? Would she expect everything to be free.

Maybe I am thinking ahead of myself. We can cross that bridge if we come to it. If, being the key word.

After making myself a calming cup of tea, I put a record on. An indie folk group with romantic lyrics. Habits from a routine I have had for months now. With my odd work schedule, I try to go to sleep as soon as I can when I get home. I grab a highlighter and my copy of Family Practice & Primary Care. She grabs a fantasy novel from my shelf. We sit on opposite sides of the couch with the music in the background and read. Her legs are inside of mine. Like a key.

She was gleaming with joy. Every time I glance up from my book, I see light in her eyes. Apparently, being able to read is rare. For reasons I don't quite understand. Something to do with not being seen by cameras and making books look like they were floating. I told her to help herself to anything on my bookshelf whenever she wants. The look she shot back said, "Thanks, I already have." That made me chuckle.

"I can buy some books that you are interested in, if you want." That made her smile bigger than I had seen before. I put my book down and pulled her towards me. Until her body curled into mine. "I know you don't sleep but stay and talk with me until I doze off." She nodded and placed her book on the coffee table. We both scooted down until she was laying on my chest. The couch creaked as we shifted.

She whispered into my chest. "What do you want to talk about?"

"What's the most bizarre death you have seen?" I swear she flinched at my question.

"Really, that's what you want to talk about."

I stoked her hair. "Call me curious." She paused. Sorting through thousands of memories.

"You would be amazed how many people die masturbating. Mostly men." She said with a laugh. "But if I had to pick the most bizarre death, I would pick the Duke of Clarence."

"Who?" I said through a yawn.

She continued. "In 1478 the duke of clarence was executed by drowning in a barrel of wine."

"Wow, what a way to go." I laughed into her hair. She was tucked up tight to my body. My brain wanted to rip her clothes off, but my body was exhausted. "Who is the most famous person you- um-"

"Reaped?" She finished my sentence. I nodded with my eyes closed. "Chuck Berry in 2017."

"Ok that's cool. Or sad." This conversation was much less awkward than I expected. Truly two people talking about their work. Her work just consists of death.

"I would say it's cool. I saw him perform in the early 60's." She nestled her face into my chest. I rubbed her back, gently pushing her closer into the curve of my body.

"60's? You're old. That could mean 1560's or 1860's or-" She pinched my side before I could finish. So, I pinned her arms to her sides so she couldn't tickle me, and she nipped at my chin like a kitten. Oh God, she was perfect. I could keep here pinned to me forever. Sleep was trying to take me under like a weighted blanket has been thrown over me. "Mila?" I said softly and she just hummed. "Will you be here when I wake up?"

The record ended. For a moment there was no sound in my apartment. Just our steady breathing. It sounded like she was breathing, although I am very tired, and my mind could be playing tricks on me.

"Yes. Unless I am called away. I will be here." The last thing I noticed before I fell asleep was her hand in mine, and that weird ring she wears that warms when I touch it.

1
Mila

Jimi returns to his work routine. I take this time to travel the globe and find reapers willing to talk. Trying to find the reapers with the oldest signatures. Those that have been on earth long enough to possibly ask the same questions. Those that might have themselves met another paranormal.

A few of them rolled their eyes and vanished at my questioning. The moment I mentioned finding an Angel or Speaking directly with Death. They seemed content with the life of a reaper and could not understand why I was poking around. A couple, however, had the same curiosity burning behind their eyes. They were more than willing to gossip. Eager in a way. Repeating lines they heard from other reapers throughout their existence. The lore behind Angels is weak. Mostly rumors and folktales. A reaper in El Salvador told me there are very few Angels left on earth. Compared to the earliest days of human civilization. He claimed most of them had been called back to the afterlife.

Those that remain on earth work behind the scenes performing miracles. Blessing the single survivor of a plane crash or curing an illness for one lucky human. It is unknown how they choose who to bless. Perhaps the Archangels decide the same way Death decides who we reap. One thing I know for sure is that Angels report to an Archangel. The same way I get my orders from Death. Archangels are beyond my grasp of communication. They would never communicate with a being like me.

Angels are known as the ones who can restore. The bringers of light and hope. They can communicate directly with our creator. Through a form of prayer. A privilege reapers are not granted. Reapers can only speak to Death and other reapers. That is what I was told. But decades ago, a reaper casually mentioned meeting an Angel briefly. Only because they were sent for the same human. A rare occurrence.

I have only ever spoken to other reapers. Or that was the case, before I met Jimi.

It was a conversation with a reaper in Louisiana that finally gave me some insight. Angels loved being worshiped by humans and can only be summoned by one. They must have no doubt in their heart. Doubt of their existence. If they pray to the image of an Angel with pure intentions, they may be blessed with a visit. A vision.

"What does it mean to have pure intentions?" I asked the Louisiana reaper who was already looking away. They tapped on their chest. A sign that they were being summoned. My shoulders sunk. I know the inconvenient feeling of being summoned when you are in the middle of something.

They shrugged and smiled. "Good luck." They said before vanishing before me.

Back in New York, I passed all the information I gathered on to Jimi. Not knowing if any of it was true. Or in any way helpful. Light rain pebbled on the windows of his studio. He asked me to let him handle it. When I pushed him to know what he planned to do, he silenced my worries with a kiss. The distraction worked and had me moving from the topic quickly.

My timing was not the best. He was grieving the loss of a young patient. His shoulders were already hanging low when I dumped more responsibility on them. I shouldn't have felt relief, but I couldn't stop the huge breath that pressed out of me. I couldn't handle adding to his pain. I pushed talk of Angels away. Watched him eat a bowl of ramen while we talked about happier things. How his Caucasian mother learned to make his fathers favorite Korean foods when they were dating. He's excited for her cooking during the upcoming visit.

Shortly after our conversation lulled and we were moving out the door. It was my intention to walk with him to work, but I was summoned to a car accident in New Jersey. I stayed away from the hospital the rest of the night. I would only be a distraction. Most people don't have their girlfriends tag along while they work. Girlfriend? Is that what I was? Could a reaper be a girlfriend? We have been spending every minute together when we are not working. Although reaping is not meant to feel like a job. We are part of the great cycle of life. That's the pitch we are sold on the first day. Lately it feels more like servitude.

When I returned to the studio Jimi was already home from work. Usually, he showers in the employee locker room, but when I appeared inside his apartment, I heard water running and steam leaking out from the partially opened door.

I quietly parted the steam with my body and stood on the opposite side of the curtain. He was humming a tune. Something I did not recognize. My face heated just knowing he was naked on the other side. I waited for him to step all the way under the water before I made my clothes disappear. Bathing was not a necessity for reapers, but I needed to be in there with him. I needed it immediately or I was going to burst.

Popping in behind him, I wrapped my arms around his waist. It made him jump and freeze until he turned his head to where I greeted him with a cheeky smile. The shower was bright with white rectangle tile and a dark grout. It seemed very New York to me. The whole studio apartment was very cliché New York. Open brick walls and tall windows. Views of tall buildings and bill-boards.

"Mila!" He said while turning in my arms and keeping us linked together. "You almost gave me a heart attack."

"I think I would know if that was going to happen." I winked. His eyes went wide when he noticed I was naked and currently pressed against his wet body. His hands found the curve of my ass and he pulled me in closer. Closing any gap between us. Our lips crashed together. I let out a whimper of pleasure. Pleasure that was building low in my abdomen. He ignited a heat in me that was never there before. A part of me that has been dormant. I broke our kiss just so I could nestle my cheek against his chest. His skin was hot from the shower. A steady beat pounded under a layer of firm muscle. "Is it crazy that I saw you this morning and I still missed you."

"Hmmm." He purred. He ran his wet hands through my hair as he pulled me into a deeper kiss. Slower than the previous one. This was even more intimate somehow. His cock lifted against my stomach as it hardened. "I missed you too. When we are not together, I feel like I am missing a part of me." I rubbed up his chest with my hands. Following the lines with my fingers. He gripped one of my hands and lifted it to his mouth. Planting a soft kiss to my palm. Jimi made a trail of kisses up my fingers, then he lingered on their tips. The soul ring warmed as metal would sitting in the sun. It always heats up when he is near.

Liquid pooled between my legs that I knew was not from the shower. I checked to see if I was feeling the water from the shower, but his body was shielding me. Water usually passes right through me anyway. He cocked his head to the side trying to dissect the look on my face.

"What's wrong?" He spoke stepping back until he could follow my eyes down.

"Just new sensations." How do I say this without sounding stupid? "I think it's arousal." This made him raise an eyebrow and give me a crooked smile. A very mischievous look that does not belong to a gentleman.

"Let me check." He moved the hand that was on the back of my neck down to the side of my breast. His thumb grazed my nipple until it peaked. My breath caught. "That's a good sign. Let me investigate further." His hand continued down my stomach until he was cupping me between my legs. I was overwhelmed with need. One finger slid between my folds. I sucked in air and tossed my head back. I tried to blink away the tingling in my head.

Jimi guided my body until my back hit the tile wall, then he stood between my feet and forced my legs apart. He captured my mouth again, this time ending our kiss with a small nibble on my bottom lip. A shiver ran up my middle.

He dipped two fingers inside me, deep enough to confirm how wet I was. My hand gripped his shoulders. I feared my legs were losing the strength to stand. I held onto him to keep from collapsing with each swipe over my clit. His kiss became more desperate. Our tongues were fighting for space while he cupped my breast with one hand and pumped two fingers inside me with his other hand. I moaned into his mouth. "Don't stop touching me."

He came undone. The center of his eyes was so dark I couldn't see the pupil. They drank in the sight of my body as he slowly pulled his fingers free from the clenching of my pussy.

He reached over and turned off the water. Then he flung open the curtain before turning back to kiss me. He slid his hands over the curve of my ass then lower to the back of my thighs. Without breaking our kiss, Jimi lifted me up. My legs wrapped around his middle. He left a trail of wet footprints to the bed.

When he placed me down, there was a slap from my hair hitting my back. I broke our kiss with shock.

"I'm wet."

"I know." He kissed me again, but I pulled away.

I placed a hand on his chest. "I mean, my hair is wet."

"Is that not normal?" He climbed over me until I was lying flat on my back. My wet hair pressed into the comforter.

"No." I shook my head. "Usually, water just passes through me. I can walk in the rain and still be dry." He was kissing my neck and settling between my legs. Not concerned by my wet hair. "Something is different. I feel-"

He caused me to cut my sentence short when he plunged two fingers inside me. I bucked against him as his thumb swirled my clit. Pressure was building in me. A vibration of pleasure that was already near its pressure point. "Jimi." I moaned. "I need you inside me."

He lifted my ass off the bed and sat back on his heels. Then he grabbed me by my hips and pulled me up his thighs until his cock rested at my entrance. My chest shook with my quickened breaths. He kept rubbing my clit. *Wait, Am I breathing? Is air filling my lungs?* My back arched as I felt the orgasm edging close. He read my need for him. As my core begun to pulse, he thrusted deep. The angle hitting a spot inside that I didn't know could feel like that. I screamed and gripped the bed with both hands. Water dripped from his wet hair onto my stomach. He kept thrusting while my orgasm clenched his cock.

"Fuck Mila." His cock deep in me. "You're so perfect. It's like you were made for me." He didn't stop playing with my clit until my pulsating muscles stopped. Then he placed both hands on my hips and slammed into me. Filling me. *He's wrong, I think he was made for me.* My body being overly sensitive and still recovering from my orgasm. Each thrust at this angle is sending me further into ecstasy. My screams are breathy and echo each thrust.

I need him this close every day. I need him to fill me, to conquer me, to use my body however he wants. I trust him more than anything in this world. More than my own thoughts. More than Death.

Jimi lifts me, squeezing my thighs and his thrusts quicken. I felt warmth inside as he spilled into me. An invisible connection vibrated between us. Like a tether. Only strengthening with the physical connection. He lingered inside as he covered my body with his. Pressing his wet chest against mine. I kept my knees spread wide, not wanting to break our connection. He propped himself up on his elbows and scanned my face. A smile twinged on my lips. He returned the smile and placed a soft kiss on my lips.

"That was amazing." I said and he twitched inside me sending a shiver up my spine. We kissed again. Slowly. It was full of longing as if we hadn't seen each other in days. He moved his body off. Sliding his cock out slowly before settling on the bed beside me.

"Come to Colonie this weekend. I know I can't introduce you to my parents, but you can see them. See what they are like." He reached down and grabbed my hand. My ring warmed. I blinked until the room was in focus. I must have heard him wrong. I could have sworn he just asked me to meet his parents. Well, I can't meet them, but he wants me to see them. To learn about them. To watch them interact.

"Ok." My voice was quieter than usual. As if it was afraid to leave my mouth. Did I just accept? What am I thinking? I don't belong in his world. If he stays with me then He will never have someone to introduce to his parents. Someone to grow old with. I've leeched myself onto him and could be his ruin. Or at least the cause of many years of isolation and loneliness.

Jimi squeezed me tight against his chest and hummed into my hair. I could feel him smiling onto me. Suddenly a wave hit my gut. *What is this? Nerves?* I am a reaper. Reapers don't get nervous.

3
Jimi

I needed something that was made in the image of an Angel. A form of worship. That is the first step for prayer aimed towards a specific Angel. I'm hoping it doesn't matter who I pray to. I only know the Christian ones, but Mila was under the impression calling the name of an Angel from any faith holds the same value.

My mother had a statue at home that would work. It was on display in our living room for most of my childhood. Her small attempt to fit in with the catholic wives around the neighborhood. I don't remember her ever praying to it. It became more of a luck charm. I rubbed its head the morning before I asked Fiona Lark to the 8th grade dance. She said yes even though we barely spoke to each other. Then it sat on my desk while I studied for my S.A.T.'s and I ended up scoring higher than expected. We gave it credit for most of the lucky outcomes in high school. I even considered taking it with me to college but decided against it. I didn't want to be a poser.

Mila was reading in the corner with a beam of sunlight landing on her book. I found myself alone in my bed. Still naked. She heard me stir and popped her face up from the book.

"Did I wake you?" she said softly.

"Not at all. The sun woke me up." It must have been around my usual time to wake up, maybe 9:00am. I spread my arm out to the empty spot next to me and padded it with my hand. "Come back to bed. Just for a moment."

She put the book down and sauntered over to me. She was wearing my sweatpants and T-shirt. "Are those my clothes?" I asked, tucking her body tight against me.

"I wish. When you fell asleep, I tried to put yours on. I could pick them up, and even got your shirt over my head, but when I walked it didn't keep up with my movements and eventually fell down." She huffed out a frustrated breath. "So, I just copied their look. They don't smell like you though, but I can pretend they're real."

"Maybe someday they will be." I moved her hair to the side and kissed her neck. I covered her hand with my own. "What's the deal with your ring?" I nipped at her ear making her squeal.

She tilted her head out of my chomping range. "The deal?"

"Yeah, why does it warm and vibrate when I touch it?" I rubbed my thumb over the ring and sure enough it heated with my touch. Her eyes watched me move over the eight-pointed star etched into the gold. Her mouth opened and closed a few times. She was pondering my question. I hadn't realized it would stump her. Or maybe she didn't want to talk about it. Or that she could not tell me. A secret to only be known by reapers. She shifted in my arms but let me continue to hold her hand.

"I didn't know you could feel it. It should only react to me, or a soul I am collecting. I wonder-" Her voice trailed off. I watched her swallow the rest of the sentence.

"How do you collect a soul?" My voice calm but still bursting with curiosity. Her eyes darted around the room.

I gave her time to think and filled the pauses in our conversation by kissing her neck. I felt her relax. Melt into the curve of my body. We fit like puzzle pieces. Something I would read on a cheesy Valentine's card. I wondered if she altered herself to fit me so perfectly.

"The souls must be recently separated from their bodies." She answered. "They separate naturally during the last minutes of life. If a reaper is not present, they would just wander around until they eventually are found and collected. You might call it a lost spirit. We gather their souls and hold them in our rings. The ring tells me when it's full. Like a sensor. Then I open a gateway to the afterlife and escort the souls through. Really, I am a fancy chauffeur."

Fancy chauffeur? Sounds kind of epic. More exciting than most jobs. I gave a shallow nod. Taking in each word she said. "What is the afterlife like?"

There was another pause, but this time I managed to keep my lips off her. Pushing down my own urges to be close to her and touch her. Denying the literal link I feel with her. A connection that is driving me wild.

"I don't know. Reapers are forbidden to pass through the gateway, and we do not die ourselves." Sadness stuck to her words, as if she was envious of dying. It made me consider if I would want to live forever. Immortality sounds nice if you could travel anywhere. The 'being invisible' part does not sound like fun. Never having anyone to talk to. How does Mila do it? She did have other reapers, but it sounds like they don't exactly hang out. They spend most of their time in solitude.

"If we find a way to make you human, what will you do?" I nuzzled my face into her thick hair. She hummed.

"More of this." She ground her ass onto my cock. *Fuck.* I was ready to bury myself in her again. There are not enough hours in the day for how long I want to be inside her.

"As wonderful as that sounds, you would have a short life in the grand scheme of things. Humans don't live that long. You can't spend all your time in my bed." I traced my fingers up her arm. "Unfortunately."

This caused her to give me an exaggerated huff. Like a child not getting their way. "Don't burst my bubble, Jimi. I am risking-" I cut her off by pulling her onto her back and I angled my body over hers. Her dark lashed hooded her gaze. Her dark brown eyes seemed bright in the morning light. Littered with gold flakes. I wanted to study her face when she said it. When she said out loud that I was worth the risk. That me, Jimin Seong, Son of a Korean immigrant and a painfully optimistic Irish woman, am worth it.

I have postponed my AANP exam twice now. Knowing the second I pass there will be a large student loan breathing down my neck. I wanted to be an NP, and I'm so close. I should be sprinting towards the finish line. But my movement was slowing down before I met Mila. Lately, I am not sure I even want it anymore. The only path I see forward is her. My thoughts are not cloudy when I think of Mila. I have only known her for a few weeks, but I am desperate to hear her say she loves me. As if I have been waiting for years. I couldn't imagine a day without her. I would challenge Death himself if I had to. If that is what I need to do to keep her.

My attention went from her glinting eyes to her full lips. Hanging on every unsaid word.

She started again, "I am risking everything for the chance to be with you. Not that I have much to risk." The last part was mumbled quietly. As if she wasn't sure I was meant to hear it. "I know it's fast to have this conversation, but I'm terrified you will change your mind. That this between us is just short fun and not forever."

I had my lips on hers so quickly that she spoke the last word into my mouth. *Forever.* The word danced across my tongue. I deepened our kiss. My hands trailed up her body. Gripping her hair, I pulled myself off just enough to say. "It feels like the start of forever." She nodded and I saw tears gather in the corners of her eyes.

She said reapers couldn't cry, but that is not the case with her. Perhaps, I am not the unique factor in our relationship. It could be Mila who is different. She is special. One in a billion.

"The start of forever." She took a deep calming breath. "Forever is a long time."

"Too long?" I nipped her nose. A giggle slipped out. I said the words in unison inside my head when she spoke. Our path couldn't be clearer.

"Not long enough." She whispered with a dip of her chin. We lingered in each other's arms. Both replaying the conversation in our minds. It was agony dragging myself up, but the day had already begun and I could only ignore it for so long.

While I was eating breakfast she was summoned away. I showered and then packed for my trip. I ran through the inevitable conversation with my mother in my head. She was guaranteed to ask if I was dating someone, and although I wanted to say yes, I can't tell her I am with a reaper that is invisible to everyone except me. That I am in the process of trying to summon an Angel to find answers how to make her human. So, she can live a mortal life with me. No, I couldn't tell her that.

I rented a car for the drive up. Usually I would take the train, but I was hoping Mila would join me. The drive was about two and a half hours to Colonie. Mila popped into the car about halfway. I had told her the route and the type of car I rented. I was in motion, and she had to concentrate to find me. She was waiting by the highway until something matching the car description passed her by. When I asked if she was afraid, it was the wrong car, she smiled and said, "Not really, I could feel it was you somehow".

Which is strange, because I could have sworn, I sensed her before she appeared by my side. That mysterious connection between us vibrating in my core.

Mila knew more music than I expected. Perhaps that was naïve on my part. When all you can do is watch and listen, I suppose you hear a lot of music. We sang together. Me poorly and her like a songbird. In the car we didn't have to hide. We could talk and belt out every song with no one watching. She kept a hand locked with mine as we drove. Our fingers staying locked with each turn of the car. I could not keep a smile off my face. She was the most interesting person I have ever met. I wanted to hear all her stories. I wanted to kiss those full lips every morning and wrap her body in my arms every night. I shifted in my seat trying not to run off the road as my thoughts became a distraction.

I needed to get my mind off her body under those clothes. Clothes that could vanish with a simple thought from her. I continued a conversation from days ago. That has been on repeat in the back of my mind.

"You said you've seen the bests and worst of humanity." I squeezed her hand. "What would you say we got right and what did we get terribly wrong?"

She turned to look out the window. Pondering my question. She let out all the air from her lungs before turning back to me.

"Space exploration. I am amazed by your advancement. It's a beautiful curiosity. I also wonder what is out there." Then she paused and her mouth turned down. "Borders. My biggest disappointment was the creation and enforcement of borders. You were always meant to be one people of the earth, but humans are obsessed with separation. They created armies to keep those who were different off their land. Humans were supposed to blend and share. Instead, they are divided and greedy. It's hard to watch sometimes."

Her head hung low. In my head she would have a funny answer, but Mila cares greatly for humans and worries their flaws will lead to deaths. I guess she has firsthand proof that they do.

I swallowed my response. What do I say to that? Defending the actions of humans was not something I am prepared for. I admit, I'd not given borders much thought. I had family members that were separated when Korea spit. One would think it is something I would have thought about. It seems now I have kept my views very small.

"I can't even imagine a world without borders. It sounds lovely. Why doesn't God or whoever intervene?" I have been wanting to ask her about God since I first met her. She mentioned the creator, and it took all my strength not to prod her for more information.

"It is my understanding that the creator did just that, create. Then they sat back and observed. The systems they put in place, like reapers, Angels, and the Natural Order pretty much run themselves. At least this is my understanding." She tapped her fingers on the back of my hand. I asked her if there was a greater purpose or plan, she just shrugged. At least we can be clueless together.

The street with my childhood home was lined with leafless trees. Large orange bags meant to look like jack-o-lanterns were filled with leaves and sat near the curbs. It was a post-war neighborhood full of bungalows with red brick exteriors. I turned into the driveway and stopped.

A thick silence filled the car.

"I wish they could meet you. My mom would love you and my dad would question how I landed such a beautiful woman." Her lips tugged upwards as she squinted at the house.

I squeezed her hand one more time before pulling away reaching for the keys.

Stepping outside, I walked around to the trunk for my suitcase. I heard the front door before I could even get the trunk closed. My mom was running with tiny steps down the stone path. She held her arms out like she was ready to catch a beach ball. Her silver blond hair had been cut short. It was shorter than when I saw her in June. Living only a few hours away was supposed to encourage me to visit more often. But as my schooling is taking longer than expected, I admit to avoiding going home.

Her cheeks immediately flushed red with the cold air. I laughed as she threw her arms around me hard enough for the suitcase to drop on the ground.

"Ma." I said in a squeezed breath. "It's good to see you too." She released me but then placed her hands over my cheeks. I heard my dad chuckle from the porch. A deep laugh that made him look like a Korean Santa in a thick red wool sweater. Grey speckled beard reaching the collar.

"You're not sleeping enough. Your eyes look puffy. And you're so pale. When are you going to be done with the night shifts?" She stretched to reach my shoulders. Inspecting me for injuries.

"Sioban, let the boy get in the house." My dad called. She stepped back to allow me to grab my suitcase. Mila was standing behind me. I checked back in her direction as I followed my mom inside. Mila gave me a faint smile then appeared next to me quickly.

"I must go. Being summoned. I will come back later." I could barely nod before she vanished from my sight.

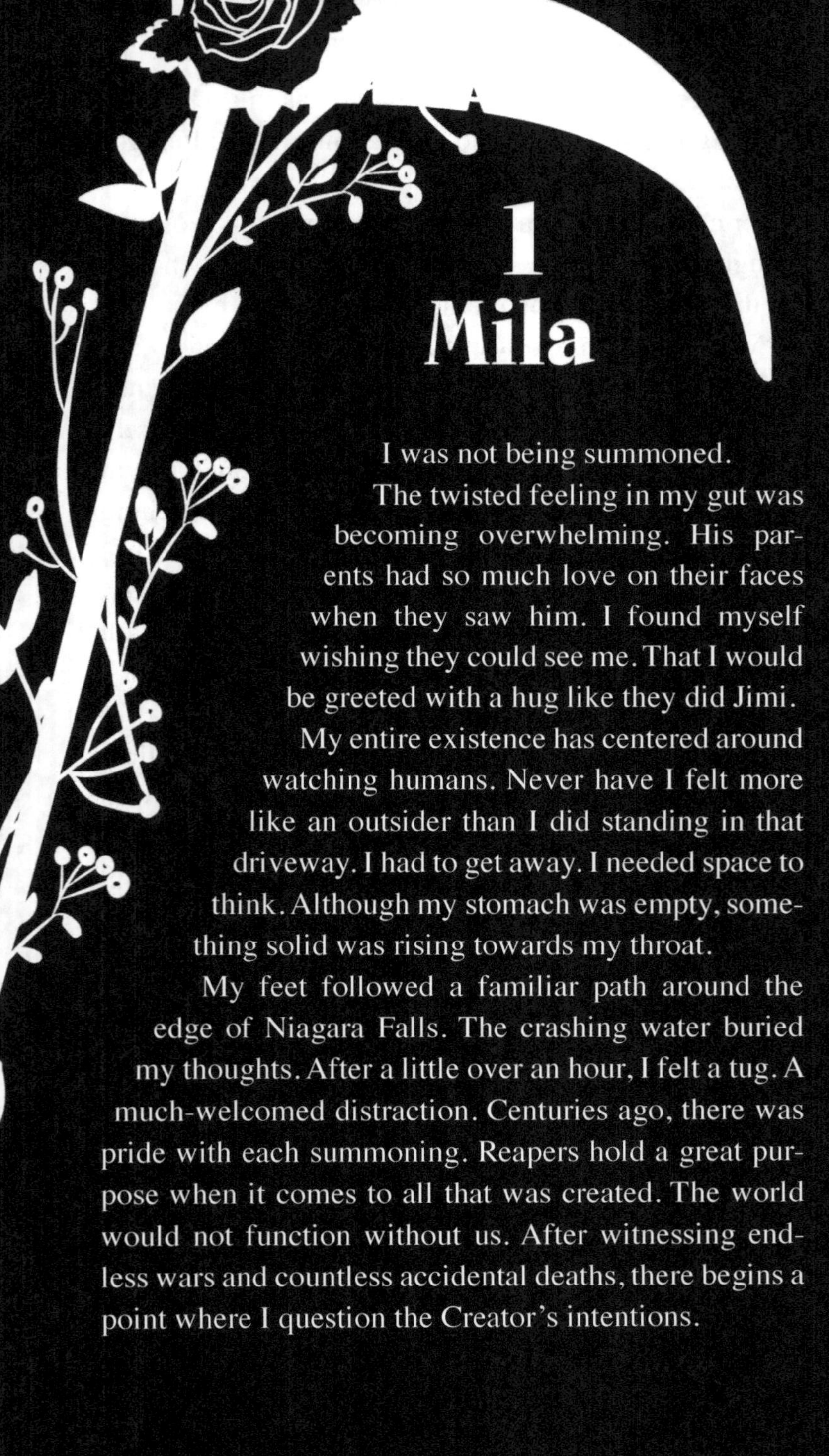

1
Mila

I was not being summoned.

The twisted feeling in my gut was becoming overwhelming. His parents had so much love on their faces when they saw him. I found myself wishing they could see me. That I would be greeted with a hug like they did Jimi. My entire existence has centered around watching humans. Never have I felt more like an outsider than I did standing in that driveway. I had to get away. I needed space to think. Although my stomach was empty, something solid was rising towards my throat.

My feet followed a familiar path around the edge of Niagara Falls. The crashing water buried my thoughts. After a little over an hour, I felt a tug. A much-welcomed distraction. Centuries ago, there was pride with each summoning. Reapers hold a great purpose when it comes to all that was created. The world would not function without us. After witnessing endless wars and countless accidental deaths, there begins a point where I question the Creator's intentions.

I appeared on a country road outside Ottawa Canada. There was a stalled SUV in the middle of the road with a frantic woman in the driver seat. Mascara ran down her face. Cries that could only belong to an infant came from the backseat. I scanned the road for a second vehicle, but all I saw was debris and a thin tire skid. I followed the direction of the tug to a ditch filled with tall grass.

Laying in the bottom was a man with a motorcycle helmet still on. His breath came out in short bursts. A thin piece of metal was sticking out of his side and blood was leaking from under his leather jacket. I have seen far too many motorcycle accidents in my time as a reaper. This man had a helmet on and probably thought he was safe. I changed into gray robes with my hood up moments before he appeared next to me in his translucent form.

"The fucking Grim Reaper? You gotta be kidding me." His eyes darted from me to his shaking body. "This a fucking hallucination."

"Just reaper, actually." I kept my arms tucked in the sleeves of my robe over my chest. "This is very much real."

"It aint my time. Can't be. I have so much shit to do. And my daughter-" he paused and removed his helmet. Dark hair was matted to his scalp. His skin was golden tan. A warm contrast to the overcast weather around us. "I promised my daughter that I would take her to Disneyworld for her birthday."

I had to dismiss his pleas as usual, but there was a twinge of pain in the middle of my chest. Another example of how I'd wish to have the power over who to save and who to take. The mention of his daughter made my throat feel tight. I gulped down the dry cold air.

"It is not up to me." His hazel eyes turned down. He bit his bottom lip and gripped the back of his neck, causing me to notice the lines of a tattoo. It must cover his back and shoulders. I found myself distracted by his beauty. His warm brown skin was rougher than Jimi's and I wondered what he would feel like run my hands over. *What the fuck is wrong with me?* This man is dying a few feet away from me and I am fantasizing about his body. I am losing control over my own mind. I am becoming unable to tamp down my emotions. This is more than curiosity.

We both turned towards the ditch as the gurgling sounds started. His lungs were pierced and filling with blood. We were about to watch him choke to death. "Can you pass on a message for me?" A common question. I used to be honest and say "no", but in later years I lie to prevent them from having unfinished business or resist me. I nod slowly. "My ma lives alone. Her name is Irma Palacios. She lives in Ottawa at 1370 Dowler Ave. Tell her I bought back father's watch from the pawn shop. That I hid it in my red toolbox in the shed."

"What's so special about a watch?" I tilted my head.

"My father passed last year. She sold anything valuable to pay for the funeral." He stared down at his feet. "I was locked up at the time. A fucking misunderstanding. I wasn't there for her when she needed me. I have been hunting down the items she sold. Hoping she'd fucking forgive me."

"Mothers tend to forgive their children." I said flatly.

"The watch has their initials on it. She gave it to him on their wedding day." His body gagged and then stopped moving. "My mom should have it."

I nodded. Maybe I will make an exception one time. I could ask Jimi to send an anonymous letter. But if I start fulfilling requests now, will it ever stop? It never bothered me so much before. It's not my responsibility and Death would most likely banish me if I tried to interfere.

I gave him a thin smile. "Take my hand. It's time."

"Promise me she'll get the watch." His eyes darted to my open palm and the glowing gold ring.

"I promise."

"And my daughter-" He started but I cut him off.

"I am sure she will make it to Disneyworld." I grabbed his hand a bit too abruptly. His face melted into a frown as he dissipated into grey smoke and slipped into my soul ring. I turned my hand over and checked the eight-pointed star. The ring felt full. That can't be possible. Unless I lost count of how many souls I have collected.

I moved quickly to the center of a secluded forest only a few miles away.

Holding my hands out I summoned the gateway. The stone arch with only a black void beyond it appeared before me. Six souls gathered next to me. Only six? Why did the ring feel full? Something is wrong with me or my ring.

As the souls walked through the void, I remembered the conversation with the other reaper. To become human, I need a soul to enter my body making it real. I called into the void. Sending a beacon from my chest begging for an unclaimed soul to choose me. A steady pulse like an invisible soundwave. I felt nothing reaching for me in return.

The last of my collected souls walked into the void and the gateway vanished like mist. Hopefully Jimi will have more luck summoning an Angel. Soon I may need to look elsewhere for answers. Or just accept this is all our relationship can be. Him a mortal human and me an immortal servant to Death.

I wandered the forest until it was getting dark, then I headed back to Jimi's parents' house.

3
Jimi

Dinner with my par-
ents went relatively smoothly.
My dad asked me if I changed my mind
on becoming a doctor instead of a Nurse practitioner. When I responded no, he audibly huffed. This
made him suggest I find a female doctor to date. Hoping
her ambition would rub off on me. Which sent my mom
on a tangent about me working late and never going on
dates.

I helped with the dishes and was grateful the inter-
rogation ended. By instinct I checked every corner of
the room when I entered it, half expecting to find Mila
watching from a corner. She was gone most of the afternoon and I wondered when she would return. If she
would return.

With my dad watching the news from the couch and
my mom settled into her knitting chair, I snuck upstairs.

There was a box tucked away in the bottom of my closet filled with items I did not take to college. This should include a certain lucky stone statue of the Angel Zadkiel. It was just where I left it. Crammed between a leather-bound journal and worn baseball mitt.

I closed the blinds and turned on my nightstand lamp. Counting on the meditation methods my father taught me to work as a prayer. The nameless reaper said I needed pure intention. That prayer in any form counts with the right intention. I crossed my legs in the middle of the bed and placed my palm on my knees. What a weird path my life is taking. Reapers, Angels, and Death themselves. Maybe I'm schizophrenic and created Mila in my head.

I breathed in deeply. *Zadkiel, I am your humble worshiper.*

Exhale. *Zadkiel, I seek your guidance on a matter involving a reaper.*

Inhale. *Zadkiel, you are wise and glorious.*

The nameless reaper said Angels liked to be worshiped and praised. Angels see themselves above all things, except the Creator. They can feel if your intentions are pure.

Exhale. *Zadkiel, you have the power to influence the greatest thing on earth, love. It is love that is growing between us. Pure and true love. We are linked. Created this way, and I need to understand why. I need to know how to make it permanent. How to make her human.*

There was a creak in my room. My eyes snapped open landing on the dark wall across me. There was nothing there. I began to close my eyes again when there was a slight breeze. The edges of my room were dark, and one wall seemed to shift even darker.

"Zadkiel?" I whispered.

A bare foot stepped out, becoming more solid as it submerged into the light. A man that appeared to be in his sixties with a gray speckled beard and hair combed back stepped forward. He wore a long white robe that was sinched at the waist with a gold tasseled rope. Honestly, it was a bit cliché. I nearly jumped when I heard a rustle of feathers behind him. Wings, he had gold wings tucked behind his body.

"Zadkiel?" I repeated.

"Yes, my child." He tilted his head. His gold wings twitched with curiosity. "It's been a long time since I have answered a call, but your light is different. Flawed." His voice had a distant echo when he spoke.

"Flawed how?"

"I needed to see for myself." His voice bounced off every wall. He moved closer but it was more like floating than walking. I froze and let his eyes search my face. They were gold, like his wings. The color was fluid like a wave. As if the gold was in liquid form. Zadkiel blinked slowly. "I see it now." He hummed.

"Is this flaw the reason I can see and speak to a reaper?" My voice childlike.

Zadkiel's eyes traced the statue on the bed. He appeared to be pleased with the likeness. Making his shoulders rise. A glow shone from his skin making my room brighter.

I might as well have been behind glass in a zoo, with the way he was looking at me. Zadkiel gave me no indication that he would answer my questions. I wondered if I should ask it again. Then his voice surrounded me when he spoke. I was still sitting on the bed, and I felt smaller than a flea.

"Child, I am afraid that reaper has been consuming your soul."

"What?" I pushed up onto my knees. A position common for Christian prayer. But I did not grasp my hands together. They remained at my side. Ready to plead or grab him. Whatever might seem necessary.

"I came to see why you felt incomplete, it all makes sense now." Zadkiel started to retreat to the shadows, and I reached out a hand.

"What makes sense?" The words came out shaky. "Wait. You can't leave without giving me some answers."

He floated closer to the bed. I dropped my hand. There was power pulsing of his body. Nausea went through me like waves as if I was inside a cabin on a boat. When he spoke the glow he generated brightened white.

"Child, you are not able to make demands of me. I am Zadkiel." He said flatly.

I pressed my hands together. "I am not demanding. I am praying for your grace. Please, what is happening to me is beyond the knowledge of a human. Only an Angel like yourself can shed light on my situation." Pun intended. I hated the groveling coming out of me. Angels have large egos and love it to be stroked. A twinge of a smile formed on his face. "Can she become human?"

"What I will tell you, child, is yes, the reaper you have grown fond of can become human. In fact, the change is already happening. She has been taking your soul for over a decade. Your recent encounters have only sped up the process."

Liar. She wouldn't do that. He must be wrong. "She wouldn't do that."

Zadkiel's gold eyes held mine. He had no reason to lie. He said every word with confidence and assurance.

"Your naïve reaper does not know, nor can she stop it now." Zadkiel raised his shoulders. "Once it is completed your body will cease to live, but she will have a mortal life."

I shook my head. It can't be. "There must be a way we can be together."

Zadkiel ignored my plea.

"Goodbye my child." He echoed before stepping back into the shadows. I jumped from the bed and ran towards him but was met with the wall of my room. *She has been taking my soul. For over ten years?* I scratched my head. *What happened then that made it start?*

I glanced down at the open box of memories on the floor. Kneeling I pulled a purple frame from under the journal. I rubbed dust off the glass with my thumb and gazed into the face of my sister. My only sibling, who died eleven years and seven months ago.

A memory flooded my mind as Mila showed up looking somber. I stuffed the picture back in the box and sighed. I stood firm.

"Were you here over eleven years ago during a school bus crash?" Her eyes went wide, and I knew her answer without her saying a word.

24
Jimi

<u>**2013**</u>

The roads had a sheen from the most recent storm. The back of the bus was filled with kids singing Christmas songs on their way home from school. Even the bus driver joined in as the excitement of the holiday break starting the next day grew. I sat next to my best friend. Pink tinted saliva sprayed from our mouths. The remnants of a candy cane hanging on our lips.

Our town was small enough that the bus was shared by the elementary and middle school. Which is how I, at age fourteen, was sitting a few seats away from my younger sister. She was ten years old. A quiet 5th grader with a talent for drawing and playing the flute. I usually sit by her on the bus, but today I wanted to trade candy and sing with my friend Bryon.

Snow had been falling all afternoon. By the time I get home there will be a fresh blanket for me to play in. I plan on building the biggest snowman in the whole neighborhood. Maybe an igloo for Jae to play in.

There was a loud screech in the road before a truck slammed into the school bus. The impact caused immediate panic. Children screamed in unison. The bus tilted. Holiday crafts with glitter and streamers flung out of hands. One student spilled an entire bag of red and green M&Ms. They hit the metal floor of the bus like rain on a roof.

My body slid off the bench and I gripped the back of the seat in front of me. My knuckles were white trying to hold on.

Just before I lost my grip, I turned towards where my sister was sitting. My view of her shifting with the still moving bus. She was already pinned under another kid with a hand reaching out in my direction.

"Jae!" I screamed. The truck was larger than average. We slid into a bank on the side of the road and lost balance. The bus fell completely on its side. It did not rock back and forth. Just smashed into the snow-covered ground with a thud. Glass had shattered from every window on the side of impact.

My head was foggy and filled with the cries of children around me. We were piled on top of each other. Our limbs twisted like tree branches from fallen trees. Slowly the kids moved until most of us were standing on a row of broken windows.

Byron balanced on the edge of a bench seat. He leaned his back on what was the floor. He held his head and groaned. *Jae!* I need to find Jae. I climbed over two seats to where she was sitting. I found her laying down. Her limp body was covered in fresh cuts.

"Oh my God, I think I landed on top of her." A student cried at me when I leaned over her. My vision blurred when I bent down. The sudden feeling of cold had me looking down at my wet shirt. Each breath stung. I lifted my shirt and noticed a gash in my flesh leaking blood. I lowered my shirt, letting it soak up more blood.

My injury was not important now. I switched my focus. Jae was not waking up even when I shook her or screamed her name.

Someone opened the emergency door, and children were exiting through the back. Only the ones with the worst injuries remained. I sat next to Jae. She has always been the small kid in her class. She was curled on the broken glass.

I was reminded of the days when she was a toddler and would sleep curled up in a ball. We surprised her with a large fluffy dog bed for her third birthday. It is her favorite spot to read to this day. I lifted my arm to signal for help, but the movement made my head spin. I sucked in a deep breath and pain shot deeper into me.

"Over here." My voice came out quieter than I intended. I waved my arm in the direction of the red and blue flashing lights coming from the open door in the back. "We are over here." I squeaked.

Other children were shouting louder than I was able to muster. I reached higher, making sure my hand was seen over the bus seat. Warm wet blood leaked down my side. I shifted so my blood would not get on my sister's body. With a twinge of pain everything went black.

Mila

2013

I arrived for a soul collection and was mortified to find a school bus on its side and a group of terrified children exiting the back. The snow was falling in oversized flakes. Sobs and wheezing filled the air.

Larger children, teenagers I assume, were carrying smaller ones. They set them down in a huddled group on the wet concrete. I moved by them looking for an indication of who I was to take.

I made my way to the front of the bus. Two souls were calling to me. I could feel it as I got closer.

The cause was a truck. It was a large truck, the kind that carries slabs of stone countertops. The crash might not have resulted in deaths if the bus hadn't fallen to its side. If the road had not been so narrow causing it to fall into the embankment. I sighed to myself.

The driver had white hair and age spots. He was already waiting in his translucent form when I approached. He was shouting and waving his arms to get the attention of a police car. Following the car was an ambulance. A firetruck was blaring their siren from the other direction. I tapped him on the shoulder. He shivered when he saw me standing in a long white hooded coat. I gave it white fur trim to match the winter weather. Plus, older people love to assume reapers are Angels, then they usually come willingly.

"They cannot see you." I said with a soft tone. My hair was a dark red, and thick curls peeked out from my hood. His eyes went wide and darted to his lifeless body at the front of the bus.

"That would mean-" He didn't finish the sentence. He just put his hands down and let his shoulders drop. "This is my fault; my reflexes are not as fast as they used to be."

"No. It was not your fault." In fact, I do not know who truly decides when humans die. Was it Death? Or is he subject to follow a form of fate?

He shook his head. "Did any of the children," he paused. "did any of them die?"

"As far as I can tell, only one." I thought the odds sounded good, but he began to sob. His temporary form could not produce tears. He paused with his hands in front of his face and finally noticed the snow passing right through his body.

"Am I a ghost?"

"I sure hope not. Take my hand. It's time to move on to you resting place." I gave him a warm smile and held out my hand with the gold ring. An eight-pointed star pressed into the top. He hesitated, as most do, then placed his hand in mine. I kept the smile on my face as he turned to gray mist and floated into my ring.

One down, one to go.

There was a tug behind me. A smaller soul, younger too. I dreaded this next reap as I appeared inside the wrecked bus and found two unconscious children. The boy was leaking blood from his side and the girl did not appear to be moving. His life was teetering. Death was still deciding if he was going to live or not. There was a definite glow coming from the small female. I waited patiently.

"Who are you?" A small voice asked from behind me. I turned to find the girl. She had straight black hair cut just below her chin. Next to her the male teens translucent form was blinking in and out.

"I am your guide." I kneeled to be at eye level. "It is time to leave this world and go somewhere peaceful."

She turned her head to look at her body. The chest was barely rising. I held out my hand. Children don't ask as many questions as adults. She reached for my palm without hesitation.

"Stop." The male teen pushed her arm down. The paramedics next to us began working on his wound. They would be the deciding factor. Determining if I would take one or two more souls. His glow faded. He was going to be saved. But she still had the signature markers all over her. A faint white glow from her dying body.

"It's her time." I threw my hood back and stood to my full height. He stepped in front of the girl's body. I pointed down. "You will return to your body soon."

"No. She's my sister." He squared his shoulders as if preparing for a fight. I smiled at his bravery. "You can't have her."

"It's not up to me, boy." I made my eyes glow white when I emphasized the last word. His translucent form was already fading. This conversation was pointless. Soon he would be back in his body, and it would be just me and his sister. He blinked away. I stuck out my hand to the little girl. "Take my hand. Your brother will be fine. He will live and you will be at peace."

She nodded and stepped closer. When she placed her tiny hand in mine. My ring warmed, she gave me the faintest smile as she began to turn into gray mist. Her teen brother was back. He quickly lunged forward trying to cover her body with his. Then he grabbed my hand. For a few seconds he faded to gray with her.

"Stop, it's not your time." I shouted and swatted at his hand. He tightened his grip. I finished collecting his sister. I couldn't help but gawk at him. He stood there holding my hand with a look of defeat on his face. I pulled myself away. The teen opened his mouth to speak but I heard the paramedics rejoicing that they got his heart at a steady rate. He vanished before me.

A breeze guided snowflakes through the back door. A shiver went up my spine. *Odd, I haven't shivered before.* I pulled the hood back over my head.

The sides of the bus were closing in on me. I longed for open air. I headed to the Empire State building. I hate collecting children's souls, and I almost accidentally took three instead of two. I stared out at the city, letting the noise of cars and people fill my head.

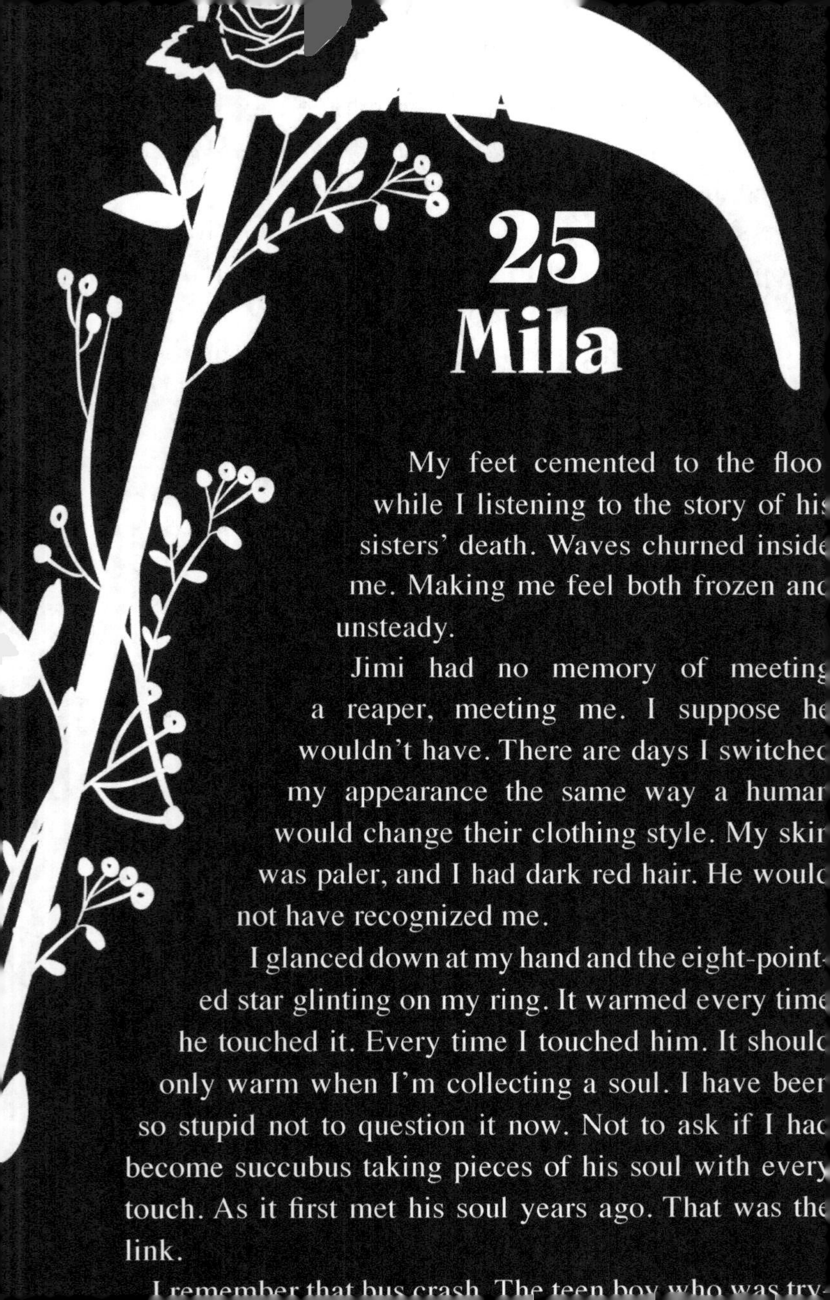

25
Mila

My feet cemented to the floo[r]
while I listening to the story of his
sisters' death. Waves churned inside
me. Making me feel both frozen and
unsteady.

Jimi had no memory of meeting
a reaper, meeting me. I suppose he
wouldn't have. There are days I switched
my appearance the same way a human
would change their clothing style. My skin
was paler, and I had dark red hair. He would
not have recognized me.

I glanced down at my hand and the eight-pointed star glinting on my ring. It warmed every time
he touched it. Every time I touched him. It should
only warm when I'm collecting a soul. I have been
so stupid not to question it now. Not to ask if I had
become succubus taking pieces of his soul with every
touch. As it first met his soul years ago. That was the
link.

I remember that bus crash. The teen boy who was trying to protect his sister. It's clear when I look in his eyes now. The same willingness to sacrifice himself, and compassion. All the things I love about him.

"Being with me is hurting you." My voice was shaky. He stepped towards me and wrapped his arms around my waist. I jumped to the other side of the room. My back against the wall. "No. Don't touch me until I find out what it's doing to you."

He took a step in my direction then let his hands fall to his sides.

"Let's not panic. The Angel came." He was moving towards me again. "Zadkiel answered my prayer. It was how I knew our connection must have been when my sister died. I'm just not sure how."

I should be honest and tell him about how he almost died. That I was the reaper who took his sister. How we spoke when he was not yet an adult. *I took a piece of his soul. What happens if I take it all? Can I even do that to someone who is not dying? Or is everyone considered dying from their first breath.*

I couldn't breathe. My chest tightened, and my heartbeat thrummed in my ear. He sensed my hesitation to stay. His face softened and eyes went wide. He moved to stand before me. Expression pleading.

"Don't run. You look like you are going to run." He tried to rub my arm, but I flinched. This made him furl his brow. "Lay with me for a while. Just relax."

He motioned to the bed. Reapers don't feel anxiety. Reapers don't get overwhelmed. What the fuck is happening to me? I moved slowly to his bed. He walked behind me and kept a hand hovering over the small of my back. *Has he figured it out? Does he blame me for his sister's death?* Clearly Zadkiel didn't tell him everything. He would be way more freaked out if he knew I stole a piece of his soul when he was a teenager. He's far too calm to know everything.

I laid my head on the pillow. My body made a genuine imprint in the bed, but I was too distraught to care more. He moved around to the other side of the bed and laid down to face me. His breathing was far too calm for someone that just met an Angel and found out their reaper girlfriend is killing them.

Although sleep is not necessary for a reaper, I still closed my eyes and tried to empty all the thoughts of worry from my head. Don't panic. Jimi's words echoed in my head. I tried to focus on his steady breathing.

Eventually Jimi fell asleep. I must have been in a deep state of meditation because I felt a tug causing me to open my eyes. A couple of hours must have passed. The moon was high in the night sky.

I stood over his sleeping body. It reminded me of the first few nights I watched him in his apartment before he knew what I was. He would doodle swirls and animals in the margins of his books. Moving his feet to the beat of music playing on his record player. I had longed to be there with him. Wondered what it would be like to be wrapped in his strong arms. Longed for his kind eyes to see me again.

I have that now. Every day this past week, I have been able to live that dream. The best part is, he wants more.

More of me. More of a life together. It aches for me to leave his side while he sleeps. The summoning tug pulls again.

I keep my goodbyes inside my head.

Exhale while I bend closer to him.

I pressed a kiss to his temple, lingering for long seconds.

Then leave in a silent blink.

26
Jimi

I have been waiting for Mila to return for five days. Two of them were spent at my parent's house avoiding conversations about my future.

I returned to my apartment in NYC half expecting to find her reading on my chair. She was not there. In fact, she was not waiting outside when I got off work or watching me from the roof across from my building.

I had time to consider the words of Zadkiel. *She has been taking your soul for over a decade.* Her reaction gave the impression she did not know. Also, unaware that she reaped my sister's soul. Something I figured out by the hurt in her eyes when I told her Jae's story. I chose not to press that part. It was not her choice who to take. That I understand.

I wonder how her taking my sister's soul has linked us together. How that event caused a part of me to stay with her.

Whatever the reason, it was making her human. Being with me was making her human. I am the solution to make her human. Me. Although, it ends with my death. Maybe we can find a way around that.

I wish she would come back so we can talk about this. I may not be ready to end my life, but I'm not ready to lose her either. My chest was hollow without her here. Fate and destiny have never been real concepts to me, but I feel it inside the deepest parts of me, we were meant to be together. That feels like fate.

Snap out of it, Jimi. I scold myself in my head. *You know Angels, reapers, and Death is real. You know souls are real. Think, there must be a solution.*

I rushed home from work after a late shift. The streets were quiet. I searched for Mila in every shadow and on every rooftop. When I reached my apartment, I didn't sleep, didn't eat. Instead, I just sat at my computer and researched. There were so many varieties of folktales and lore. I remember Mila saying there was a bit of truth in all of them, and the only thing that mattered was *intention.*

I successfully summoned an Angel. Maybe I can summon a demon. They are notorious at making deals according to tales from around the world. I needed something they would trade for. Most legends have people trading first born children, or women to be used as brides. Then there is the most common commodity. Souls.

My soul is incomplete. I would rather have it used by Mila than traded for a demon. There must be another option out there. I could try to get a message to another reaper. She went to a reaper when she needed answers. Perhaps they would have empathy for the situation.

On my knees I rummaged through a box of old art supplies. A hobby that started when I was very young. I have been too exhausted to keep up. The days of wanting to be an illustrator are long gone.

I pulled out a sketch pad of thick watercolor paper and a box of pastels. A gift from my mother that still had plastic on it from two Christmases ago. The wood floor creaked under me as I shifted to a better position. I forgot to raise the thermostat as the temperature outside has been dropping. A minor punishment to myself until I get Mila back. Why feel warmth if it's not because of her.

My hands and forearms were covered in black smudges. Probably a few places on my face also. I sketched her face repeatedly. I traced the lines of her full lips that were burned into my memory. I tried to catch the warmth of her brown doe eyes, but her beauty went beyond a 2D drawing. I became frustrated with the brown looking too dull. She has a way of stripping me down with one look. Seeing deep inside me where I like to hide. I sketched fervently and threw the rejects into a pile near the wall.

When satisfied with the likeness, my body collapsed onto my couch, and I fell asleep.

I followed death around the hospital like a leech. If there was someone on life support and their health was wavering, I would visit them. I would call out into the spaces of their room that seemed empty. Hoping a reaper was waiting there.

"If there is a reaper here waiting to take this soul, please tell this reaper," I held up the sketch of Mila. "That I am looking for her. That she needs to come back. I need her to come back."

There was never a response, but even if the reaper was there and speaking, would I even know.

I spent every minute between tasks looking at patients' charts. Trying to predict who would die. A calm voice came over the intercom, "Alvarez code blue, 214". I flinched with excitement. A man that was on another floor was having cardiac arrest.

I rushed down the stairs two at a time. Then barreled into room 214. Dr Alvarez and a nurse were already performing CPR, but a voice in the back of my mind hoped it didn't work. Hoped there was a reaper waiting nearby.

"What are you doing here, Seong?" Dr Alvarez shouted over the high-pitched beeping of machines.

"I was nearby and thought I could help." I pulled my hand from my pocket where it gripped the sketch of Mila.

"Jimi?"

The voice calling my name was familiar. It was Serena. She was assisting CPR and staring at me with confusion.

"Prepare the AED." Dr Alvarez instructed. Serena was watching me with wide eyes wondering why I was on this floor to begin with. Why was I not moving swiftly like a trained nurse should?

I grabbed the cart and pulled it towards his body. Serena was lifting his hospital gown to expose his chest. I handed her the first pad, and she placed it on his upper right side. The next pad went on his lower left side, just below his armpit. I glanced back into the empty side of his hospital room. The hairs on the back of my neck tingled.

We connected the cables and stood back from his body. Quietly I moved further into the room. Hoping the shadows would conceal me. "Clear." Serena called, as the short countdown on the AED changed its glowing red numbers. I slipped the paper from my pocket and held it open against my back. "Clear." All I could do was hope a reaper was behind me. I had written the words 'looking for this reaper' on the top of the page.

Odds were against me if this man lived. I have never wished for death, and I wondered if humans were greedy and evil. I feel greedy now. Wanting to put my own desire to have Mila above this man's life.

"Call it." Dr Alvarez pointed to the straight line on the screen. He hung his head and violently ripped the sanitary cover on the CPR mouthpiece off. Tossing it roughly into the waste bin.

"Calling it at 11:38pm October 16th, 2023, for William Roberts age sixty-three." Serena began to fill out his chart as the Dr. pulled a sheet over his head. I folded the paper and placed it back in my pocket. Before Serena could question why I was there, I slipped into the hall.

27
Mila

I have been wandering around the Oregon coast between reapings. Trying not to stay in NYC. The temptation to see Jimi is too strong. The best thing for him is if I leave him alone and not risk taking anymore from him. Maybe in time his soul will fade from me. Maybe in time he will become whole again. If I stay with him, he will have no chance of a normal life. If he lives at all.

The moment I was flooded with the memories of the bus crash, I knew it was not a blessing that we found each other. It was a curse. I was a curse set upon him because I was sloppy during a collection. My stupid mind thought I would be worthy of being an exception to the rules. That Death would allow me to have love. To feel pleasure and live in the delusion that I could be human with him. Have a life with him.

I tightened my hands into fists, wishing I could feel pain from digging my nails.

All this time I was stealing from him. Slowly killing him. I'm a sickness.

I held my fingers to my lips thinking about his kiss. My core heated when I remembered the orgasms. The moments of passion that tricked my mind to believe I was human. That every sensation vibrating through me was proof we were meant to be together. Not proof that I stole a piece of him when he was a teenager. All lies in my head.

I wanted to bury myself in the sand and hide forever. How could I be so stupid? So naïve. I got lost in his deep brown eyes and crooked smile. I forgot what I am. I am a reaper. A child of Death. A conduit for dying souls. I don't get to have a home. I don't get to have a lover. We were created to live in the shadows and wait until summoned.

Jimi was good. I have seen evil people in this world. He wanted nothing more than to help people. He was a wonderful son and a loyal friend. He accepted the darkest parts of me.

I turned, making divots in the sand, and was shocked to find someone staring at me. I should have sensed the other reaper sooner. My voice inside my head was too loud. It blocked out my reaper intuition.

I paused only for a moment before continuing my stroll down the beach. They appeared by my side and kept pace with me as I walked. I uncurled my hands and tried to look at ease.

"I don't see many other reapers in my territory." She spoke with a slight Mid-West accent. A fun choice for someone who could make their voice sound like anything. "When did you get summoned here?"

In truth, every summons I had for the past five days has brought me back to New York. Part of me was hoping for a shift. That Death would station me somewhere else. Giving me less reasons to be in the same city as him. Where I might be tempted to see him. To hurt him.

"I wasn't summoned. I just like to walk the beach to clear my head." My voice lacks warmth. Her short blond hair bobbed as she nodded. Her signature was not recognizable. I have not met this reaper before.

She slapped her leg in a comical way. "Rats. I was hoping you were taking my place, and I could go somewhere else. I have only been here."

"You've been in this area for hundreds of years?" My mouth gaped open. I have been fortunate enough to see many parts of the world. Boredom would overtake me if I stayed in one spot for that long. Even with my history, I take every chance I get to travel. To watch the sunrise from rooftops in a new city.

"Oh gee, no." She swung her arms like a child as she walked. "I did my training in Minnesota. I have been on the Oregon coast for only five years."

"Five years!" I almost choked. "I have never met a reaper so young. I didn't think Death was creating more reapers to be honest."

She beamed. Her childlike smile made more sense now. Did I have that youthful glow when I first arrived? I was more eager then. Excited to please Death and do a good job. There was an inherent need to make Death proud of me. A feeling that has faded over the years, I admit.

"I heard a handful of reapers have disappeared in recent years. Not sure what the cause is though." She blabbed.

"Interesting." I said mostly to myself. That must mean reapers are either finding a way out or dying. Maybe I am not the first to find themselves linked to a human. There could be humans walking around that used to be reapers. It sounds too farfetched. I think I am just grasping for answers in the dark. I kicked a shell causing it to tumble in front of me. The mist and drizzle of rain caused the beach to be empty. The only two visitors here are us reapers. Leaving no footprints as we walk.

"What's the rest of the world like? I can't wait to be stationed somewhere else." She spoke with strong O's and flat A's. A habit she had to of picked up in Minnesota. I have always liked the Midwest dialect. It feels inviting and reminds me of casseroles.

"You know you can leave whenever you want. You weren't told this during training?" She shrugged at me. "Death will summon you back if you are needed for a collection or he might summon you somewhere else, if you appear nearby a person near death. They often choose the closest reaper."

She was looking around the beach as if waiting for Death themselves to show up and contradict me. I smirked at her ignorance. I remember being new. Being a young reaper excited to see the world. Now I feel like I have seen everything but have still not lived. Until recently. When Jimi looks at me, I feel alive. I feel whole.

"I think I would like to see the Eiffel Tower and the Taj Mahal." Her eyes sparkled and it appeared she was walking on her tiptoes. As if her excitement would cause her to float away.

"The Eiffel Tower is a good choice. I remember it being built. Amazing human engineering." She grabbed my arm to stop me from walking and turned me to face her. There was only pressure where she gripped me. No warmth like when… I shook the thought of Jimi from my head and focused on the young reaper.

"You were there when it was built?" She beamed. "I am so jealous. I am fascinated with building design. They call it Architecture, right?"

I nodded. "You should go check Al Hamra Tower in Kuwait or Marina Bay Sands Hotel in Singapore. There is a skyscraper shaped like a giant sailboat in Dubai."

I rambled off three of my favorite buildings. Then immediately thought back to the simple roof across from Jimi's studio. I held back the frown and matched the face of joy she wore.

"I guess it's not that busy here. A little travel shouldn't make Death mad. Thank you, reaper." She dropped my arm and bounced once in the sand.

"Mila."

"What?" She blinked rapidly. "You have a name?"

"Yes, Mila." My gaze went towards the overcast sky. "I gave it to myself."

"I think I would like to have a name." She made a yellow rain jacket appear on her body and slid her hands into the pockets. "Maybe I will travel and name myself after my favorite building."

Is this what a parent feels like when they are proud of their child? I never understood why we didn't have individual names. Was Death so worried of reapers being unique. That we would be harder to control if we felt special. "That's a lovely idea." I said.

"Thanks for the conversation, it has been ages since I had someone to talk to. I am going to hop over to Paris for a bit."

She took a few steps away and raised her hand to wave.

"Have fun. Walk into a bakery, the smells are divine." I shouted. She gave me a quick smile and was gone.

I found myself alone again. Just the Mist and me. And my thoughts of Jimi.

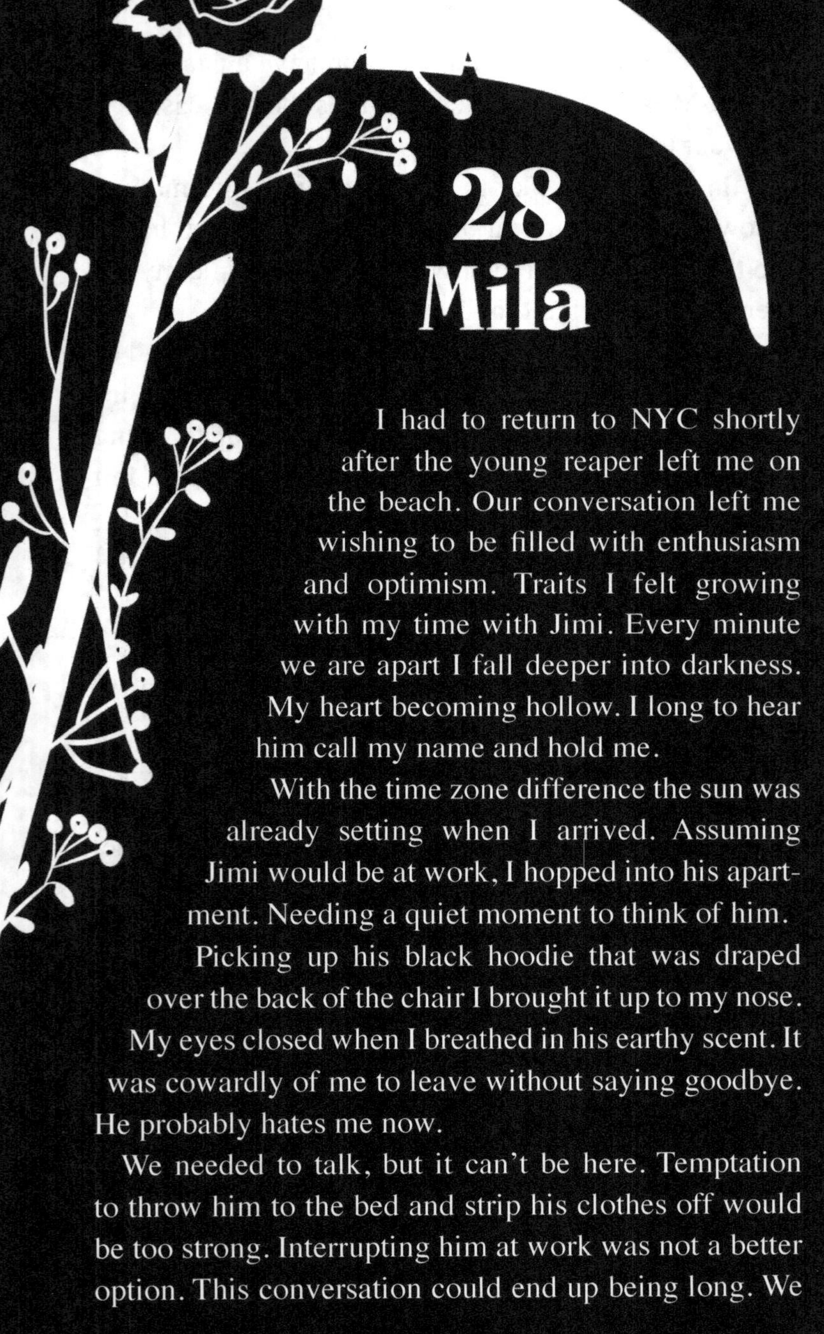

28
Mila

I had to return to NYC shortly after the young reaper left me on the beach. Our conversation left me wishing to be filled with enthusiasm and optimism. Traits I felt growing with my time with Jimi. Every minute we are apart I fall deeper into darkness. My heart becoming hollow. I long to hear him call my name and hold me.

With the time zone difference the sun was already setting when I arrived. Assuming Jimi would be at work, I hopped into his apartment. Needing a quiet moment to think of him. Picking up his black hoodie that was draped over the back of the chair I brought it up to my nose. My eyes closed when I breathed in his earthy scent. It was cowardly of me to leave without saying goodbye. He probably hates me now.

We needed to talk, but it can't be here. Temptation to throw him to the bed and strip his clothes off would be too strong. Interrupting him at work was not a better option. This conversation could end up being long. We probably stand on different sides of the issue. Whether to stay away from each other or risk his life. He needs to know that I love him and that is why I can't risk it. *Love. This is love. I love him.*

That is why I need to stay as far from him as possible and just hope everything rights itself. Hope his soul returns to him and I go back to things as they were before. Before I was seen. Before I was touched. Before I was Mila.

I turned to read the work schedule pinned to the fridge. It was Thursday. He traded days and does not work tonight. I spun around in a panic wondering if he was in the apartment. There was nowhere to hide in his studio, and the bathroom door was open. I did however, notice an empty bottle of peanut butter whiskey lying on the coffee table. Picking up the bottle I noticed the stack of drawings beneath.

An image of my face was created with lines and smudges of charcoal. Repeated from different angles. Dozens of them. Some were only partially finished. Others on crumpled pieces in a pile on the floor. This answers my question of 'I wonder if he was thinking about me'. A beep chimed from the couch. His phone lit up with a picture of Governors Island as the background. He must have taken it from the ferry ride back.

"Where did you go Jimi?" I said aloud as if the walls would answer. If only I could find you the same way I would find another reaper. Maybe I can. If I try to grasp onto our connection in my mind. Maybe I can find him. I closed my eyes and recalled the memory of the vibrations that travel between our bodies when we touch. The heat he creates in me. I felt a tug, different from being summoned. It was pulling me up. "Up?" Then I thought of the roof and began to worry when I squeezed the empty bottle in my hand.

In an instant I'm on the roof of the building. Jimi was standing dangerously close to the edge with his arms out like wings. Gusts of wind were whipping his black hair in every direction. I approached slowly and stopped about ten feet behind him.

"What are you doing Jimi?" I asked loud enough that my voice wouldn't be swallowed up by the sounds of the city below.

I could have sworn his shoulders relaxed. Jimi didn't even turn towards me. His feet stayed on the ledge. There was a slight wobble in his legs. How long has he been out here? Clearly taunting Death. Pressure pushed on my chest making it hard to breathe.

"Is there another reaper here?" He slurred. *Jimi won't jump*. I keep telling myself. But he might be drunk enough to slip.

"No. Just me." I didn't even have to look around. There was no glow on his body, and I did not sense another reaper nearby. My feet inched closer to him.

Panic was building inside me. *What if I didn't see a reaper because I am here? I am the reaper. Fuck.* I took each step slowly. He watched me over his shoulder.

"I wasn't going to jump." He brought his arms down to his side and dropped his head low. Defeated.

"Then why are you up here, Jimi?" I was behind him now. He turned around on the ledge to face me. His movements were smooth for someone that reeked of peanut butter whiskey. His eyes were red and puffy. It broke my heart to see him this way. I did this to him.

His cheeks were pink from the cold. The denim jacket he wore was not warm enough after the sun disappeared over the horizon.

"I was running out of ideas." He said flatly.

I swallowed. "Ideas for what?"

His lips tugged up into a short-lived smile. "I have been trying to track down reapers to get a message to you."

"Message received." I motioned to the ledge where he was still standing. Dangerously close.

"This is not my message." Anger laced his words. My breath hitched. He has the right to be mad at me. I took his sister, I have been stealing his soul, and I left while he was sleeping without explanation. How do humans do it? Handle all these strong emotions. Handle relationships. I don't know what to say to fix this. I don't know if I should fix this. He is safer if I walk away. Jimi would thank me in the future because he would have a future.

"You left."

Can words punch you in the chest? His tone made my entire body tense. I couldn't think of the right words. My expression softened. Pleading for forgiveness.

I lifted my hand towards him, then switched it for the one without my ring. "I am here now." He grunted at me. "Please come down. We can talk."

"Talk? I poured my heart out to you, Mila." He frowned at my outstretched hand. "I never talk about losing my sister. With everything you do, everything you are, I figured you'd be empathetic. And there was more I wanted to say, but you just vanished. Zadkiel dropped a bomb on me. I'm not dumb." He looked at the street below. "Well not all the time. I am smart enough to figure out what is going on. You vanished. You ran away."

The wind pushed tears to slide across my face. I wiped them away with shaky fingers. "I am sorry. I knew that if I stayed, I would hurt you."

He pushed down a laugh. "You left and it hurt me."

"You don't understand, Jimi." I stepped close enough for him to reach my hand if he wanted. "Being with me is killing you."

He placed a hand in mine. Jimi leaped off the roof's edge and landed directly in front of me. He pulled my hand tight against his chest. My breath hitched. I shouldn't be feeling the air. Real air entering my lungs. It was cold and biting. With his free hand he cupped my cheek and forced me to look up to him.

"I already know." He pressed a kiss to my forehead. "I know what is happening between us and I think I know when it started." He kissed my cheek. His lips came off glossy from my tears.

"Jimi, I can't risk your life. You deserve-"

"I deserve to have a say in whether we are together or not." His lips finally landed on mine, and I let out a quiet whimper. He pulled back far enough to speak but his words went right into my mouth. "You cannot come into my life and let me know you, crave you, taste you – and expect me to forget you. Mila, we are fucking linked together, literally. I can feel you with every breath I take. You fill my thoughts when I'm awake. You haunt my dreams when I sleep. Don't you fucking vanish again."

I nodded obediently.

Jimi cupped my face with both of his hands. My eyes burned as tears flowed. A sensation I am still getting used to. That unfamiliar pounding in my chest returned.

My voice cracked quietly. "Okay."

"Okay what, Mila."

"Okay, I won't run away." I pushed up onto my toes to meet his lips. We crashed together. Heat rising between us. His tongue twisting with mine. The taste of whiskey still lingering on his tongue.

I kept my hand with the soul ring pinned behind my back. His hands traced down my body, gripping my hips hard. Without breaking our kiss, he nudged me backwards, towards the door to the roof.

I'll let him guide me. Lead me anywhere. This perfectly imperfect human. This mortal being full of hope and anger. This wickedly sexy man who has spelled me into submission. I won't run away Jimi. I will fight for us. I will find a way.

I tripped when my leg slammed into a chair. It was hidden in a vale of shadows. Jimi caught me before I could fall. Gripping me close as we hovered over the seat.

"Should we stay a while longer." Jimi turned me around so he could sit on the chair. He patted his lap, signaling me to have a seat. I placed my hand on my hip and scanned the thousands of windows around us. I do not fear being seen, but that doesn't mean someone wouldn't look out and spot Jimi on this roof. I am pretty sure there are laws against what his eyes are suggesting.

"I guess we are enough in the dark." I lowered myself onto his lap, straddling him so our faces were aligned. "Aren't you cold though?"

He shrugged. "Surprisingly, no."

"Doesn't that alarm you?" I asked. His hands ran up my back. One trailing higher until he gripped my hair.

"What alarms me is that you are not wearing a skirt. This would be a lot more fun." A crooked smile formed on his face. He leaned forward, placing a kiss on my neck as he pulled my head back.

"You know I can just make my clothes disappear." I laughed. He moaned his response.

"Yes, please do that."

I gripped the back of the upholstered dining chair and grinded onto his body. His cock hardens beneath me, and I pressed my body onto it. Pressing my lips to his I let the world melt away. Ignoring our differences and the imminent threat to his life. Allowing myself to live deep in his kiss. My back arched when his hands roamed from my waist to my thighs. His hands flexed, kneading my muscles. He was distracted. It was the perfect time to make my clothes vanish like a breath.

The moment he realized he was gripping skin his cock twitched. I laughed, ending our kiss. Jimi looked where our bodies were touching. I was completely naked sitting on his lap. Instantly angry at the fabric between us. There was hunger in his eyes. Desperate need.

"Fuck, you're beautiful." He moved his hand to my ass and pressed his hard cock into me. "I think I dreamed you into my life."

My head fell back, letting him have more access to my neck. "Maybe the other way around. I have been on this earth way longer than you."

His tongue trailed up my neck until he placed a kiss on my jaw. A light thrumming appeared under my skin. A pulse. It felt like blood pumping under my skin. Surging through my veins. Reacting to his tongue.

"You have a point." One of his hands cupped my breast and squeezed. He lowered his mouth to my nipple. He sucked and tugged on my peaked nipple with his teeth. There was a twinge of pain. "If I was created for you, what would you like to do with me."

"Do that again." I moaned. He swirled his tongue around my nipple before grasping it between his teeth and tugging. It hurt. *I felt pain.* Part of me loved it. I craved more. A wet spot was forming on his jeans from where I was rubbing. Real wetness like before.

My hands worked the button and zipper on his jeans until his cock sprung free. My hands wrapped around him tightly and I stroked. Gripping him tight from base to tip. Heat lightly warmed my palm, and I realized it was the ring.

"Fuck, I'm sorry. Wrong hand." I pinned my hand behind my back and gazed at him through my lashes.

"It's fine. We just have to get used to it. Imagine you have one arm." He laughed quickly then worked my body in controlled motions. His hands tight on my ass while I slid over his cock. I needed him inside me. I couldn't wait any longer.

I pushed up on my feet until I was hovering over him. His hard cock pulsated in my hand as I lifted it towards my entrance. Slowly I lowered myself on him. Taking him inch by glorious inch. My head was dizzy with pleasure. I moved my hand with the soul ring back to the frame of the chair. Grateful for something to stabilize me.

I found myself full of him and seated once again. My hips moved in a slow rhythm. I began to raise myself up and he held me down.

"Easy." He hummed next to my ear. Our lips met with sloppy intent. A mix of gasps and licks. My core tightened when his fingers slid between us, stopping to circle my clit. I let out a groan into his mouth. His lips tugged up at my response.

Jimi continued to circle my clit. Dipping down to find my own juices, then using them to slide over my clit. Flicking it until I feel my inner walls flex.

"Yes, Mila." He started rocking up into me. The sensations were becoming overwhelming. My nipples are still red from his teeth. "Come for me."

His words pulled me over the edge. My thighs clenched around him. I covered him with dripping proof of my orgasm. He pumped harder. Thrusting until I was lifting and falling repeatedly. A scream escaped my mouth. My breasts bouncing with each strong thrust.

"Jimi." I moaned, hoping the sounds of the city would drown me. Forgetting in the moment that I was not human. That no one could hear me, but him. He growled a response. My sweet compassionate Jimi, a powerhouse between my legs. There was nothing shy about him here. He saw what he wanted and took it. "Jimi, I love you."

I'm not sure why I said it. I kept my eyes shut, too scared to see his expression. He pulled me tighter until my breasts pressed against his chest still covered in clothes. He tried to kiss me, but we were both frantic with pleasure. His thrusts became erratic, and moaning my name as he spilled into me.

Jimi huffed out a low breath and gripped my hair in his hands. I stayed on his lap while our juices mixed and dripped between us. Gathering a bit of courage, I opened my eyes. He was breathing heavily and looking at me like I was a vision. Moonlight reflecting in his brown eyes.

Cupping my face with both hands he placed a gentle kiss to my lips. "I love you too." He whispered. Something inside me was doing flips.

Then a chill on my back. The sensation of cold I have never felt before. I shivered causing him to pull me closer. *I won't leave you again Jimi.* I said inside my mind. I will find a way to make this work. I need you. Always.

I shivered again and he looked at me with concern. He too was trying to think of ideas. Not wanting this to end. This feverously hot connection between us.

29
Jimi

Three amazing days of the closest thing to a normal relationship we could have passed by in a blink. Mila would leave for an assignment and return to my apartment. We would walk to my work together. Me with my earpiece on display so people don't think I am talking to myself. Before I stepped inside, she would kiss my cheek, look up at me through her thick lashes, and say "I love you, Jimi." *She loves me.*

We spent our time together watching movies or researching folklore. By the off chance there is a solution that makes her human and keeps me alive. It seems impossible to keep her soul ring from touching me forever. And that's how long I want to be with her. *Forever.*

On my break at work, I fell down a rabbit hole of Reddit forums. People around the world claiming encounters with Angels, demons, and what they call The

Grim Reaper. One woman in Ecuador says her young son was dying and that she prayed for an Angel, but what answered was a demon wanting to make a deal. Her son recovered almost overnight from his illness. The woman never admitted to what she traded for his life. I wondered if I had anything a demon would bargain for. *Would it really hurt to ask?* I took a few screenshots of evocation methods on my phone. I have no way to know which faith or culture has the correct method. Some called for bones or special bowls that I have no idea how to find.

"What are you up to?" I didn't hear Serena walk in. I have melted into the tan couch in the back of the break room. Staring at my phone with a half-eaten sandwich next to me.

"Nothing." I slid my phone into the pocket of my scrubs. Last thing I need is Serena to see me researching lore of demon summoning around the world.

Under the sandwich sat an unopened textbook and notebook. Serena scanned them with her eyes. "Studying for the ANCC exam?" I should be. My textbook has remained closed all week. My mind has been elsewhere. I frowned down at the book and notepad. Collecting them on my lap so there was room for her to sit. My father had already sent me the $395 I would need for the certification exam. Although I am not ready. Not just for the test itself, but for a new chapter in my career. It felt like growing up when I have so much I want to do first.

I need to get out of the city more but have had no one to travel with. Now, I have Mila. She has been practically everywhere. I couldn't think of a better tour guide. I blinked away thoughts of Mila, realizing I was ignoring the friend before me.

"Back to nights again?" I said, changing the subject from the exam.

She sat next to me, leaving very little space between us. "I was filling in day shifts for a nurse on vacation. She returned yesterday and I am stuck with my low seniority shift in the ER once again." She loosened her body and rested her head on the back of the couch. The familiar look of exhaustion for hospital staff. "I did miss your face. So, that makes nights not so bad."

I forced a smile. I like Serena. I do. But things have changed since I saw her last. Or rather things need to change between us. I tapped the book and cleared my throat. "I only have two more months on the night shift before I switch to Clinical Management training."

"Lucky." She nudged my arm.

I rolled my eyes. "Lucky? I will spend less time with patients and more time in the office. I hate paperwork."

"You knew what it meant to be an NP when you started the program, Jimi." She stretched her neck from side to side and her hair swooshed like a horse's tail. "Requesting tests, ordering prescriptions, and studying medical history can be fun too. Think of it like being a medical detective."

"Can't I skip that and stay the fun nurse who plays games and sneaks treats?" I slumped.

"Oh, you're the reason I found a rice crispy wrapper under Johnny's pillow." Her mouth twisted to the side.

I faked a whistle and looked at the ceiling. "I have no idea what you are talking about." I let the clicking of a clock fill the lull of our conversation. "You still dating that doctor?"

"Dating? Ha." She covered her face with her hands. "Turns out he tries to hook up with every young female resident. We went on one group date and one solo date. Lucky for me it didn't go that far."

I nodded. She turned to face me, placing a hand on my leg. "He didn't scratch that itch." My body stiffened. *Should I mention I am dating someone? Do I tell her I am madly in love with a paranormal entity that might accidently kill me?*

Gently I placed my hand over hers with the intention to move it off. She slipped out of my grip and moved it higher towards the waist of my pants.

"Serena, not now." I stopped her hand this time and removed it. She pouted. Usually that would work on me. Her blond bouncy ponytail and bright blue eyes. Now all I could think of was Mila. The depth of her dark eyes. The way she fits so perfectly curled against my body. Her expressions when telling me stories of what she has seen. "I just started seeing someone."

She scooted away from me like I was suddenly toxic. Her eyes went wide, and her mouth gaped open. She dramatically blinked. "Tell me everything."

"No." I scowled playfully. "It's new and I really like her. Telling you about it feels like a jinx."

"Ouch." She slapped my chest. "I thought we were friends."

"Be real. We never see each other outside hospital hook ups. And before that it was dorm room hook ups." My smile was too much like flirting and I let it fade from my face. Serena is a habit I will break.

"I thought about it once, ya know." Her eyes darted around the room as if avoiding mine. "Having something more with you."

"Of course, you did, I'm fucking sexy." I grinned.

She smacked my chest again with the back of her hand. "Most of the guys at our school were creeps, you were nice. Remember Halloween 2018? A group of us went to the haunted carnival in New Jersey."

I nodded.

"Well, Jessica had been encouraging me to cross the line from booty-call to girlfriend. After a foot long Zombie juice, I was determined to make a move. I think I even said a prayer asking for a sign. Can you believe that?" She chuckled then continued. "Anyway, I pulled you away from the group. I definitely got my sign."

"Wait, What?" I sat up more alert. "I don't remember anything special about that night."

"I am not surprised. You were drunk too. I dragged you into a fortune tellers' tent. Hoping she would say we were meant to be, or something." Images of that night flashed in my head. Her friend screaming at her boyfriend because he got cotton candy in her hair. Trying to hold in my laughter. Serena leading me away by hand. One of the few times we ever held hands.

The scent of funnel cake lured me in the opposite direction of the dusty red tent she pulled me into.

I scratched my head. "Oh yea, Madam um… Madam Martisha. I don't remember what she said that was so crucial."

"I do. I can still hear her creepy voice." Serena made her voice lower and raspy. "This young man has already been claimed by something very powerful. To walk with him, is to walk with death. Then I accused her of faking her accent and she tossed us out of her tent. No refund. Just a cryptic message."

"Holy shit." I froze.

"I know right. I was so freaked out. Madam Martisha said she saw a dark future for you and anyone you love. I was gullible and decided it was best to keep you at a distance. For the most part."

I stood up and gripped my study materials tight to my chest. Then I tossed the sandwich in the trash and pulled my phone from my pocket. "Holy shit."

My legs wobbled as I took a few steps away from the couch. Murmuring to myself *"Holy shit, holy shit"*.

"Where are you going?" Serena called after me as I briskly walked towards the door.

"I have to finish my shift" *Then I need to find a carnival psychic.*

30
Jimi

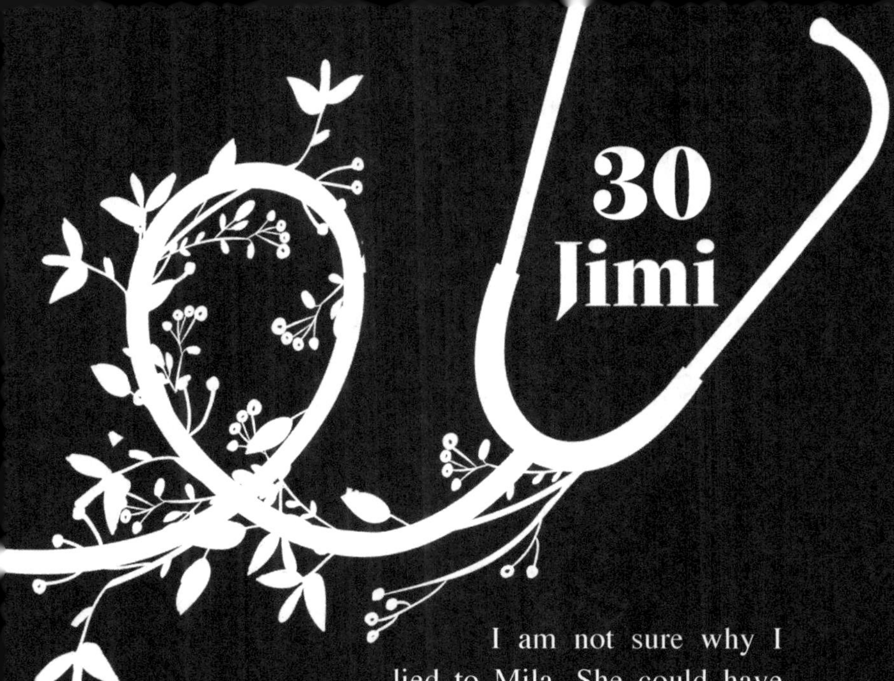

I am not sure why I lied to Mila. She could have come with me while I tracked down a psychic from five years ago. This seemed like a gamble. I didn't want to get her hopes up. Who would have thought a woman working at a carnival might have real insight to the things I know exist in the shadows. Angels, reapers, and Death themself.

(We know demons are real) Why wouldn't demons be real? Is she sees these things, then perhaps she knows how to summon one. Fuck, maybe she knows a less deadly solution.

I feel like a fucking idiot taking a train into the Bronx to speak with a psychic. Someone who sells various crystals and bushels of dried herbs. It screamed the word "scam". I would think it was a scam if Serena didn't remind me of the ominous reading, she gave us years ago.

She said, "I walked with death". Most people would assume it meant people would die around me, but I understand it now. I walk with Mila. She works for Death. A conduit she calls it. I wonder if she knew how accurate her reading was.

Her website allowed me to schedule an appointment. I took her earliest slot. Work ended at 2am. I stayed at the apartment with Mila until it was time to leave for the Bronx. I told her I had a dentist appointment, and it would be weird for her to tag along. She joked about making me laugh in the chair while he poked sharp objects in my mouth. I may have snapped back about putting something in her mouth as payback, but that made her raise her eyebrows in a way that made my cock twitch.

It was a few minutes before 8:00am. I should be in bed. My body is exhausted, and I am surprised I didn't fall asleep on the warm subway.

My breath fogged the glass as I leaned in to press the brass doorbell. She lived and worked out of a short row house. The red brick had been painted white years ago and was peeling in areas.

A sign hung over the front window. Madam Martisha – Spiritual Guidance & Fortune Telling.

This should be the most ridiculous thing I've ever done, but a few weeks ago I summoned an Angel in my childhood bedroom. A face peeked from behind the fabric covering the door window. I grinned too eagerly. The door creaked open. She was walking away from me as

I crossed the threshold. I saw her disappear behind a beaded curtain into a connecting room. I shut the front door behind me.

I shoved my gloves into my pocket and unwrapped my scarf, so it hung free. "Madam Martisha?" I called.

"Yuh time starts now, come in bowy." She grunted while she lowered herself into a red tufted chair. I recognized her thick island accent. Jamacia, if I had to guess. Across the table from her was a single wooden dining chair. The frame was carved with swirls, and it reminded me of the chair on the roof of my building. My cheeks flushed as I moved to sit down.

There was a fire going in the corner. One of those old-fashioned black wood stoves. The room was stuffy and filled with incense smoke.

Madam Martisha had dark skin with wrinkles around her eyes and speckles of grey in her tight curls. Her hair was pulled up on top of her head with a silk head scarf wrapped from the back and tied in the front. Her eyes were cold. When she narrowed them at me fine lines formed at the corners like sun rays. For a moment I thought she recognized me. I went to speak but she lifted a palm.

"Mus bi urgent tuh si mi bright n early." She lifted a scrap of fabric the size of a handkerchief and revealed a tarot deck of cards. "It seems yuh already kno whaa is missing."

"Yes. I know my soul is not complete. That's not my priority."

"Wah cud be more important dan making yuh soul whole again?" She squinted and placed the deck in front of me. "Cut di deck, please."

I split the deck in half and watched as she placed them together again, then laid four cards down.

I went to speak and again she stopped me. "Mi see. Love." She tapped her finger on a card. "Dis love is wah mek yuh nuh whole."

"Let's just say, she is not of our world. We have a connection, a link. I'm grateful for it, but it also might kill me. Literally."

"Most love cyna be described dat way." She chuckled. "Wah makes yuh special?"

What makes our love special? How about she's a fucking reaper and immortal. While I am a boring human that works in a children's hospital. There's the part where she reaped the soul of my sister when I was 14 and apparently, I tried to stop her while in my spirit form. Which forever caused a link to her when a piece of my soul was suck into a unique ring she wears.

I blinked slowly. "Let's just say she works very close to death, and I work to prevent it." Would she think I was crazy if I told the truth? After all there are images of mythical things all over this room.

"Aks di question on yuh mind bowy?" Madam Martisha placed her hands flat on the table. She squinted over her tortoise shell glasses to look at me. I gulped.

"Is it possible to make a deal with a demon to save someone's life?" I paused and waited for her laugh. The silence thickened. A loud pop from the fire made me flinch. She slowly went up to the window. Closing the curtains, lighting a bundle of what I assume was sage, and grabbing a piece of rolled paper from a clay jar on a shelf.

I didn't try to speak this time. I let her settle back into her chair and watched with patient eyes. Another pop from the fire had my body tense. She cleared her throat.

"Yuh, tis possible. Mi can nuh pramise who well answar yuh call." She rolled the mini scroll on the table. "Sum people get confuse wit angels and demons. Both put dem own interests firs, yuh understand."

I nodded slowly. "Has this worked?"

A closed smiled filled her face. She tapped one of the tarot cards, Temperance, a winged figure pouring water from one gold chalice to another.

"Aks yuh angel fren." She winked. "Dis nuh yuh firs time callin di beyond. But fir wah yuh want, yuh well need blood."

"Blood?" There was too much smoke in the air. My winter clothes were smothering me, and I found myself desperate to get outside.

"It all here." She held the scroll towards me. I tugged at the collar of my sweater. My hand reached out to grab it and she pulled it back.

"One tousand dollars." She waved the scroll. Smoke from the incense in the room parting in the air. "Nuh refunds."

"You got to be kidding me. A thousand dollars for a spell or whatever, that is probably a scam." I stood up and my head blurred for a second. I had to brace myself on the table.

"It well wuk fir yuh, cuz yuh already touched."

My eyes focused on the paper she held like a wand in my face. Without thinking I reached into my pocket and pulled out my wallet. "Fine." I said through my teeth.

She pulled out a Square reader that was conveniently nearby and attached it to her phone. My heart was racing as I watched her scam me out of one thousand dollars. I am paying for a chance at answers. Not a guarantee. Would Mila try to talk me out of this? Does one thousand dollars mean anything to a reaper?

She handed back the card with a toothy smile. Her teeth were stained yellow from years of tobacco and coffee. The scroll rested between her fingers like a long cigarette. This better be worth it. I just dropped half a months rent on this piece of paper. My fingers were damp with sweat when I grabbed it. I removed the gloves I shoved in my pocket and slid it in.

This room was going to kill me before Death could. The air was getting thicker by the second. I stumbled through the beaded curtain and paused with my hand on the doorknob. The brass was cold, and it snapped me alert.

"Thanks, for meeting me." I opened the door and sucked in a wave of cold air into my lungs.

"It wus mi pleasure." Madam Martisha called from her porch as I rushed away. "Good luck wit di lady deth."

31
Mila

Jimi returned from his dentist appointment completely exhausted. He made a cup of tea but fell asleep before it finished steeping. He left the TV on to a channel with people answering trivia questions for money. Something I bet most reapers would be good at.

I pulled his arm over me and inhaled his scent. Bergamot and citrus. I wished I could bottle it and take it with me when I am summoned far from here.

My fingertips grazed over his arm. Stroking him into a deeper sleep. I have never been so relaxed. My movements slowed. My mind must have been distracted, because I blinked, and I missed an entire question on the show.

I adjusted my body so that I was lying next to him instead of sitting. I continued to brush his arm. My eyes were heavy. A weird sensation.

I blinked.

The room was darker now. The Tv was playing a family sitcom. I sat up abruptly.

"What just happened?" I asked into the room.

Jimi rubbed his eyes. "What?" He grabbed his phone from next to him and checked the time. "I still have a few hours before I need to leave for work."

My chest rose and fell rapidly. Those were definitely stars in the sky. *How long was I on this couch?*

"Jimi." I turned towards him and waited until his groggy eyes focused on me. "I think I fell asleep."

"Maybe you needed rest." He yawned and reached around to rub my back. It should be calming, but my mind had a million questions. Things were changing too fast.

"You don't understand." I twisted the ring on my hand. It was warm. As if it had been sitting in the sun. "Fuck."

I hopped off the couch. Clenching my hands into fists. I am so stupid.

"What's wrong?" He was sitting up now. I paced in the middle of his studio. The floor creaked as I moved around. I made one more circle before stopping to face him. His dark brown eyes studying me. Patiently waiting for me to explain why I am freaking out. I should just vanish. Save him the inevitable tragedy that comes with being with me.

"I was lying next to you, and I think I touched you with this." I held up my left hand. The eight-pointed star glinted in the moon light pouring in. "Then I fell asleep. Still touching you. I am a reaper. Reapers don't sleep. That means I took more from you. Fuck."

Jimi stood and grabbed my arms, pinning them to my side. He pulled me against his chest. The rhythms of our chests moving together. "Calm down. Look at me, Mila" I tilted my chin to look up at him. "I am still here. I feel fine. I don't feel any different. I promise."

"You are fine, until you're not." I turned my cheek from his dark begging eyes. "I should have stayed away."

"Don't say that."

His grip on me was firm. He would not let me slip away. Or he would try. I could vanish from his hands if I wanted to. I shook my head.

"Jimi I am killing you." I sucked in a quick breath. Pressed this close to him I could have sworn I felt the cold air fill my lungs. A tear fell from my eye. Jimi loosened his hands enough for me to bend an elbow. I wiped the tear sliding down my cheek and lifted my wet palm to him. "This should not be happening. This is a sign that I am killing you."

I tried to shift away from him. I was moments away from a flood of tears. Jimi slid one arm behind my waist. Keeping me pressed against his body.

"Feel this." He took my right hand and pressed it firmly on his chest. My palm vibrated with the steady thump of his heart. I closed my eyes and let the beat consume me. Let the world drift away and focused on the thrumming beat. His voice went low and he spoke so close to my ear I could feel his breath. "See. I am still alive and strong. A little tired, but no more than anyone working night shifts in a hospital."

He grabbed my chin and forced my head up. My hand still resting on his chest. Afraid his heart would stop if I moved it away. "Jimi-"

"Look at me." He whispered. I complied and opened my eyes. His dark eyes were bright surrounded by all the shadows of his apartment. Rain began to hit the window. He lowered his face until our lips were a breath away. "I am not done fighting for you. For us. We have gone way past want. Do you understand? I need you."

I sucked in air, and it was tight in my chest. More tears slid down my cheeks. I couldn't speak. Words evaded me. I nodded as he pressed a kiss to my lips. I will never deserve him. Deserve this love. But I will take every day I can get with him trying to make him feel as I do. Whole, and with purpose.

His fingers gripped my hair as he held me in place to take the kiss deeper. My lips were wet from tears. I tasted salt when we moved our mouths together. I moaned.

Salt?

I pushed him back and touched my lips.

"I think I just tasted something." I yelped.

Pointing to himself, "Me?"

I shook my head. "I think it was a tear." I swiped my finger across my wet cheek and wrapped my lips around it. I squeaked. "Tears are salty, right? I think I'm tasting salt."

"Holy shit." He said with arms out in surprise.

"Quick give me something else to taste." He smirked devilishly. I placed a hand on my hip. "Something classified as food, Jimi."

"Fine." He walked to the kitchen and grabbed his favorite snack. These tiny oranges he was always munching on. I plopped myself on a stool to keep myself from bursting with anticipation, but my toes still tapped on the metal bar.

I squeaked again when he placed the small orange in tiny sections in front of me. Slowly I picked up one crescent shaped piece. Pausing to see if it would fall through my grasp. Instead, I felt the squishy texture of it between my fingers.

I opened my mouth and let my tongue hang out. Jimi was grinning from ear to ear. When the orange fruit hit my tongue, I froze before clasping my mouth shut.

"Oh-my-fucking-God." It was like nothing I have ever experienced. My eyes went wide. I sucked in my cheeks trying to get the juices out. Pressing it against the roof of my mouth. Jimi chuckled.

"You have to chew it. Like this." He popped a piece into his mouth and began to grind it with his teeth. I copied him. Orange tinted drool slipped out of my mouth, and he laughed. "Try with your mouth closed first."

I have watched humans eat for centuries, but never had I thought about the logistics of it. I pressed it with my teeth until the texture was smooth and my mouth was full of juices. I went to grab another one.

"Swallow first." He tilted his head up and I watched his throat bob. Jimi opened his mouth to show me the fruit was gone. "It didn't occur to me until now that I needed to teach you how to be human."

I swallowed and plopped two more pieces into my mouth. I scanned the kitchen wondering what else I could taste, but I felt the tug.

I groaned. "I am being summoned."

"That's okay. We will meet up after work." He pushed the rest of the orange bits towards me. I shoveled them into my mouth, and he laughed. "I have an idea on what you can taste next."

He walked around the island. Smooth as Hell, he spun the barstool to face him. I wiped a bit of liquid from the corners of my mouth. I was conflicted between asking for another orange and the seductive look he was giving me. Jimi pushed my knees apart and stood between my thighs.

"Oh yea?" I cupped his cock through his sweatpants. He grabbed my hand and brought it to his lips.

"Trust me I am looking forward to that, but I have something else in mind." He leaned down to kiss me, and I could taste the fruit on his tongue. I felt the tug again. Worst timing ever.

"I have to go."

"Go to work." He smiled and placed a kiss on my forehead. "I love you."

I hopped off the stool. "I love you too."

32
Mila

I collected a soul in the Upper East Side of Manhattan. A heart attack. Not very eventful. He was over eighty years old and lived a very fulfilling life according to the dozens of travel pictures and awards that lined his mantel. Afterwards, I wanted to head back to Jimi and catch him before leaving for work. Maybe, walk with him, but there was another tug.

"Another one. So soon." I said to myself. Blinking I allowed the tug to pull me where I needed to go. Traveling this way has always been like being pulled at the waist by a tether. Almost like being pushed through a water slide. I opened my eyes, and I hadn't moved. "That's strange."

I closed my eyes again and focused on the tug. I have never struggled to move before. Could I be tired? Reapers don't get tired. Although, many things have been happening to me that are not typical for reapers. My body jolted with resistance. This is usually a fluid motion. The same way I move around with just a thought.

My feet wobbled when I landed on the Franklin D Roosevelt boardwalk. I stumbled to my knees. Colliding with the rough wood planks. Dizziness circled my head like a wave then settled low in my stomach. My insides were trying to crawl up my mouth.

What is happening to me? Did Zadkiel have it wrong? Am I the one dying?

The thrumming under my hands drew my attention upwards. Commotion rattled the boardwalk as a group of people were running and shouting. They were not shouts of joy, but fear. It was dark, but streams of white Christmas lights connected the poles illuminating the edges.

"Are you okay?" an unfamiliar voice asked.

I found another reaper looking down at me. Standing I padded off my clothes. They smirked knowing our clothes could not get dirty and it was just for show.

"Yes, I just-." I was going to say 'tripped', but how could a being able to move through objects trip? So, I let my sentence fade and attempted to direct their attention away from me. I tilted my head towards a part forming in the crowd. "They sent two of us. Is this a mass casualty event?"

The reaper began to walk, and I kept by his side. He wore a black suit with a black shirt and tie. A little dramatic for my taste. "I think this is your typical angry man that can't handle his woman moved on. They both are glowing. Are you new? Maybe Death didn't think you could handle it."

I scoffed. My nails bit into my palm as I formed fists with my hands. "I am not new, reaper. I can handle collecting many souls without missing a step."

"Okay, okay. I get it. You've been around." He put his hands up. A sign of surrender. "I don't know why Death sent two of us. It's not like they tell us anything, other than where to go and when."

I could handle it. Two souls, that's nothing. But I have been changing. What if the reaper is here in case I can't collect. In case I make a mistake. What if Death knows I am glitching in a way. Changing from being the pure reaper he made me to be. I swallowed down my questions and tried to focus on the chaos erupting before me.

At the end of the boardwalk was a skinny Caucasian man with a backwards red hat and ripped jeans. He was pointing a handgun towards a female. She had her body pressed against the railing, creating as much distance as possible.

We walked matching each other's strides. Then we both stopped about five feet away. The noise of the boardwalk faded around us. A bubble of tense emotion blocking it out. I shifted as a blur moved in the corner of my eye. The man's translucent form popped up first. His eyes darted from us to where he stood aiming a gun at his ex-girlfriends' body.

"What the fuck is this?" He said.

"We are about to see you commit murder. Then suicide, if I had to guess. Although somehow you die before her since you're here first." The reaper said coldly. I glared at the man, making my eyes go eerily white to creep him out. Sometimes I enjoy invoking fear in people. Perhaps if I become human, I should get a job in a haunted house. The translucent man started shaking.

I flinched when we heard a gunshot. Accidently vanishing for a second. My instinct being to flee, even though I cannot be injured. The woman fell to the ground. Her hands holding her abdomen.

I snarled. "You're a shitty shot. You deserved to suffer, not her." My feet led me towards the woman's side. Her cream puffer coat was filling with blood.

There was another gunshot behind me. This time he had placed the barrel under his own chin and died instantly. The other reaper was convincing him to take his hand. I was hoping he would be gone before she showed up. Unfortunately, she appeared behind me. I whirled my head around. She gasped at the horror.

The woman cupped her hands over her mouth. Concealing her screams. Her eyes darting between her body bleeding out and the translucent form of the man who shot her. I moved to stand before her. Trying to block the view of her assailant.

"Oh my God." She screamed into her hands.

I placed my hands on her shoulders. "Don't look at him. Look at me."

"Am I dying?" She said sucking in air. I nodded. "Can you still save me?

"The choice has already been made. I am sorry."

She pointed down the boardwalk. Three cops were

running with their guns drawn. EMT's were waiting to be waved over. I knew by the time they confirmed the gunman was dead she would have bled out.

The reaper had finished collecting the soul of the scum of a man. He saluted me then vanished. The woman whimpered in fear when she saw him disappear.

"Look at me." I said again, drawing her attention towards me. "You don't have much time. Look how harsh this world is. Where you are going there will be peace. No more pain."

Sugar coated lies. Reapers are too good at them. We have no knowledge of what waits for the dying.

She sniffled, unable to cry in her current form. The cops were checking his body and discovering there was no pulse. The EMT's ran over, but by the time they reached her side it was too late. We watched as her eyes glazed over and her hand slid from her abdomen and fell onto the blood-soaked wood of the boardwalk.

I held out my hand with the soul ring ready to take her. Her body shook in tiny quakes. I motioned for her to grab my hand. She slipped her hand over mine and I gripped it tight. The way you would when introducing yourself. It made me want to tell her my name. I have a name. But I kept my thoughts to myself. I gave her a small smile before she turned to gray smoke and was sucked into my ring.

This is the part where I leave and turn my back. My feet were glued down as I stared at their bodies. He probably thought he loved her. She might have told him she loved him once. I scrubbed my face. There is so much I don't understand. So much I fear about the future with Jimi. *I fear? I am afraid? A reaper is afraid?* There was too much chatter around me, my head was spinning again.

I made myself move.

I have observed humans seek specific locations when needing comfort or to ease a spinning mind. A temple or building around their faith. Perhaps just a quiet spot next to a river. Reapers are drawn to the beach. The space where dry ground meets crashing waves. The ocean has a way of resetting our thoughts with the moving tide. I have always been drawn to the view of cities from above. Another way I am different, I suppose.

It is becoming harder to keep a wall up around my emotions with people dying in my sight. So much pain. Part of me wants to comfort humans. Wants to save them. I understand the circle of life. That everything living must die someday. But my heart aches still.

My legs dangle off the edge of a NYC skyscraper. Carnegie Hall Tower. The building doesn't have a restaurant or lookout spot for tourists. Allowing me to be completely alone. High above the noise of the city and just below the dark clouds threatening to storm.

I spun the ring around my finger anxiously and thought about what it meant to die. If I become human. If by some miracle, I become human. That means I will die, someday. It also means I would live.

I sucked in a deep breath. A chill spread through my lungs. Cold, I can feel cold now. I licked my lips. They were rough and had a slight citrus tang. I can taste it now. I can get dizzy now. I can cry. This is happening too fast. I need more answers. I need a plan, before I take so much from Jimi that he dies in my arms.

It is time to see my boss.

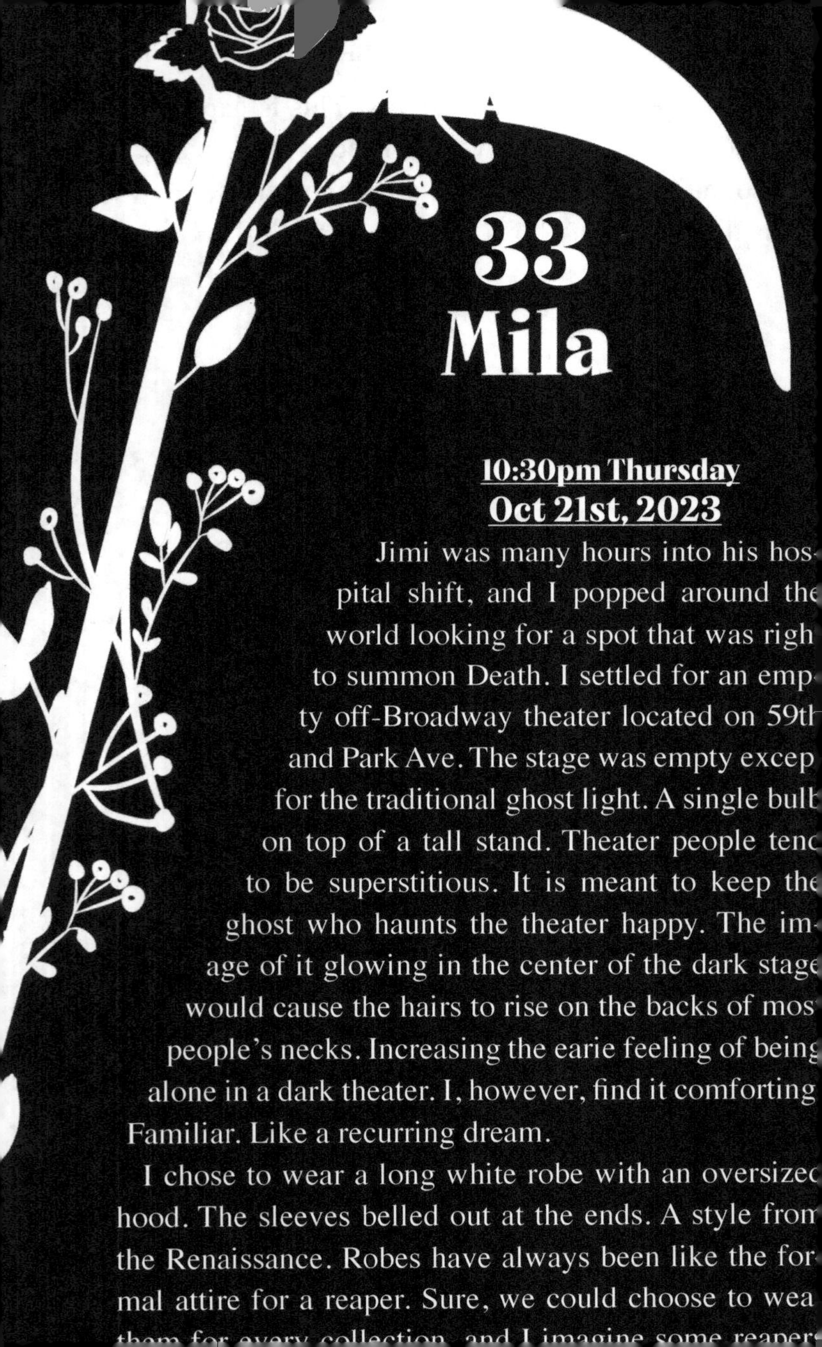

33
Mila

<u>**10:30pm Thursday**</u>
<u>**Oct 21st, 2023**</u>

Jimi was many hours into his hospital shift, and I popped around the
world looking for a spot that was righ
to summon Death. I settled for an empty off-Broadway theater located on 59th
and Park Ave. The stage was empty excep
for the traditional ghost light. A single bulb
on top of a tall stand. Theater people tend
to be superstitious. It is meant to keep the
ghost who haunts the theater happy. The image of it glowing in the center of the dark stage
would cause the hairs to rise on the backs of most
people's necks. Increasing the earie feeling of being
alone in a dark theater. I, however, find it comforting
Familiar. Like a recurring dream.

I chose to wear a long white robe with an oversized
hood. The sleeves belled out at the ends. A style from
the Renaissance. Robes have always been like the formal attire for a reaper. Sure, we could choose to wear
them for every collection, and I imagine some reapers

do, but it is not necessary. I choose these now to honor Death. They are a white version of his own. The fabric gives me the appearance of a ghost on this empty stage. Unimpressed by the single bulb meant to keep me away. I smile to myself at the image.

I was hoping to figure out a solution by myself. Find a way to get my soul. Humans often say, "Do it now, ask forgiveness after". Once I started tasting and feeling cold sensations, I knew my time was running out. It won't be long before I steal the last piece of Jimi. Before I kill him.

A shiver went up my spine. I rolled my neck. Body language I have observed when people are about to try something hard or go into battle. Hopefully not the latter.

It is not completely unheard of for Death to speak to their reapers. We are their employees after all. Our rings give us direct contact with them. They allow Death to track us anywhere in the world.

I've just never had a reason to call on them, until now. An image of Jimi flashed in my mind. His crooked smile and soft eyes. His lean body and the way it felt pressed up against me. I would give anything to have many years with him. Years of his laughter and stupid jokes. Years of his touches and soft lips.

I shook my head and focused on the task at hand. A conversation with Death. Possibly the most important conversation of my long existence on this earth.

Standing in the middle of the stage, I lifted my arms out to my side. In theory, we can call Death with just a thought, but I decided to speak aloud into the darkness.

"Death, I am your humble servant. I have dedicated every minute on this earth to your work. I have helped you keep balance. I-" The words got stuck in my throat. I took a breath and counted to five in my head. "I have never wanted more than to serve you. I have always done what you asked of me, and never asked for anything in return."

The air was thick and flat. Not even a slight breeze from the heaters. I expected to find him behind me. When I looked around, I saw no one. I was still alone on the stage.

The hairs on the back of my neck stood up. *That's new.* Then a strange tingling sensation formed low in my stomach. *Nausea?* Are my nerves causing this or is Death on their way.

I opened my mouth to speak but the shock of the light-bulb going out caused me to shriek and pull my arms in. I spun my body around in the darkness. The air grew even heavier. Weighing me down to where I stood.

I could feel a presence nearby, but the only light was from the two green exit signs in the back of the theater. I squinted at every shadow, waiting to find a form appear.

"Death?" I asked the darkness. The light bulb flickered then shined brightly, as if answering my question. I rocked back on my heels. Feeling unsteady. There was movement from the corner of my eye, and I whipped my head to the side. The heavy velvet curtain moved like a slow wave from the top down. I held my breath.

Suddenly I was terrified. Suddenly reminded how small I was in the large world. How powerless I truly am. Every bit of power I have was gifted to me by Death. That I am nothing without them. I gulped down the stale air.

Heavy footsteps appeared before I saw their source. Each step had an echo of chains rattling, but in fact there were no chains in sight. A shiver ran up my spine.

With each footstep a large form became more solid. They wore black robes that draped onto the floor. Behind them were large black wings. The feathers had a sheen like polished knives. I instantly took a step back. They towered over me by a couple feet. My hood nearly fell off when I looked up into the black void where a face should be. My heart was racing in my chest so loudly I am sure they could hear it. Death stopped about ten feet from where I stood, but their power engulfed me. It filled the entire room like sonar pulsing off their body.

"Are you frightened of your creator, reaper?" Their voice was both male and female. It was ancient and caused a flutter in the back of my head. I couldn't help but tremble.

"Yes." My voice was a cracking whisper.

They hummed and slowly shook their head. I was so shocked when they appeared that I almost missed the scythe. The real scythe mentioned in all the legends.

It was larger than I expected. A wooden staff of twisted tree branches with a long-curved steel blade. Their hands were translucent black, like a shadow wrapped around white bone.

My feet couldn't move, and my hands formed fists. The tension was clouding my thoughts. I am struggling to remember what I intended to ask.

They answered my call. This is really happening. Death is standing before me, and I forgot everything I needed to say. Death tilted their head. Observing my every tremor.

"You don't have to say anything." Death's voice echoed in the empty theater. They tapped the scythe once on the stage. "I have wondered how long before you would call on me."

Death was waiting for me to call on them. I feel like I might be sick. *Could a reaper throw up?* I feel like I might vomit. The power pulsing from where they stood, choking me.

"You have? You know what has been going on?" I finally spoke, but the words came out naïve and childlike. I adjusted to stand straight. I loosened my hands and tried to imagine Jimi was standing next to me. Tension eased in my shoulders.

"Although you do not see me, reaper. I watch all my children. I have been feeling your changes." They tucked in the black wings swiftly. I flinched.

I could not tell by their tone if they disapproved of the changes. Unsure where they stand on the matter, I decided to first address the negative effects.

"My changes are killing a human." I wanted to say Jimi's name but chose against it last minute. Does Death care about humans individually or are their lives just a series of tallies on a chalk board. Are they only concerned with the greater balance. I crossed my arms across my stomach. Suddenly feeling a chill.

Death started walking in a circle around me. Keeping the black void where a face should be in my direction. "Humans die constantly." The rattle of unseen chains following their movements. I stood in the center with the ghost light and turned my body to face them. "This human is special to you."

"Yes. He-"

"Jimin Niall Seong, I have been watching him also." Death interrupted.

I gasped. "You have?"

Death stopped walking and hovered over me. Closing the distance to less than five feet. I stared up into the endless void under their hood. It reminded me of the void I see every time I open the soul gateway. Could they be the same? Do souls reside within Death themself.

"Ever since there was a shift in his soul many years ago." Their voice deepened. "When you were very sloppy at the collection of his younger sister."

I shrunk my body down even smaller. The shadows in the theater were closing in on me. Or maybe it was shame.

"It was a mistake, but now that we have found each other-" I gulped. "I need him, and he needs me."

The silence after my confession sat between us in the thick air. Death stood perfectly still. Not even a ripple of black robes or a rustle of feathers. My palm felt damp, and I rubbed them against my robes. Their hood tilted lower slightly. As if watching me awkwardly wipe my hands.

"I know little reaper. Why else do you think I kept sending you to that hospital." Their wings flared and tucked back in. Wind lightened the air, and I sucked in a breath.

"You wanted us to find each other? Did you know what it would do to him?" My heartbeat was pulsing in my ears. Pressure was building in my chest like I was going to burst.

"Once the connection was established years ago, I made a choice. I could have stripped the soul from you and returned it to him." That ancient voice bouncing off every corner of the theater hit me twice with the echo.

Confusion filled my thoughts. "Why didn't you?"

Death tapped their scythe once more and took one step closer. Although they appeared to float, each step was loud and was accompanied by the rattling of invisible chains.

"You have watched humanity evolve for many years, and I believe you truly love them. As I love all humans. Not all reapers are capable of love. Some may say the same about humans." They paused but with a pulse of their power I knew not to respond. To just listen. "When you made the mistake on the school bus, I decided then. I wanted you to have a taste of the human world. Decided you deserved it."

"You decided to let us keep the connection." I whispered in shock. My heart is not mad that Death toyed with me like a puppet. Jimi was in fact a gift. A blessing.

"I decided to watch his life, and when he was ready for love, I sent you in his direction." Death tapped the scythe on the stage floor. Snapping my attention upwards. My trembling stopped but there was a burning in my chest when I gazed into their black void. "I also took him the day of the bus crash, but sensed his purpose was greater than most."

"His greater purpose? To save lives and heal others." I suggested.

Death tilted their head again. I watched their grip tighten on the twisted wood of the scythe. "Some paths are beyond my vision, little reaper. You think of yourself as a chauffeur to souls. I am not much different. I decide the destination and time, but once they arrive all entities have free will."

Death truly has been in my thoughts. That's creepy. They probably are hearing me think this right now. As if in response, Death chuckled low. A deep rumble came from their throat. I probably didn't need to ask this aloud, but it won't feel real unless I do.

"Does he have to die?" My voice cracked.

"No." It echoed around my head. Quick, as if the answer was waiting. My shoulders released the tension keeping them up. "I can restore it, but it will break your connection. You will no longer experience the changes within you. You will go back to being what I created, a reaper. Nothing more."

A reaper. Nothing more. Immortality filled with servitude. Surrounded by death and suffering and sadness. A tool. A conduit. A reaper. Nothing more.

I gave a shallow nod. "I just want him to live."

"If that is what you wish, little reaper." Death did not tap the scythe this time. Instead, they scraped it across the floor until it was tucked against their body.

Yes. Jimi is a human that deserves a long and beautiful life. Jimi should have love that can live in the light and not hide in the shadows. My eyes scanned the dents and scratches in the wood floor. I closed my eyes and focused on the lingering taste left by the small orange fruit on his lips. Trying to brand it into my memory.

I would never have that again. Never feel him again. He would never see me again, but he would live. Slowly I lifted my gaze.

"Would you consider granting me with my own," I paused. I was like a child asking a strict parent for permission to do something dangerous. Death opened their wings, waiting for me to finish the question. "my own soul? To make me human."

A lump fell to my stomach. My vision blurred and I realized my eyes were filling with water. I pinched them and a few drops hit the stage floor.

"I considered it." They continued their circles around

me. The taps from the Scythe bouncing off the back of the theater like a drumbeat. "You would make an excellent human."

My lips tugged up at the corners and my cheeks flushed. I think this is pride. A result of hearing their praise. I blinked and more tears slid down my cheek.

This could be it. Death can restore Jimi's soul and grant me my own. We could live and be happy together. Death shuffled their wings wide enough to get my attention. I recovered from the happy thoughts of what a life with Jimi could look like. The air thickened again.

"Little reaper, I do not have a soul for you." Death's words are like a knife to my gut.

My shoulders fell forward, and I leaned on my knees. A sob broke through dropping tears onto the stage. The sound of rattling chains stopped in front of me. "Please." I begged.

"I am the one who takes souls, not who can give them. That role belongs to-" Death shook their arm, and the sounds of metal chains filled the air, "My own master, and he is not very gracious."

I fell to my knees. Inches from Death's robes. Countless people have cried in front of me. Begging for the life of their loved one. I never expected it to feel like this. Like I was being torn from the inside. Like a waterfall opened from my eyes.

I peered up from where I knelt. My white robe billowing around me in a rumpled circle.

"Please. If you cannot give me life. Then restore his. I cannot risk killing him. I love him." I gripped the fabric needing something to tether me to this spot. Instinct had me wanting to go to a skyscraper and scream knowing nothing could hear me. Then run into Jimi's arms and savor every moment with him.

"I know you do, little reaper." Death placed a boney hand on my shoulder. "I will give you until sunrise before I restore his soul. Say your goodbyes."

I sucked in a scream and sobbed harder. My hand reached out to grab Death's robe and they vanished. My palm hit the rough stage floor.

That was it.

Only a few more hours.

Only enough time to say goodbye.

34
Jimi

11:00pm Thursday
Oct 21st, 2023

Never have I stolen anything from the hospital before. Yet, I found myself smuggling a bag of blood tucked into the waistband of my scrubs. Rolled up in my pocket is the scroll from Madam Martisha. Where she had written clear instructions how to summon a dark spirit. I gave up hoping it could be anything other than a demon. It hit me when I swiped the blood. I am really doing this. I am about to summon a demon.

The elevator down to the basement seemed to hum louder than usual. Taunting me for my crazy behavior. The security guards switch shifts at 11:00pm. They usually are distracted for the first five minutes. Passing off reports and any important information. I kept checking the time on my phone. *Move Jimi, get past the cameras.*

I take my chances that they are not looking at the tiny

box in the upper right corner of the monitor labeled basement-3. Where I am currently walking suspiciously. This area has nothing other than storage of broken equipment. My breath quickened as I sped up my steps.

Located on the opposite end of the employee lockers and around two corners. I found myself alone in a dimly lit hallway with lights flickering around me.

"Great. This looks like a horror film." I mumble to myself. "A great place to summon a demon, and maybe die."

I opened the windowless metal door to the broken equipment storage room and shut it quietly behind me. There were broken beds, wheelchairs, and random office machines piled around the room. In the middle, I laid down the white bed sheet that was tucked under my arm. It has a plastic back and is usually used under patients that might soil themselves. The last thing I needed was a janitor asking why blood was smeared all over the floor.

Unraveling the scroll, I read the instructions carefully.

Step 1: Draw a pentagram on the floor with human blood, make sure it's large enough for something to stand inside.

I found the use of the word *"something"* disturbing. Not a human or person, but just something. A shiver ran up my spine.

After searching the room for something sharp. I was able to puncture a small hole in the blood bag with a broken pen. The hole was small enough that I could control the slow stream. I then carefully drew a pentagram as it dripped. This might be the grossest thing I have ever done. I placed the leaking bag in a trash bag and looked down at the red pentagram.

I laughed at myself. "This feels so cliché."

**Step 2: Write your desire on a piece of parchment and burn it.*
Place the ashes in the center.

The first part of this I completed before entering the building. I would have set off the smoke detectors and I was not ready to explain what the hell I was doing to the hospital staff. Mila stopped visiting me during work. She didn't want to distract me and said a normal couple did not see each other if they worked separate jobs. If I had waited to do this at home, she would have tried to convince me to stop. The mere hint of demons made her scowl. She was bitter enough when I summoned an angel without her. Claiming I am poking forces I don't understand. Forces she doesn't completely understand.

I took out a snack size plastic bag full of ashes. I had written *"For Mila to become human and myself to keep my soul. Then we could be together"* before I burned it. I sprinkled the ashes in the center of the pentagram. Careful not to step in blood. My heart was going to burst from my chest and my hands were clammy.

**Step 3: Repeat four times*
"Ego te, Moloch, clamo ut pacisci. Libenter ad te
venio"
Then wait.

I do not speak Latin, but I did use a translation app this morning and was not too worried by what it said. I am not certain if Moloch is a name or a species. At this point its small potatoes.

I cleared my throat. "Ego te, Moloch, clamo ut pacisci. Libenter ad te venio"

Nothing happened.

"Ego te, Moloch, clamo ut pacisci. Libenter ad te venio" I repeated.

While reciting the phrase the second time the lights flickered. *Oh yea, I am definitely doing something stupid.*

"Ego te, Moloch, clamo ut pacisci. Libenter ad te venio" During the third time a breeze passed by me in the windowless room. That was unsettling.

I hesitated. I could stop now. I could clean up and walk away. Maybe I should have done this with Mila. My tongue was stuck to the roof of my mouth. I had to mentally pry my lips apart to continue. "Ego te, Moloch, clamo ut pacisci. Libenter ad te venio"

At the end of the fourth time the blood had started to glow. Like embers of a fire. I took a step back, needing distance from the bed sheet. I shoved the instructions in my pocket. *Fuck, I might die tonight. There's probably a reaper behind me laughing at my stupidity.*

The ashes began to float up and spin caught in an invisible tornado. Goosebumps covered my arms and neck. The lights were all flickering until all of them went out except for the light directly above the pentagram.

Here we go.

A woman appeared in the center. She had the body of a swimsuit model and was wearing shiny black pants that appeared painted on. The back was completely exposed. The muscles on her back flexed as she rotated the angle of her body. She looked at me over her shoulder with a big smile. I froze when I noticed her teeth were sharp and her eyes red.

She whipped around her icy white hair, and it seemed to float behind her as if there was no gravity in the room. Her top was made of silver chains draped over her breasts like a necklace with a hundred layers. She had two sections of hair twisted into nubs at the front of her head. They mimicked horns. I shivered at the realization; she was a demon. Madam Martisha knew what she was talking about. She was speaking truth years ago at the carnival and about this ritual. I summoned a fucking demon. She nodded as if hearing my thoughts.

"You're, um," I hesitated. "a demon. Sorry I don't know what to call you."

She ran her tongue under her sharp teeth then smiled. The ashes had turned back into a solid piece of paper in her hand which she was using to fan her face.

"Moloch. You call me Moloch." She had a sultry tone. It made my cock unintentionally twitch, and my eyes perk up. She winked as if knowing the effect of her voice. I adjusted my stance wider. Keeping a strong appearance. Everything I read about demons said they will find any loophole to screw you over in a bargain. I needed to keep my request simple and clear.

"I want to make a deal." I stated, puffing out my chest.

"I bet you do." Her head dipped looking me up from my feet before locking her red eyes stopped on mine. "You are a good-looking specimen. Come closer so I can have a better look."

"You can look from there." A note on the bottom of the instructions that appeared to be written in a hurry like an afterthought told me not to enter the pentagram once the ritual began. I assume that means Moloch cannot leave, and I cannot be touched unless I enter.

"Don't you want a closer look at me?" She ran her hands over her exposed sides and down her hips.

"You're not my type."

"You're no fun." She pouted. "I picked this body just for you."

"I'm sorry you wasted the effort." I crossed my arms over my chest. "You read my request. Are you willing to make a deal?"

The faster I get this over with the better. I just need a simple yes or no. My visit from Zadkiel felt far better than this. Even though he was smug and hardly informative. Moloch is looking at me like I am a late-night snack.

Moloch closed her red eyes and tilted her head back.

She sucked in air through her nose like a hound trying to pick up a scent. When she stopped her red eyes narrowed on me.

"A reaper, you call Mila, wants to become human. You need your shattered soul made whole, and you want to be together. How sweet." She said reading the scrap of paper. The last part was full of sarcasm. I rolled my eyes. "These are big asks. Do you have anything worth bargaining for?"

I gulped. This is the part I was unsure of. "What would you want in return?"

Moloch brought the paper to her nose and sniffed. Gross. She then flicked out a sharp tongue and tasted the words written. "Your soul when you die would be nice." Moloch casually answered. A sinister grin tugged at her lips.

"I figured you would say that. What does that mean? An eternal life in hell?" I scoffed.

"Humans are so narrow minded." She lifted her arms to run both hands through her hair. The chains slid over her breast exposing the underside. I kept my focus on her red eyes. Ignoring her pathetic attempt at seduction. Sensing my thoughts again her eyes darkened as she spoke. "Hell is not a place. It can be many things. And no, you would work for me."

"Work for a demon? Like possessing or killing."

She lifted her hair off her body and let if fall like in slow motion. It was amazing that she was even here. That I was speaking to a real demon. I hid the excitement from my face and tried to remain stoic.

"I am more like your reaper lover than you think." She held up her hand with sharp black nails and on the middle finger sat a black ring with a star in the center. "I occasionally collect the soul of someone trying to break a deal. You may think of me as sinister, but my deals are fair. And sanctioned by powers you would only understand if you worked for me."

I tried to think about all the conversations I have had with Mila about nuance. Good people die just as much as bad. Sometimes bad people live long lives and other times a child is taken too early. The choices are beyond my understanding. There is nuance in everything. Maybe even woven into the deals with a demon.

"Mila will be human with a soul of her own. I will keep my own soul intact. And we can be together." I repeat my words in my head double checking. They were simple and clear. I couldn't find a loophole. Maybe I should specify the number of years we get together. Although I am pretty sure Death is the only one who can decide when a life is over. "Then when I die, you get my soul, and I will for work for you."

She nods. "It could be that easy." She reached out her hand with the black ring. I stared at it, contemplating the deal.

"Fifty years." I said."

"What?"

"You can have my soul for fifty years, then you must send it to wherever I was meant to spend my afterlife." I must of hit a nerve because her jaw tightened.

"Two hundred." She crossed her arms to mirror me.

"Seventy-five." I remembered how Mila said a century goes by fast in an immortal life. I was hoping that was true.

"One hundred and fifty years." Moloch's red eyes flared bright.

"One hundred years. Final offer." I widened my stance. Moloch glared at me. I feared eyes would catch my scrubs on fire. She slowly unfolded her arms pressing the paper between her hands like she was praying. Her hands rubbed together until the paper returned to ash.

She clapped her hands free from the ash and stuck out the hand with the black ring once more.

"One hundred years of service to me when you die. You will have your soul intact. Your reaper, Mila, will be human with her own soul. The deal will begin at sunrise." Her face was flat. Gone was the sinister smile. Nothing more than a business transaction now.

A hundred years of servitude was worth it to live a lifetime with Mila. To travel with her and love her. Make a million memories with her. I wanted to sit next to her in a theater and watch her eyes widen as the curtains opened. I needed to feel her skin pressed against mine every day. I need her kiss. Need to celebrate every inch of her body.

I blinked slowly, trying to think of a reason not to make this deal. I took two steps closer to the star made of blood. Making sure to keep my feet outside the lines. When I placed my hand in hers the hesitation grew.

"Deal?" Her sultry voice enveloped me.

"Deal." I copied.

The bulbs in the room began to flash like strobe lights. The hand I was holding suddenly felt large and rough. I stumbled back pulling out of her grasp. Tripping, I landed on my butt staring up at a different demon.

No, same demon, new body.

This one was male with large horns that curved back. His skin was grey like ash and his eyes were shining like embers of a fire. Moloch laughed with a deep voice then vanished. All the lights turned on leaving me alone on the floor with a pile of ash, a bloody pentagram, and a deal with a demon.

35
Mila

I paced around Jimi's studio apartment feeling what I assumed was anxiousness. I knew He would not be home until around 1:45am. I bounced around a few rooftops, but traveling was making me tired. Instead of pacing, I decided to curl up on his couch and read a book. His cat nestled near my feet. Still not aware of my presence.

The front door shut and woke me. *I was sleeping again.* His eyes went wide, and he ran over to me. Without a word he leaned down and kissed me.

"God, I missed you." He said between kisses.

"You saw me this afternoon." I laughed. He silenced me by deepening our kiss and tossing the book opened on my chest onto the coffee table. He must have showered at the hospital. There was a slight hint of pine on his skin. It was nice, but it made me miss his usual cologne.

"Mila, you look exhausted. Lay down with me for

a couple of hours. Theres somewhere I want to go at 6am." Jimi pulled me towards the bed. He kicked his shoes off and tossed his coat and scarf onto a chair.

I stared down at my feet, wishing my shoes to vanish. I must be tired, cause the are not vanishing. My brow scrunched until lines formed between them. I have never struggled to control my appearance before.

Jimi's hands were on my ankles before I noticed him kneeling before me. He rubbed the back of my calves.

"Are you alright?" He asked in a low whisper. I watched as his fingers un-tied my boots before pulling them off. He tossed the boots behind him, but they vanished before striking the floor. I scoffed at the irony. They felt real on my body. He could touch the laces when I was wearing them. Then we are both reminded that they are not real. Just an illusion.

"My mind is foggy." I frowned. "I have never struggled before. I have never been tired before."

"You're changing." He crawled on the bed and pulled me up to his chest. He curled my body into his as he laid us down. His mouth was tucked against my neck. I closed my eyes and focused on his warm breath. He murmured into my hair, "It's a good thing."

I wanted to tell him the truth. That I made a deal to restore his soul, and at 6:45am he will never see me or touch me again. I plan to travel as far from here as I can. Hopefully Death will keep me stationed far from Jimi. I don't think I could resist the temptation to watch him all day. I need to be far and kept busy.

He set an alarm on his phone before pulling a blanket over both of us. Heat from his body warmed my back. It was so much more pleasant than the cold I felt earlier.

I was going to miss feeling things. Feeling him.

A mechanical sound mimicking birds chirping woke me. I was still wrapped in Jimi's arms. He groaned and reached back to turn the alarm off.

One more hour until sunrise.

We got dressed for the cold weather and headed out of the apartment. I wanted to hold his hand, but there were plenty of people already outside. I almost forgot I was invisible to all but him. After a few blocks we ended up on the side of Bryant Park. I recognized the smell immediately. We were walking towards the bakery.

As we got nearer to the door an employee flipped the sign around, "open". I beamed and followed Jimi inside. He held his hands behind his back. I interlaced the fingers of my right hand with his. He squeezed.

"Can I help you?" The short red headed woman asked from behind the counter. Her apron was covered in flour and various colors of frosting.

"I'll take six of your famous chocolate chip cookies, two apple fritter donuts," He peeked at me. I was on my toes trying to look over his shoulder at the sweets in the glass case. "And one red velvet cupcake. It's my girlfriend's birthday."

"My birthday?" I whispered into his ear.

He smiled but quickly turned to the worker so she would think he was smiling at her. She nodded and began packing his order.

I wandered over to a large case full of decorated cakes. Symbols to celebrate birthdays, weddings, or graduations. All things I would never experience. According to the clock behind the counter we only had forty minutes left.

Jimi paid and walked out. I was too slow to follow through the door, instead I just appeared outside. Traveling made my head spin for a second. He had a look of concern. Lips pressed in a thin line.

"Let's take these to our bench."

I nodded slowly, trying to clear my head.

I tried to walk as close to him as possible. Savoring every moment of his body warmth. Branding his scent to memory. Thirty minutes and he will have his soul back. He will go on living a full and long life. Without me. I am not a blessing to him the same way he is to me. I am a succubus. A curse.

The air was cold enough that a thin layer of frost had formed on the bench overnight. It was the bench we had our first date. Before he knew what I was. Before we understood our connection. Before I knew I was killing him. He pulled two cookies from the bag and inspected our surroundings. The park was mostly empty this early. Still dark with scattered light posts. A few people cut through to subway stations and were in too much of a rush to pay him any attention.

Jimi handed me a cookie and flashed a goofy smile.

I lifted it to my nose and inhaled the scent. Sweet and almost nutty. It was warm against my fingers. I opened my mouth and took a bite. It sat on my tongue for a few seconds before I remembered to chew. Each bite sent a wave of melted chocolate bits over my tongue.

Humans are so lucky. Food is incredible. Tasting is incredible. I should have begged Death for a few days more. Or perhaps Jimi didn't have any longer. Maybe Death knew Jimi was at the end of his rope. That I was only a few touches away from killing him.

I tried to push aside my worries and focus on the last minutes I have left with Jimi. And this amazing chocolate chip cookie. I moaned and shut my eyes.

"I will never get tired of hearing that." Jimi chuckled.

36
Jimi

It was hard not to stare at my phone. I researched the time of sunrise on my way home from work last night. Then I checked what time the bakery opened. Sure, she would be human soon and can try everything, But I wanted to have this moment to remind us forever. This bench is where I had my first date with her as a reaper. This bench where I will have my first date with her as a human. The beginning of our life together.

When she tried the apple fritter, she moaned at the flavors of cinnamon and cooked apple filling her mouth. That perfect mouth. There were just enough people in the park that I was unable to grab her and lick the frosting from the corner of her lips. Not without looking like a schizophrenic.

Soon, I have to keep telling myself, I won't have to

hold back. The air was stagnant. A calm before a storm. In the distance there was a glow from the sun casting colors into the clouds.

The sun will be above the horizon in a few minutes. My heart was pounding in my chest, and I wonder if Mila could sense my eagerness. Can she sense something big is about to happen?

"It feels like snow." Mila said with a mouthful of the last bite of fritter. "I can smell it.

"You can smell the snow?"

"Oh yea, there is a very distinct smell in the air right before a snowstorm." She folded her hands in her lap and stared down at them. "Jimi, I need to tell you something."

"I need to tell you something too." A sliver of the sun was above the horizon now. Butterflies filled my chest. "You go first."

She turned away when she spoke. I noticed she was watching the sun rise also.

"I spoke to Death." she said quietly.

"Death? Like the big guy in charge."

Mila nodded. "He agreed to restore your soul to you."

"And what about you?" I already made a deal for my soul. Frustration filled me. *I already took care of it. Does one deal become void? Do they cancel each other out? What did she give up for her deal with Death?*

"There was nothing he would do for me. You get your complete soul back, and I go back to the life of a reaper. No more connection." She was fidgeting in her lap. "The last couple months knowing you have been amazing. More than I could have dreamed. More than I deserve. I-" She paused noticing she was breathing out white breath that matched my own. She shivered. "What is happening?"

Mila grabbed her chest. The way one would having a heart attack. Her big doe eyes filled with fear, and she gazed up at me. I think she is in pain.

"That's what I wanted to tell you." I pulled her into me, I should have been more prepared for her to become human on a cold morning. Her leather coat was hardly warm enough. "I made a deal too."

"You made a deal? With who?" Her voice cracked.

I swallowed hoping that what I was about to say didn't anger her. "With a demon. Moloch."

"What?" She tried to stand out of my grasp, but she fell onto my lap. Unstable on her feet.

"You're becoming human. We should have stayed in the apartment. It's too cold out here." I took the beanie off my head and put it on her. I should have thought this through more. I glanced around the park. The sun illuminated everything, and we were no longer hidden in the shadows.

"Jimi, it hurts." Mila pressed her palms to the side of her head and buried her face in my chest. I rubbed her back hoping the friction would heat her up.

Strange grey smoke seeped from her ring and slid down my throat. I drank it in. The smoke tasted like nothing but was warm inside. My chest heated and I gasped.

"Mila." I cried. Her clothes vanished. All but the

beanie on top of her head. Her skin was instantly red and covered with goosebumps. She remained in a state of shock, still holding her head. Shivering.

I took my coat off and forced her into it. Zipping it all the way to the front. Her teeth were chattering.

"Shit, shit, shit." Someone might walk by and see a naked freezing woman in the park. I took my shoes off to remove my socks. I laid her down on the bench while I put my socks on her feet. Her bare legs were shaking and getting blotchy with red marks from the cold.

Once I had my shoes back on, I scooped her up in my arms and ran. My apartment was only a few blocks away. My own breath making clouds as I ran. *Not your best executed plan Jimi. I scold myself.*

This was my deal with Moloch. It seemed to work. She was human. I could tell by the concerned looks we received as I ran. Everyone could see her. She was human, and a part of me that was missing had returned. It slithered down my throat like a smoke snake. We have everything we want. I kissed her forehead.

"We are almost there." I entered the door code quickly. "Hang in there."

I took the stairs up to my studio two at a time. Ignoring my own freezing body and numb arms. Focusing on the only thing that matters. Her.

37
Mila

Splashing water and a muffled voice tell me I am not alone. Not that I fear Jimi would leave me outside to freeze to death. I pinched my eyes shut when Jimi was carrying me. The cold air was so intense I thought it was peeling away layers of my skin. I must have passed out. The last thing I remember clearly was talking with Jimi when I was suddenly overwhelmed. There was a tightness in my chest, and I think my clothes disappeared. I tried to teleport away, but it made my head throb. I have never had pain inside my head before. It blasted me in waves of pain behind my eyes. Even now. I feel like an anchor has been attached to me.

I changed.

I feel different.

I could tell the moment it occurred.

The sun became too bright. Each breath had my chest

filling with cold air. Burning from the inside. I felt the bench freezing under me. It was terrible. No wonder humans wear so many layers.

I expected to go back to being like I was before. A reaper as I was meant to be. I expected my deal with Death to come to fruition once the sun rose. Then it clicked in my mind that Jimi made a deal to make me human, I couldn't react before pain took over my body. It happened too fast for me to ask what the terms of his deal was.

He made a deal with a demon. Those never end well. I should have known he would try something stupid to save me. I would have done the same thing for him. I also made a deal, but Death seems more credible than a demon. Although, saying that statement in my head sounds like I am also making assumptions. Assuming Death has no ulterior motives. I suddenly feel like I understand nothing.

Opening my eyes, I found myself in Jimi's bathroom. Every inch of my skin is tingling. I am partially laying down in his porcelain tub. Warm water is rising around me. My frozen fingers ache under the water. I gasped. Jimi leans in, already kneeling at the side of the tub.

"Thank fuck." He placed a hand to my forehead and then smoothed back my hair. "I thought I was going to lose you for a second."

I flexed my fingers under the water. A dull pain had formed in each knuckle. My skin looked blotchy with flourishes of red all over it. I can't change it. I can't force my skin to look a certain way. I am powerless. I adjusted to sit up straighter. I feel heavy. Weighted down.

"I feel everything." I panted. "Is this really happening?"

He nodded slowly and glanced down at my body. Jimi stopped the water and watched me in silence as I flexed my hands in front of my face. I must look ridiculous to him. An alien that just possessed a body.

My expression pleaded at him to say something. Anything. I need to make sure he is not regretting this. I really need to ask what he traded for this, but now I am transfixed on the sensation of water on my skin. On the air and how it sends chills down my spine when it touches my wet shoulders.

"The sun rose, and you turned human, just like the demon said would happen." He stroked my hair. "I inhaled some weird grey smoke that I am pretty sure came out of your ring. Then all your clothes disappeared. I wasn't expecting that. I rushed you here as soon as possible."

I blinked rapidly. His soul was in my ring this entire time. I carried part of him with me for over a decade and didn't suspect. If I didn't get his soul, who's did I get? Or maybe it is mine. The one that Death kept from me to have me be a reaper. A reaper in eternal servitude.

My tongue is stuck to the roof of my mouth. "My throat." I rasped lifting a wet hand to my neck.

Jimi ran out of the room. Leaving me alone to settle in this body. A body up until today was just an illusion. Something I had created from a mix of women I had admired or found beautiful. But now, it is mine. My real body. My body feels sore, achy, and for some reason my fingertips are wrinkled.

The warm water had the numbness leaving my toes. I wiggled them under the water. To be sure I am no longer a reaper, I tried to imagine myself across the room, but my body remained in the tub. I lifted my hands one by one watching the water drip off my fingertips. This is strange. Slowly, I turned the gold ring until it slipped over my knuckle. My breath caught and I sat up straight.

I blinked tears free as I held my soul ring in front of my eyes. Looking through it at the sunlight coming in from single square bathroom window. It was a regular ring now. A piece of jewelry that holds no purpose other than being beautiful. Not much different than myself, I suppose. Just a ring. I laughed for one beat. Just a woman. I am just an ordinary woman now. This thought made my chest flutter with excitement.

Jimi returned with a tall glass of water and a bendable straw. He knelt by the tub and brought the straw to my lips.

"Drink some water." I wrapped my lips around the straw and sucked. It had almost no taste. Although, something lingered in the water. A hint of flavor. Not sweet like cookies or tangy like the tiny oranges. "Swallow." He laughed when I was holding the water in my mouth for too long. Sloshing it between my cheeks.

I finished the whole glass in many long gulps. My

head was no longer spinning. Jimi pressed a kiss to my forehead. I grabbed him by the shirt and pressed my lips to his before he could move away.

"I love you." I said into his mouth.

"I love you, Mila." He kissed me again this time slipping his tongue into my mouth. I stood in the tub guiding him to stand with my grip still on his shirt and keeping his lips on mine. "I would do anything for you."

"You've already done too much." I will ask him about the deal later, now all I can think of is how I am standing naked against his body. He didn't seem to mind that I was dripping water onto the floor and drenching his clothes.

On shaky legs, I stepped out of the tub. He deepened our kiss. His hands gripped my hips tightly. I shivered with the sudden cool air over my warm skin.

"That will take some getting used to."

"What will?" Jimi brushed my hair back to kiss my neck.

"Being cold." I answered. He smiled onto my skin.

"Wait till summer. You will be desperate to feel cold." He trailed his hands from my lower back and rested them on the curve of my ass. I pressed my body harder into his. I felt his body before, but every inch of me feels overly sensitive now. The roughness of his denim against my skin. The Dripping water streaming from my hair.

I let him lead me out of the bathroom. Never breaking our contact. The back of his legs hit the bed after a few strides. I peered up at him. No longer cold. I felt like I was being warmed from the inside out. Can he feel how eager I am? Desperate to try out this new body.

My hair continued to drip water. His cat came close to rub against us and was quickly appalled by the water. They ran to the safety of the sofa. Jimi's grinned hard enough that it made lines branch out from the outer corners of his eyes. I could look into those dark eyes forever. I could live on those lips and bask in his touch.

"Well, new human. What would you like to do first?" He gave me that crooked smile that causes flutters in my core.

I moved around him to sit on the bed, laying back until I was only propped up by my elbows.

"I have a few ideas."

Jimi started at the inside of my knees. Placing soft kisses on my skin. He moved up to my thighs. My skin was cool from still being wet from the bath, but my core heated with every kiss. A streak of sunlight was peeking through the clouds casting its light on the bed just for us. Snow was silently falling. The first snow of the season. Earlier than usual.

Jimi had a record playing on his console. One of the folky rock groups he likes. It was utterly normal, and yet I am waiting to be awoken from this dream. Waiting to feel a tug inside that will pull me away from here. But it's strange, I feel no connection. I only feel me.

He kissed the curve of my thigh where it meets my core. My stomach tightened. My breathing was choppy, and I wasn't sure if I should be trying to slow it down. Is it possible to breathe wrong?

"Relax." Jimi said, noticing the stiffness in my body. I dropped my head back and shook it. Loose wet stands of hair gliding over the bed. I looked down at him kneeling between my legs and smiled. A signal I was attempting to relax.

He grabbed my thighs and forced them apart. I opened wider to him. Allowing myself to be on full display before his face. A drip slid down my entrance. I wasn't sure if it was from the bath or the heat that was rising in me.

My eyes rolled back in my head as he licked up my center in one long swipe. I arched off the bed. With one hand gripping the comforter and the other tangled in his hair. I let out a breathy moan.

"Jimi." His name on my lips made him go ravenous. He circled his tongue faster around my clit. I thought I was going to float off the bed when a finger slid inside me. "Jimi."

I forgot all words except his name.

He pumped his finger, curling it to hit a spot inside that made a wave of pleasure surge through me. I loved him. Loved the way he looked at me. I love the way he treats me. And I most definitely love the way he touches me. Every touch heightened somehow. Like my sensitivity dial has been turned up. Before I had this human body, he felt incredible, but now I think this might be what heaven is like. Laying here with my wet body sticking to his bed while he licks the most sensitive parts of me. Making me wiggle and lift my hips up as if I am going to burst from too much pleasure.

Every swipe of his tongue grew more intense. Building a pressure low in my abdomen. He slips a second finger inside. My thighs clench around his head. A low chuckle vibrated from his mouth onto my clit. I released his head from my thigh and let my knees fall further apart.

He removes his fingers quickly to pull me to the edge of the bed. My legs draped off. Thumping as they hit the floor. A sound escapes me. A squeak? I feel less in control of my body also. My breathing, the sounds I am making.

I am empty without him inside me. Lonely without him touching me. Jimi smiled. Coy and sensual. I must have been making a weird face. A face that is pleading for him to continue to touch me. His lips are slick from my juices. I think I whimpered when he stuck his tongue out and ran it around his lips. He shut his eyes for a moment savoring me. I could feel my face blushing.

Kneeling, he lifts my thighs until they rest on his shoulders and continues to devour me like I was his last meal.

His fingers pump in me quickly as his tongue makes a pattern of fast licks and slow sucking on my clit. I buck against his face. My ass nearly falling off the edge of the bed. He moaned with his mouth on me. The sensation had me come undone. My stomach clenched and I screamed his name. Wave after wave of pleasure surged through me. My inner walls tightening around his fingers. His tongue lapping up my release. I gripped the bed so tight I thought the fabric would tear.

My climax stopped and I suddenly was too sensitive to be touched. I have never had this feeling before. I pulled him by the hair until he let up. His smile was greedy. A drip trailing down his chin. He lifted a dry finger and wiped it off only to place it inside his mouth. It might be the sexiest thing I have ever seen. I was finally able to breathe when he removed his fingers from inside me.

"That was incredible." I panted, letting my head fall back onto the bed.

I stayed at the edge of the mattress, unable to move. Legs no longer on his shoulders but hanging limp. I don't think I could move them if I wanted to. Jimi pulled his shirt over his head and undid his pants. I was nervous to keep going. My body was still recovering from the orgasm. Before he removed his boxer briefs, he placed a pillow from the couch between my feet on the floor. I raised my brows with confusion.

"For your knees." He said plainly.

"My knees?"

Jimi leaned over me on the bed and kissed me. His lips were still slick with my release. I opened my mouth and let his tongue slide inside. The taste was new. A mix of salty and sweet.

His arms wrapped around my waist and pulled me off the bed until I was kneeling on the pillow.

"Turn around." He said patting the bed with his hand. "Bend over and watch the snow fall."

39
Jimi

The most beautiful sight was before me. I don't mean the fresh snow falling outside in large flakes. I mean the glorious olive-skinned Goddess that is bent over and dripping in front of me. I removed my boxer briefs, throwing them across the room which made her laugh when they landed on the record player causing the music to stop. Her laugh was beautiful, but I was ready to hear her scream my name once more.

I ran my hands down her back. Small goosebumps appeared as I trailed my fingers. I loved seeing her skin react to my touch. Small things that didn't happen before. Before she was human. Like goosebumps and flushed skin. The most perfect shade of pink.

She's mine and I am hers. From this day forward. As long as this world will have us. I am going to enjoy every chance I get to touch her. Every conversation. Every kiss. I breathed in the scent of her arousal as she waited bent over my platform bed.

Enough moments have been wasted staring at Mila's back. I grabbed my cock from the base and lined the tip to her entrance. She was so wet. So ready. Before pressing inside, I rubbed forward gliding over her clit. She shook with pleasure. I slid my cock back and entered her slowly. Thrusting in only a few inches. Letting her stretch around me.

"Please. Jimi." Her voice was airy and full of need.

"Please what?" I teased.

She bucked back onto my cock. Trying to push me inside her. I leaned onto my heels, denying her any more than the inches I was giving her.

"Please take me." She begged. "Fill me."

She couldn't see the smile on my face showing how pleased I am with her words. Proof that she is perfect in every way. My hands roamed from her sides over the curve of her ass. I gripped her hips tight and pulled. I filled her with one hard thrust. She cried out in pleasure. I removed my cock until just the tip remained inside and thrust again.

We filled the apartment with sounds of my body smacking her ass followed by her screams. My name is like a song of worship from her. As she belted "Jimi" loud enough I was sure a passerby in the hall would hear.

My muscles tightened while I buried my cock deep inside her. *Fucking perfect.* Her inner walls are clenching around my cock. Evidence of her pleasure. It's still not enough. I need her to come completely undone under me. I need this to be the best first day a human could ever ask for. *I wonder if I can make her come again.*

Reaching around with one hand I find her clit. Still sensitive from when I was sucking on it before. She grips the bed until her knuckles turn white.

"That's it, Mila, come again for me." I pumped inside her all the way to the base of my cock while my fingers circled her clit. Pressure building inside me. Not just in my balls, about to explode. But deep in my chest. I grunt out "I love you."

"I love you too." Her voice cracking and high. Her body clenches down on my cock. The muscles in her back tense.

"Fuck." I throw my head back and pumped a few more times before my own release comes. Her inner walls are squeezing me. Milking out every drop I have to give. We both stopped pulsating at the same time. I collapsed on top of her. Our bodies sticking together with sweat and the remnants from the bath. My cock going limp inside her. Lingering in its version of heaven.

I could live here. I could die here. Covered in proof of her pleasure and completely elated. Pressing a kiss to the back of her shoulder I roll off. She still doesn't move.

"Are you okay?" I asked calmly, hoping I didn't hurt her. She turns her head to face me and pulled her arms to be tucked under her body. Her face was flushed pink. *Beautiful. She is truly beautiful.*

She nods and licks her lips. "Everything is perfect."

I slapped her ass as I stood. She let out a squeal that made me grin. "Let's get cleaned up. We have a big day." She scrunched her brow. "It's your first day as a human."

40
Jimi

I made her a plate with scrambled eggs and toast while she took a quick shower. I pulled up a YouTube video made for toddlers explaining how to use the toilet. She slapped my chest and didn't think it was funny. "I've seen people use the bathroom. People can die anywhere you know." She snapped at me.

Secretly I was grateful that I wouldn't have to teach her everything it means to be human. The next few weeks might be the worst case of mansplaining ever. *Will she get a period? I have no idea how to talk to her about that. I wonder if there is a YouTube video to explain.*

I do, however, need to get her some clothes. Right now, she is wearing a pair of my sweats and a hoodie. Hunched over my kitchen island eating like it's Christmas morning.

She seemed thoroughly distracted eating and typing things into the search bar of my laptop. A good opportunity to slip away.

I left her in the apartment and ran down the street to a small store called D2. They have a random mix of household items and clothing. Nothing fancy, but I am low on funds after giving one thousand dollars to Madam Martisha. A fee that has proven to be worth it. Maybe I will send her a holiday card with a photo of Mila and me. After all Mila can have her picture taken now.

Returning to the apartment with two large bags, I found her sitting cross legged on my couch petting Nabi. His fluffy white fur was moving between her fingers. He was purring. Happy for the attention.

I guessed her shoe size at the store and went with a pair of knock off Uggs. Hoping they wouldn't fall off if a little too big. I picked out a warm winter coat. A deep red that will be amazing next to her tan skin. An assortment of sweaters, leggings, and sweatpants that wouldn't fall off her body.

She smiled the entire time trying everything on. I sipped my coffee and took in the sight of her joy. Spinning like a child. It was overwhelmingly cute.

"I like this." She said pulling out a tan trench coat."

"It was on clearance, it's more suitable for spring. The red one is warmer." She pulled the tag off the trench coat and scoffed.

"I will wear this soft tortoise neck sweater underneath." She beamed a smile at herself into the full-length mirror hanging outside the bathroom.

I laughed. "Turtleneck."

She shrugged and finished getting dressed. Gray fleece leggings, black turtleneck, and black boots. *Exquisite.* My phone made a ding. A new text message blinked at the top of the screen.

> Hey man. Been a long time.

> Is this business or pleasure?

> Both

> I need a foreign passport.

> Italy. No questions asked.

> Do I ever ask questions?

Jorge was a college friend. But he transferred from NYU to MIT after two years. He lived with Dante and I for over a year. Providing us and other students with ID's or other documents. He told his parents the extra funds came from tutoring, but creating a scannable fake ID was very lucrative.

I considered asking him for a New York ID for Mila, but she has no paper trail in the states. Or anywhere. I thought it we made her from Italy people would question her less about not knowing things.

> What do you need from me?

I need a photo of the person with
a white background. An address to
put on a work visa. Assuming you
need that too.

Yes

Give me a week.

I will have a courier bring it to you.

Thanks man. I owe you.

Owe me?

I will send the bill to your Venmo.

I laughed and noticed Mila was no longer twirling in front of the mirror.

Of course.

I owe you several rounds of beer
also.

Beer – My favorite type of tip.

Mila was staring out the window with her palms pressed to the cold glass. I walked to her. Wrapping my arms around her waist, I breathed in her hair. She was really here with me. This was real. This is just the beginning.

"I keep waiting to be summoned for a reaping, but there's no tug inside." Her tone almost somber as if she was missing the tug, as she calls it. She turned to face me. My arms remained around her. "I don't know what I am supposed to do now."

I kissed her full lips. Pressing her body flush against mine. "What would you like to do?"

She bit her bottom lip and studied me through her lashes. I melted inside. I'd give my soul again to have her look at me like this forever.

"Can I stay here with you?" I nodded. "I would like a job. I know that's not very exciting, but it would make me feel useful."

I hummed and kissed her forehead. "Where would you like to work?"

"A theater." She said without hesitating.

"You're in the right city for that."

Her eyes glinted.

I brushed a strand of hair behind her ear and placed a kiss on her forehead. "You might have to start as an usher before you can make it backstage where you want to be."

She nodded.

"Okay then." I pulled her away from the window and grabbed our coats off the chair. "I need a photo of you to send to my friend for an ID. We can pick up a few job applications afterwards. Which I will help you fill out. Maybe lunch. I am thinking Korean. And of course, we need to get your own key to the apartment. Your home."

"Home." She repeated in a whisper that was meant for herself. My lips tugged up.

"Yes, Mila. Home."

41
Mila

The flavors from the bibimbap still coated the inside of my mouth. Onion, ginger, soy, and so much more. Jimi took me to a small restaurant with a mixture of scents floating in the air and painted screens hanging on the walls. I have been to restaurants before, but never as a patron. I have never had a server look directly at me and ask what I wanted to drink. I blurted out wine like a weirdo. Jimi had to chime in and order tea for the both of us. I guess I never noticed people don't typically drink wine in Korean lunch spots at 11:30am.

He presented me with a bowl that was filled with colorful vegetables and marinated meat. *Completely divine*. It was hours ago, and I am still thinking about the new flavors.

I think eating is my new favorite thing. How do people stop? I want to try everything. I want another chocolate chip cookie. As if reading my mind, we stopped by the bakery on our way back to the apartment. The woman behind the counter remembered Jimi and wished me a belated happy birthday. Assuming I was the girlfriend he spoke about. I blushed and tucked my body close to him.

I never considered myself shy. Reapers never hid from each other. Out in public I keep catching myself trying to shrink my body down or hide behind Jimi. As if I shouldn't be seen. As if I am breaking the rules. It will take time to get used to being seen and spoken to. Being acknowledged. Time I have now, thanks to Jimi.

We stopped at a small bodega with dusty shelves after lunch. It had cellphone accessories and miscellaneous electronics. The store employee smelled like pastrami and body odor. I should have been completely miserable tucked in an odd corner in front of a wall. But I was bouncing in my oversized boots as he took a quick photo of me from the shoulders up. He told me not to smile. I was shaking, I was so excited.

Walking away from the bakery, Jimi pulled a wallet sized photo from his pocket. The store was able to email a digital copy to his friend, but he asked for a copy for himself. It was the first photo of me ever taken. Nothing special. Just a solid white background. Jimi said it was the most beautiful picture he'd ever seen. My cheeks flushed.

Back at the apartment, I studied the single filled out online job application, with the word "submitted" in red at the top. Humans must do so many tedious tasks. Things I will have to get used to. Filling out paperwork.

Paying bills. Not all of the responsibilities are annoying. Nabi seems to like me even more after I filled his food bowl with the stinky contents of a can.

Jimi showed me how to log into his laptop and phone. He let me tinker around on the internet explaining the things I should not click on or download. Then he laughed when I searched "What is download?"

"I will leave these here for you while I am at work." He tapped the phone sitting on top of his laptop. We had to put his email and phone number on the application. I know how phones work, in theory; I just have never used one. Same with computers. I remember watching them being invented. They went from large machines that took up a whole room to a small device that can fit in a pocket.

I kept staring at the phone. Willing the theater to call. My insides twisted in knots.

"Give it time. You literally just applied." Jimi rubbed my back softly. "You probably won't hear from them for days."

He threw back the rest of his coffee. He had to work in a few hours and was operating on very little sleep. I played with the newly cut key that sat on the counter. I have no intention to use it tonight. The key to a place to call home. A home with Jimi. The man who sacrificed to clear a path for me.

I am still angry about the deal he made. But we are stronger together. We are clever and can find a way to make the deal work for the both of us. Stand firm and make a new deal if we must.

42
Mila

One perfect day, turned into two, then three. And now I am on day four already of being human. Jimi had to go back to work, and I struggled to let him get the necessary sleep during the afternoon. I had so many questions and wanted to do a million things in the city. So, I let him nap and I wandered around.

It takes forever to travel now. I used his metro card to take the subway to Battery Park. I was bumped and pushed by strangers on the subway car. It was wonderful. A scream-ing child dropped their stuffed elephant. I picked it up and handed it back to the child. The mother looked at me straight in the eye and thanked me. Who would have thought being seen could feel like this. Like I matter. Like I am part of this world for once. I have been taking every opportunity to talk to people. In line getting slices of pizza to bring to Jimi for dinner. At a local bookstore. I had no money to buy anything, but I still asked the shopkeeper to tell me about all the new releases. As soon as I have my own funds I will be back.

There is still no word from the theater that I applied to. Jimi is not worried. He claims I might have to apply to many jobs before I find one, and not everywhere hires a foreign person. I am more foreign than they will ever know.

Tonight, Jimi does not work. We are going on a double date. Just like in the movies. It is not the first time I have seen his best friend and his girlfriend; I watched them at the bar last month. This time I can actually stick out my hand and introduce myself.

"Does this look alright?" I walk out of the bathroom to find Jimi sitting at the kitchen island. He is lit up with shades of pink and orange as the sunsets beyond the windows.

"You look beautiful. I have no doubt all eyes will be on you." He wore jeans that were cuffed at the bottom and a faire isle sweater that looked like it belonged on a much older man. He paired it with his favorite denim jacket.

I fidgeted with the waist of my dress. It was long sleeve and crossed in the front. I am forced to wear leggings under it due to the season, but it's not bad. I will have to figure out what my style is. Before I just copied looks from what I saw around me. It would be so nice to still have that ability. I would have copied the look from a high-end store window display for tonight's double date. I also would not have been affected by the cold.

We walked hand in hand to the sushi restaurant. Jimi would pull me in close when we passed people. I am still improving on my instinct to get out of people's way. Before I would just let them pass through me. It took me rudely bumping into a few people to really grasp the concept.

Dante and Nina beat us to the restaurant. She was flashing a stunning diamond ring at Jimi when we walked in. Nina bounced up from her seat.

"Look." She held up her hand and pulled Jimi into a tight hug. "You are really stuck with me now." She released him and eyed me standing behind.

"Hi. I'm-"

"Mila!" She pushed Jimi aside and grabbed me by the shoulders. I was startled by her friendliness. "Hot damn you are gorgeous."

My face got warm. "Thank you. Congratulations on the engagement. Jimi is very excited."

Nina tapped the top of a chair to indicate for me to sit down. She walked around to her seat. "This is Dante. My fiancée." She drew out the last syllable of 'fiancée' while rubbing his shoulder.

Dante had the air around him like he belonged in an old movie playing a greaser. An Italian male stereotype from the 60's. Everything except the tattoos on his knuckles. Those screamed "I want to be a rock star".

"It's nice to meet you." He reached across the table to shake my hand. I smiled and repeated what he said back to him but with more awkwardness.

Jimi slipped a hand behind my waist, and we eased into conversation.

It was magical. Better than I could have imagined. I haven't witnessed anyone die in four days. I can go anywhere with Jimi in public. We don't have to hide affection or even the fact we are in a conversation. There has been no sign of Death or Moloch. And in addition, not having the love of my life at my side, I think I might be making my first two friends.

On the walk back to the apartment I practically recited everything Nina said to me. Even though Jimi was sitting next to me during the whole thing.

She talked about wedding plans and how Dante had only one request. For Jimi to be the best man. Nina invited me to go dress shopping with her and a group of friends. That way I could coordinate with Jimi's suit and tie. It was all so exciting.

The only thing that shut me up was Jimi ripping off my clothes and pulling me into bed back at the apartment. A welcome distraction.

Day five and six were just as perfect. I got a library card yesterday. Humans can just borrow any book they want for free. I have been inside a library before, but I didn't know they were free. What a luxury.

My face is in a book while I sit at the kitchen island. Jimi is having breakfast, which for most would be a late lunch. He has been making me practice cooking so I can make food while he is at work. I am still trying to master cracking eggs without tiny pieces of shells landing in the pan.

He kissed my cheek and peaked over my shoulder. He made small circles on my back with his palm. His breath smelling like coffee.

"New book?" He asked.

I nodded. "It's written like historical fiction, but it has vampires. I am really enjoying it."

Jimi turned away from me. My back already cold from his hand leaving. I jumped in my seat with the crash of his coffee cup shattering on the floor.

"What's wrong?" I stood behind him already shaking. He didn't answer. He was frozen in place. His socks splattered with coffee. He moved a finger to point before him. I moved to his side and followed where he was pointing.

"What" I don't see anything." My eyes darted from his finger to the window. He was frozen with pure fear.

"Death." He said pushing out a slow breath.

43
Jimi

I turned around to find a tall, hooded figure standing in the middle of my studio. He had dark gray, almost black, wings stretched out wide. First, I noticed the large silver scythe, then the dark empty void under his hood. He had no face. Nothing but darkness. I knew who he was before he spoke a word.

Knew it like it was implied by the universe. Written on the air around us. There was no denying, this is Death.

I ignored the coffee cup falling from my hands and the way my socks felt wet. I was frozen. Pinned in place. Mila was talking to me, but her voice was underwater. All I could do was point and managed to get one word to escape my lips. "Death."

"Death?" Mila shrieked. "What are they doing here?"

I shook my head and slid half a step back. My feet finally able to move. I tucked Mila behind me and kept my body facing the towering figure.

"Jimin Niall Seong, it's a pleasure to meet you." Death's voice was like gravel on my eardrums. My cat, Nabi, perked up and ran from the couch to the bed. Also sensing something unwelcome in my room. Why is he here to see me? Mila is the one who used to work for him. "The man who took my reaper from me."

"I didn't take her." I crossed my arms over my chest hoping it would hide my nervous shaking. "I gave her the chance to live. That's all she wanted, and it was what Mila deserves."

"What are they saying?" Mila gripped my bicep with both hands. Her eyes were already glossy.

"He is saying I stole you from him." I huffed.

"You made a bad deal, Jimin Seong." Death tucked in their wings, and I heard the faint sound of rattling chains with their movements. I looked at where he stood and saw no metal.

"I'm alive, and Mila is human. It seems like a good deal to me." I slipped an arm around her waist and pulled her in tight. She clenched her fists. Her eyes darting from me to the center of the room.

"Why can't I see you?" She asked into the room.

"Demons know there must be balance. If I lose a reaper, I must create a new one." Death's words echoed off the brick walls until they surrounded me where I stood.

"He said he must create a new reaper to replace you." I whispered into Mila's hair.

"So, make one. I know you can." She pleaded. "Why can't I see you?"

Death ignored her and continued. "When a life is given or taken not according to fate, it must be corrected." His hood tilted slightly Like a predator studying prey. A shiver ran up my back. "Mila cannot see me because I am not here for her."

"You're here for me?"

"What? They're here for you? What is going on?" Mila pushed off my body and stood before me with her arms wide. "Death, take me back. Don't do this."

Death took a loud step forward until he was inches from her. She still could not see them and didn't flinch when they lifted a boney hand to hover over her forehead. Their wings twitching.

"Nonsense Mila. This is your chance to live a full life. To experience all the things, you were curious about." I grabbed her hand, the soul ring now absent. An afterthought she discarded next to the soap dish in my bathroom. Judging by the way her shoulders fell, she heard them speak.

I could feel her guilt. See her pain. I pulled her back to stand next to me. Wrapping a hand around her waist once more. *We stand united,* I told myself.

"Jimi, I don't want a life without you. It's not worth it." She began to sob. Her chest was heaving. Still getting used to this human body.

"Plead all you want, my child." Death tapped his scythe on the floor. I could tell where he was focused. The void under his hood was angled towards me. The voice with many layers of old and new, male and female, seemed to move through the room like waves when they spoke. "I've been watching since you called upon my brother Zadkiel. You gave us plenty to discuss, and a decision was made after you foolishly struct a deal with Moloch. You sealed your fate," They turned the tip of the scythe to point at Mila, "and hers."

"I just wanted us to be together." I raised my voice trying to project power I do not have. They didn't even flinch. I reached to grab her hand. We became a circle together. Hands linked in front and arms wrapped in back. Mila squeezed my hand. Our fingers interlaced so tightly it could bruise.

"Please Death." Mila cried.

The void where a face should be shifted in her direction, but he still did not address her directly. Instead, He took a few steps back until his wings nearly touched the large window.

"I was loyal to you for over seven hundred years. I never questioned my purpose. I answered every summons quickly. I-" Her voice was shaking with each word. "Please give me this one thing. Please."

Mila bowed her head in submission. I squeezed her waist and placed a kiss on top of her head. I could feel his answer before he said it.

"I am giving you a gift. I will let you keep the soul that Moloch took. It belonged to a human that died far too young and never lived a full life. It might as well get some use." Death spread their wings. I could see the window and bricks through their body, as if they were slowly fading. "But the price for it will be paid by the one who made the deal."

"No." Mila cried, her eyes darting to mine. She heard every word he said. Heard them echo off the walls and attack her from all sides.

"It's okay." I rubbed her back. *But it's not okay.* I just have no idea what to say.

Death faded further. He was no more than a ghost now. "You have until the next sunrise."

"No please." Mila gripped the fabric of my shirt and cried into my chest. I could not speak or move. I was frozen in time.

"Make most of your life, little reaper." They whispered. I blinked and Death was gone. The faint sound of wings and chains echoed off the walls until there was just silence.

"Mila, I-" What do you say to the woman you love when you have hours left before you die? Should I apologize for sealing my death in a deal so she could live? I would do anything to have a life with her. "I'm sorry. I fucked up not asking if there were consequences for the deal, but I am not sorry you get to live."

"You should have told me your plan. I would have stopped you." She twisted my shirt in her grasp.

"You would've been back to being a reaper and I would have to live my life knowing you are there. Knowing I couldn't have you." I shook my head.

I tilted her head up with her chin. I did this. I caused this pain in her eyes. I fucked up.

"You still won't have me, Jimi." She said through clenched teeth. "Death is taking you from me and we will still be apart."

"Fuck. I know. I'm sorry."

"Sorry?" She pushed against my chest but didn't let go of my shirt. "I don't want apologies. I just wanted you."

I swallowed the lump in my throat. "I did this for you. I just wanted you to live. Deep down I think all I wanted was to know you got to have a life. With or without me."

"Then you are stupid." She tried to yell but her voice cracked into a cry.

"I'll accept that." She was shaking her head, opening her mouth but no words came out. I pulled her in close until there was no gap between our bodies. "I love you more than anything in this world. Let's not waste these moments together being angry."

Tears streamed down her face and her dark lashes held drops waiting to fall. I pressed a kiss to her full lips. I should fight for her, for this. I deepened our kiss. Mila let out a whimper and the sound broke my heart. I am about to hurt her worse than I could have imagined, but she will live beyond me.

I began to pray inside my head. Reciting every Angel I have ever heard by name. Hoping, wishing, pleading for a miracle.

44
Mila

Jimi called the hospital and claimed he was sick. He was not going to spend our last ten hours together at work. I wanted to spend that time in bed holding each other. Or begging another Angel for help.

I suggested we head out to the woman who gave hive the instructions to summon Moloch, but it was almost night and he didn't feel like barging in past business hours.

As the hours went by, Jimi was less urgent to find a loophole. He seemed content to give up. Which made me become numb. I had no clue what to say or do. I paced around the studio or sat on the bed and rocked with my knees tucked under my chin.

His focus was frantic. He insisted on emailing the landlord and getting my name on the lease. The landlord responded quickly. Excited, Jimi had a serious girlfriend. The response would have been odd if the landlord didn't know Jimi's father.

Then he set up something called auto pay for the next two months' rent. He was panicking that I was going to end up homeless. Consumed with logistics after he was gone. Every mention of him not being here had be sinking further into myself.

"Can you walk away from the laptop for a second and just be with me?" I was sitting crossed legged on the bed. His cat purred next to me as I scratched behind his ears.

He didn't look up from the glowing screen. It was the middle of the night, and no one was responding to his emails anymore.

"You will need to check my email first thing after I-" He paused, "After I am gone." The keyboard clacked under his stressed typing.

"Don't say that." I mumbled.

"Do you remember how to log in?"

"Yes, Jimi. I remember how to check your email, and use your phone, and use your debit card. I am not worried about all that." I patted my hand on the bed. "Please, take a break and just be near me."

Jimi's eyes were glazed over when he glanced away from the computer screen. My chest ached at the sight. His deep brown eyes turned down. He slowly slid off the stool and sauntered over to the bed. With a numb expression he laid back. I curled up next to him, my head over his heart. Each beat was a tick in a dreadful countdown. His arms came down to cradle me.

For hours I prayed for an Angel. I kept my pleas quiet and didn't want Jimi to hear. To know I was breaking into pieces inside. When he saw me the first time, I should have kept my distance. Should have been content with the role I played in this world and not longed for change. He wouldn't be so close to death if I had stayed away.

"I took out all the contacts from my phone expect my closest friends and my parents. If you need help, promise me you will call them." I nodded onto his chest, unable to make words. "I changed my employee records to have you as my domestic partner. I am not sure how long it will take to have HR approve it."

"Can we not talk about this." I held back a sob.

"I need to know you are taken care of. That you will be safe without me." His hand lifted to brush the hair from my face. I choked on a shaky breath. He soothed me by stroking my hair. I let the rising of his chest lift my head. I was so tired. My body was physically weak, and my mind was having a hard time completing thoughts. *Is this normal for a human? Can a human die of a broken heart?*

"I can't just sit here and wait for you to die." My eyes already puffy from crying squeezed out a single tear.

"Part of me died years ago when my sister did. I have been living like a ghost ever since. Doing the bare minimum to survive. I never had a real purpose. It should have been me who died in the bus crash."

"Don't say that." I pushed up on my elbow to look down at his face. There was a sad smile tugging at his lips.

"I think you were my purpose, Mila." He smiled bigger and I shook my head in response. "I can't explain it, but I feel it deep in my-" He tapped his chest, "soul. My soul that is mine to do with as I choose, and I would trade centuries of servitude, for you to live if I had to."

I was crying again. I didn't understand how a human body could leak so much. His shirt was growing damp with my tears. Jimi rolled me over onto my back. He wiped the wetness from my cheeks and kissed the corner of each eye. Then he kissed each cheek. Lingering for a few breaths. I wanted to freeze time when he kissed my lips, but it was quick. Leaving me with a soft memory.

I need more time.

I need more time.

"It stopped snowing. Let's get bundled up and be first in line when the bakery opens." He sat up and tugged me off the bed. "We can get cookies and watch the sunrise from our favorite bench."

45
Mila

<u>**6:50am Saturday**</u>
<u>**Oct 23rd , 2023**</u>

The news stations will have headlines about the record snow fall so early in the year, but it will all be melted by afternoon. Right now, it covers the ground like a blanket of despair. Here to remind me that I am completely alone and the man I love is dead.

Moments after the sun lifted above the horizon, Jimi fell off the bench into the fresh snow. My screams earned the attention of a man walking his dog. I didn't notice him calling the ambulance. I didn't notice the EMT's running up to us. My hands shook and my mouth remained agape. Everything was happening in slow motion.

Cars barely move. The city was waking up before, but now it's moving behind a haze. Nothing exists except Jimi. His unmoving body aglow from the rising sun.

If I am patient, maybe I will wake up from this nightmare. Death just wanted to teach me a lesson. Soon I will blink and find myself back on the roof top watching him through the window. Debating if I follow him to the bar.

I will find myself back to reaping souls and he will go on to save many lives. He was meant to bring joy to those with illness. He was meant to save them, not me. Not sacrifice himself you me. Not this.

"Miss?"

My attention darted to the fingers snapping in front of my eyes. An EMT stood with a concerned look on his face. I nodded.

"Do you have a ride to the hospital?" He asked.

I shook my head. My hand tightened around Jimi's cell phone and wallet in my coat pocket. He gave them to me a few minutes before falling over. I pressed my lips together and blinked at the EMT.

"You can ride with us." He hovered his hand over the small of my back and encouraged me towards the ambulance. Inside the ambulance the silence was deafening. No machines were beeping. They were not trying CPR. Jimi appeared to be sleeping. He looked at peace.

Sliding onto the bench I lifted his hand. It was so cold. Before we left the apartment, I grabbed my ring from the dish. I had the intention of throwing it into the ocean. I was going to curse Death and I never wanted to see a reminder of him again. Looking at the ring now, I missed the way it used to heat up when we touched. I slipped the gold soul ring off my middle finger and put it on his left hand. The spot I would have wanted to declare my commitment to him if things were different. If we had more time. I placed a kiss to his knuckle as the ambulance jerked forward.

"Miss, what is your relationship with the deceased?" The EMT asked.

Reaching out I gently stroked his cheek. No longer flush. The movement of the ambulance rocked his body. I placed my hand on his chest to steady him.

"He is my love. My reason for living." I lifted my head, making eye contact with the worried EMT.

"Miss, would you like to speak to a counselor at the hospital?"

I shook my head. "No, I will be-." I couldn't finish the sentence.

Fine? Will I be fine?

He is the reason I have breaths to take and food to taste. The source of the most powerful love I've ever known, and the most devastating tragedy I have witnessed. He gave me the most powerful gift. This human body.

"I will be fine." I assured the EMT. "I will be just fine."

46
Mila

<u>Three Years Later</u>

"Mila, the prop table looks like something is missing."

I dodged a rolling rack of costumes, trying not to drop my armful of props. Plastic wine glasses made to look full. Hollow books and various hats. "I'm here Mr. Henley."

Carefully, I placed the props next to a set of coffee mugs and a vase of fake flowers on the folding table located just off stage. Double checking everything was in the correct order for the prop manager.

"You've been backstage for four months, drop the formalities. Mila." He waved a hand and walked away staring at a clipboard.

"Yes, Elliot." I called towards his back. I begged at the start of every new production for almost three years now to work backstage. The only job I was qualified for in the beginning was as an usher during shows. Unfortunately, that didn't pay very well to keep Jimi's apartment.

My first year as a human was one struggle after another. I never thought food was so expensive. My friend Nina and her boyfriend Dante helped me switch the utilities into my name after the heat was shut off in mid-January. I tried not to blow through the money Jimi left behind. Most of the time I wore his shirts and jackets. Even now, I prefer anything he wore over new clothes.

My forged documents allowed me to get a shelf stocking job at a nearby grocery store. That paid the bills the theater job could not cover.

I spent my free time in the library. Reading out in the open for all to see. I absorbed any resources about theater production or set design. Dante suggested I read about financial planning. Said to me with a snarky tone when he had to help me set up bills. But I took the advice. It was torture.

Dante was immediately alarmed when I called him from Jimi's phone the morning of Jimi's death. He rushed to the apartment with Nina. She stayed with me for the first two nights while Dante met with Jimi's parents. Nina fed me when she noticed I stopped eating. Food had seemed to have lost its appeal. I was content to let my body wither and die.

I am not sure how long a person is supposed to grieve. I suppose as a reaper you only see the immediate moments around a person's death, and not the impact on those who knew them. It's wild to think of the thousands of people whom I witnessed die. And yet, there is only one death that sits on the edge of my mind every morning. One death that weighs heavy with every footstep.

I signed my name on the paper resting on the prop table. I am just a prop assistant. Backstage has always felt like a home, and I am just grateful to be a part of it. My signature was sloppy, but I am filled with pride every time I write it.

Jimi wanted to give me an Italian last name on my passport. He claimed it would help sell the story that I was an immigrant. I threw that idea out the window. I had a plan of my own.

How his eyes widened when I asked to take his last name instead.

"Jorge is making it look like you are here on a work visa from Genoa Italy." He said swinging my hand in his. We were walking to a store that offers photo services for passports. It was my first day as a human. "We need to sell the story that you are Italian. Since you will be stuck with that pretty Italian face forever. And since there is no trace of you in the US."

I blushed. "I don't want an Italian name."

"What do you want? Don't pick something crazy." He flashed me the crooked smile that I loved so much.

"Seong." I watched him from the corner of my eye. Waiting for the rejection. A lump sat in my throat.

Jimi stopped moving down the sidewalk and pulled me into an alley. Out of the way from the crowds of pedestrians. His eyes were wide and I couldn't tell if I offended him.

"Seong?" He repeated it like a question. I nodded. There was a twisting in my stomach. "You want my last name?"

"Yes."

"Do you know what people will think?" Jimi braced his hands on my shoulders and studied my face. I nodded. "They will think you are my wife."

"I know." I gulped down air.

"Would you want that?" He brushed my hair off my shoulders and cupped my face with his gloved hands. I nodded again. I blinked back tears. Why was my body wanting to cry? This is the happiest I have ever been.

He leaned down and kissed me for long minutes. The world faded to silence around us. I lived in this kiss.

"I am yours, Mila Seong, and you are mine." He kissed me again.

"I am yours, always, Jimi Seong." We smiled on each other's lips.

As his arms wrapped around me a phrase sung in my head. As if sharing my thoughts, he spoke it aloud before I could.

"Til Death do us part."

Epilogue

It took me a few years to track her down since she moved from my old apartment. Moloch restricted my movements in the beginning, but now I am free to roam the earth as I please mostly. Working for a demon consists of a lot of busy work. Guarding the souls trapped in Molochs prison, watching humans that made deals with us, and contracting new deals.

The first half of my decade of service has been spent in Moloch's prison. Death tossed my soul to Moloch like a bag of trash. Having my committed servitude begins immediately. I didn't even pass through the gateway Mila told me about.

I hovered around with no form or sense of time. I became a cloud of what I once was. What I will never be again. A human.

Once Moloch released me from the iron box, I came to call it, he burned five marks onto my back. Turns out, even in this form I can still feel pain. One mark would appear on the anniversary of my bad deal for the next ninety-five years. Something to look forward to. Sort of.

I would make the deal again in a heartbeat if it meant Mila would end up here. Standing on a stool placing ornaments on a Christmas tree. With no clue I am watching her.

Two small children decorate the lower half while music plays on my old record player. I couldn't help but smile seeing a piece of me remains in her home. Even though I am not the man currently making dinner for her in the kitchen. Even though those are not my children.

That is my cat, however. My fluffy white fur ball that is currently asleep cuddled up with a child's stuffed toy.

"Nabi, you have completely forgotten me haven't you." I mumble. "Enjoy your cushy life with my woman."

I pushed down jealousy that was rising like a fire inside me. Being around nothing but demons has awoken some changes in me. I visit Dante and Mila to try and hold on to a part of me I fear is slipping away.

I watch Mila like she lives in a snow globe. My nose pressed against the glass of her living room window. She moved into his Tudor home and became the world's best stepmother. On my first visit here, she was building canopies over their beds to make them look like castles and pirate ships. The walls in their bedroom were painted with scenes of a forest straight out of a fantasy book. A decade working in a theater brought out her true artistic talent. She flourished in set design.

I faded my body through the wall and entered her home. If they only knew that an almost demon stood a mere five feet away.

That's what I am becoming the longer I do this job. A demon myself. I was bothered in the beginning, but again, the changes inside make it easier to accept.

I understand what it felt like for Mila as a reaper. Being on the outside. Always watching and not partaking. The main difference between how we exist in the world is that a demon can be seen by anyone. Not by our choosing but by theirs. Humans just need blood, the right words, and our name.

When I began training on earth it occurred to me that Mila could summon me. I rushed to find her. I looked everywhere. If I could just get a message to her that I was here. That I was watching. Waiting

My apartment was empty when I searched for her there, so I went to the theater where she worked. That is when I saw her walking out hand in hand with a golden-haired man. I hated his tweed blazer and tortoise shell glasses. He made her laugh, and my body felt like it was burning up.

Moloch sensed the change in me and pulled me back to his gap world. It's like being stuck in a shadow of earth. Everything is faded except for the demons that reside there and the iron brutalist structures. I assumed it was Hell when I first arrived. That caused Moloch to laugh deeply. *"Jimi, you could never imagine what Hell truly is."*

His words still haunt me. When he pulled my tether after I saw Mila with the man, I was greeted with a list of warnings. A cold reminder that I was in servitude for ninety-five more years. That Mila was human now and would only live out a human life span. That there will forever be a separation between us, and I should move on. Never.

I *was* warned to look and not touch. Or I would be thrown back into the iron box.

"Look but not touch. As if I could touch her anyway." I scoffed, saying the words aloud in her living room.

Mila finished decorating the top of the tree and walked down a narrow set of stairs to the basement. This basement is creepy, and that is coming from a literal demon in training that is currently haunting her. It was dusty with cobwebs in every corner. If I listened closely, I could hear a slow drip of water. It almost sounded like there was a well buried below. Great, there is probably a monster living in it. I wanted to warn Mila to be safe there could be creepy things down here. Then I chuckled because I am the creepy thing down here.

I followed her as she moved around a series of boxes to get access to red plastic tubs marked "holidays".

I tried to smell her hair when she moved in front of me, but that is not a privilege demons have. I would willingly add more years onto my contract if it gave me one more night with her. Without that pesky man upstairs to bother us.

Mila stopped moving and crouched down to study a cardboard box. The writing is faded and hard to read. I shifted to be across from her, and my lips tugged up when she lifted the flap. The words "Jimi's – Do Not Throw Away" were written on it in faded black marker.

I crossed my legs and placed my chin on my fist.

"*Are you thinking about me Mila?*" I said aloud knowing she could not hear me.

She dug through the box. Her eyes began to get glossy, and she sniffled. Wiping a dusty hand across her cheek.

"*Don't cry my love.*"

I lifted a hand to brush the single tear off her cheek, but I just passed through her like smoke. I wondered if I still lived in her thoughts as much as she does mine. Our short time together plays like an endless film inside my head.

"Oh Jimi." Mila said softly while lifting my old denim jacket out of the box. She lifted it to her face and inhaled.

"*I'm here.*"

Mila continued to move the contents of the box around until she froze. "What is it?" I leaned over the edge of the box and peered inside. Crushed on the very bottom was a small scroll of tea-stained paper. An item that cost me a thousand dollars when I was alive and started this path to my hundred years of servitude.

My eyes widened when she lifted it out slowly. I shifted to my knees. As if in prayer before her. Her slender fingers slid off the red ribbon. She took a deep breath before unrolling the paper.

"That's right, Mila." I said nodding.

"Jimi." She said my name with layers of pain embedded in her voice.

"Yes, my love."

She studied the paper, still not able to hear my voice.

"Could I see you again Jimi?" A tear fell slowly from her cheek and landed on the paper. She rolled it back up and tucked it into her cardigan pocket.

"Yes." I answered from habit.

Mila stood and I mirrored her movements. Every part of me wanted to scream that I am here. It was no use. Demons can't intervene without being seen unless directly summoned. Maybe she will try to summon me. *"Please Mila, try"*. I would like to tell her that I still love her. That I regret nothing.

She placed a hand over her heart. "Thank you, Jimi. For this life."

I gave her my crooked smile that I know she loved so much. It always made her cheeks flush.

"Oh Mila. I hope you enjoy every minute you have on earth because I have already made arrangements." I chuckled to myself. *"The living may have you for a few decades, but I will have your forever."*

THE END

Relive the love story of Mila and Jimi by listening to the official Spotify playlist.

ABOUT THE AUTHOR

Rena Rene Mangold grew up in a small town in Oregon. Where she developed a love for theater, fashion, and writing. She attended a fashion school in Los Angeles. Rena kept a writing journal filled with outlines of movies, plays, and novels. To Touch A Reaper is her first published work. After deciding her dreams could not hide in the shadows any longer.

When not writing, she spends time with her husband, two kids, and hound dog in Utah. Playing video games or hunting for cool rocks.

Find her on TikTok and Instagram @she.rhino